MW01122828

IN THE WAITING ROOM OF FORGIVENESS

IN THE WAITING ROOM OF FORGIVENESS

Stephen B. Lourie

Library of Congress Number:		00-192226
ISBN #:	Hardcover	0-7388-3903-5
	Softcover	0-7388-3904-3

The people and incidents that occur in this book, with the exception of historical facts, are completely fictional and in no way should be construed as having taken place.

This book was printed in the United States of America.

United Middlesex Limited

To order additional copies of this book, contact:
Xlibris Corporation
1-888-7-XLIBRIS
www.Xlibris.com
Orders@Xlibris.com

To
Audrey
who helped
me on important
lesson.
Love
Stephen

To Frank, Mary and Jeffrey

1

"Come on, Hans, we're due on the soccer field in half an hour. Where the hell were you?"

"I was in church, Friedrich."

"In church? On a Wednesday? You never go to church during the week. Have you committed some horrible sin?" Friedrich replied facetiously.

"You went to church when your parents were killed and you haven't been back since their funeral."

"Don't be a wise guy, Friedrich. If you must know I went there to pray."

"But why in the middle of the week, Hans?"

"Friedrich, have you forgotten that I'm getting married next week?"

"Fool, how can I? I'm your best man."

"The truth, Friedrich, is that I'm scared shit about marriage."

"I can understand that, Hans. I think many men go through the same thing. You love Lily, don't you, Hans?"

"Friedrich, what the hell do I know about love?"

"I don't know," replied Friedrich, "you tell me."

"What can I say," countered Hans, "I've had plenty of sexual encounters, but marriage is nothing I've even considered and now I'm hooked and scared, Friedrich."

"Don't you want to marry Lily, Hans?"

"Yes, I need her. When I'm with her I seem complete. When I'm not with her things just don't seem to go right. It's being with the same woman for the rest of my life that scares me. What if she changes?"

"Idiot! Of course she'll change and so will you. None of us stays the same, Hans."

"I know, but what if I want to go to bed with someone else, Friedrich?"

"So? There's nothing to stop you, Hans. Have you done anything to her yet?"

"What...what do you mean? What the hell am I supposed to do to her, Friedrich?"

"Kiss her, fondle her breasts. Make love to her, whatever."

"For god's sakes, you loon, she's a nice virgin girl from a fine family."

"Yeah," replied Friedrich, "you got lucky. Lily von Mendelssohn-Bartholdy from a Jewish family, and her father Solomon—one of the biggest bankers in Berlin."

"She's Protestant. Felix Mendelssohn-Bartholdy's parents converted and Felix married a Huguenot pastor's daughter. I don't care what religion she is. As my wife she'll be Catholic. But getting back to what I said Friedrich, what if I want to go to bed with someone else after we're married?"

"Look, Hans, don't be so damned innocent. This is 1912, a new century. We're German military officers. We can do what we want. Gosh, in France this purity act is passé. Look at all the goings-on in Paris. I'm sure engaged couples sleep together."

"Yeah, Big Shot, but this sure isn't Paris."

"We're going to be late for the game."

"Yes, yes, *Herr* Count Friedrich, the Great . . . the Great Pest that is!"

2

Creeping vines covered the bottom perimeter of the small country church. The building now surrounded by rather unkempt grounds was adjacent to the family cemetery. The area surrounding the family estate, however, was well manicured—as if each blade of grass was cut by hand, so that none dared to be taller than the other. This was the House of von Wallenstadt—where religion now seemed to be an accessory. The family had always been devout. The women in particular went to the family chapel on a daily basis; the men attended perfunctorily on Sundays, and occasionally at other times to petition God to gratify their material wants. Even on the warmest of days the family chapel would emit a chill from the stone walls, as if winter hibernated there all summer. The chapel was nestled on a hill behind a clump of trees It was close to the city of Konstanz, just north of the Swiss border. This first day of summer of 1912, the building's solemnity was brightened by the marriage of Hans von Wallenstadt to Lily Mendelssohn-Bartholdy.

Lily stood at the rear of the church waiting for the processional. Her thoughts returned to her first meeting with Hans. He was at the front of the aisle remembering the same occasion. It was Christmas eve, 1911 at Boernicke, twenty miles east of Berlin—the family mansion of Lily's uncle, Ernst von Mendelssohn.

"Hilda," Lily asked her cousin as they peeked through the second floor banister rails, "who is that attractive, tall, blond man speaking to Count Friedrich?"

"That's Count Hans von Wallenstadt, Lily."

"He's got such a sad look about him, Hilda."

"I guess it's to be expected—his parents were in a coach with his father's brother, wife and young child. Something scared the horses—some dogs I think—and they bolted as the coach was making a turn. Everyone but the baby was killed, Lily. Von Wallenstadt is taking care of his little cousin."

Lily felt immediate empathy for the man.

"How tragic," replied Lily, "not to have parents. I would have loved to have known my mother and to have had brothers and sisters. She had to die to give me life."

"You have me," said Hilda, "and I couldn't love you more if you were my own sister."

"I know that Hilda, forgive me. I'm just feeling a bit sorry for myself and Count von Wallenstadt too, I guess. After all, we're grown women now, Hilda—eighteen years old—and I guess you're never too old to miss your mother, even if you've never met her."

The girls descended the staircase regally, relishing the spotlight as all eyes turned to them.

"Kitten," said Lily's father, Solomon, "all of the guests are waiting for you to play the piano."

Lily sat at the piano and glided through a Beethoven sonata. She had followed in the footsteps of her famous ancestors Fannie and Felix Mendelssohn-Bartholdy, and she was an accomplished pianist, well known in German concert halls. After the performance Lily mingled with friends and relatives until the high point of the evening, the lighting of the candles on the Christmas tree.

Hans watched Lily as all assembled sang "Hark the Herald Angels Sing," that indicated the evening's celebration had come to a close. At that point the von Mendelssohn-Bartholdy family gathered as a group to wish their departing guests a good night and a happy Christmas. This was the time when Hans saw the opportunity to meet Lily. He approached Friedrich and asked:

"Do you know *Fräulein* Mendelssohn-Bartholdy, Friedrich?"

"Yes," he replied, "her father does business with mine."

Hans with utmost seriousness said:

"Would you introduce me to her, *Herr* Big Shot?"

"Aha, Hans, you are captivated by *Fräulein* Mendelssohn-Bartholdy?"

"No, no," Hans responded with a vehemence that of course meant yes.

He walked with Friedrich to the spot where Lily stood chatting with Berlin's cognoscenti.

"*Fräulein* Mendelssohn," said Friedrich, "I'd like you to meet my friend Count von Wallenstadt."

Lily smiled warmly and said, "It's a pleasure to meet you, sir. I've heard of your tragic loss and I'm truly sorry. My mother died at childbirth. I never knew her, but I miss her. I'm fortunate to have papa who's been a father and a mother to me."

"*Fräulein* Mendelssohn," replied Hans, "When I heard of my parents' death along with my uncle and his wife, I couldn't believe it or accept it. I felt abandoned and deserted; then I felt more alone than I've ever been. I felt angry, so angry at them for leaving me. Now the realization of what's happened has settled and I mourn them. I have no other family except my father's brother, Josef. He lives in Windhoek in Southwest Africa. The only person left is my uncle's son, Paul, who survived. I will rear him and give him enough love to compensate for his lack of parents."

The openness of this stranger who confided such personal feelings impressed Lily. Most men would put up a tough front, she thought, but here is a person who realizes and expresses his feelings—how refreshing and honest.

3

"I understand, *Fräulein*, that you're going to give a concert in Zurich next month. I'll be there. I would be honored to have you and your father visit at my home for a few days."

"Thank you," responded Lily. "I'll talk to my father and let you know."

Hans drew a calling card from his vest pocket, penned his address on it, kissed Lily's hand, looked at her intensely and said:

"I shall look forward to it, *Fräulein* von Mendelssohn-Bartholdy. Please do not disappoint me."

Hans smiled at Lily, clicked his heels in a military fashion and joined Friedrich.

"How did things go with *Fräulein* Mendelssohn-Bartholdy?" he asked as they departed.

"I found her to be a sensitive, caring young woman," Hans replied. "I now know why her piano performances are so exceptional."

"I think you're smitten, m' boy," countered Friedrich.

"Papa," said Lily after the party ended, "Count von Wallenstadt has invited us to visit for a few days after the Zurich concert. I found him to be very warm and caring. We discussed the deaths in his family. He is so alone. I would like to go."

"That's sweet of you, Kitten. You may be able to give the lad some consolation. Count Friedrich's family does business with my bank and they've often mentioned the von Wallenstadt family. Maybe we can cheer up the boy."

Lily wrote to Friedrich the following day:

Berlin, 20 April, 1911

My dear Count von Wallenstadt,

Thank you for your kind invitation to visit after my Zurich performance. My father and I are pleased to accept.

Cordially,

Lily Mendelssohn-Bartholdy

As Hans read Lily's acceptance, he began to feel the sadness that had perpetually weighed upon him since all of the deaths in his family. He recalled Lily's elegance, her charm and their mutual sympathy for each other's circumstance. The sadness, however, was soon replaced by feelings of anticipation.

The next month Hans met Lily and her father after the concert. They had supper at the railway station and boarded a late train and arrived at Konstanz the next morning.

"Lily," said Hans as they strolled through the von Wallenstadt garden, "I have such admiration for you. You're not like other German women—shy, retiring and usually uneducated in the ways of the world; you give me more than you realize. I'm really going to miss you when you've gone."

"You're sweet to tell me these things, Hans. You can see me in Berlin or you can visit if you're near any place where I'm performing."

Hans took advantage of this opportunity almost all of the time.

"Papa," Lily said, "I've fallen in love with Hans."

"Is he in love with you Kitten? Has he proposed?"

"No, papa, I can tell that he wants to, but he's shy. He still mourns his parents' death and that may have something to do with it. How do you feel about it, papa?"

"Kitten, he's a wonderful, young man. You two get on marvelously together. I'd be proud to have him as my son-in-law."

"Ah, thank you papa, thank you," Lily exclaimed as she hugged her father.

"But, Kitten, he hasn't proposed and we don't know what's going to happen."

"But, papa, I love him so. I'll be heartbroken if he doesn't. He's sympathetic, not like most German men. He's handsome, courtly, and treats me as an equal—not condescending to women, with false charm and an uncalled for paternalistic attitude. He has rank and station and I imagine that he would show as much respect for the char as he would for the Kaiser."

Hans and Friedrich were involved with military duties in East Prussia that precluded any Berlin visit.

"Friedrich," said Hans, "I can't stand being without Lily anymore. I'm going to ask her to marry me."

"About time you ninny, about time," said Friedrich as he grabbed Hans' hand and shook it endlessly.

Lily received the letter several days later. She read it to her father:

> Konstanz, 6 June, 1911
>
> My darling Lily,
>
> The longer I'm away from you, the more I miss and need you. My love for you is driving me crazy. Will you be my wife?
>
> Hans von Wallenstadt

"Well, Kitten, better late than never."

"Papa, I'm going to send him a telegram."

"A telegram? Isn't a letter sufficient?"

"No, papa. I love him and I don't want him to be anxious waiting for my reply." She sent the telegram.

"Hans," said Friedrich with surprise, "this just came for you."

"A telegram, Friedrich, the first I've ever received."

"Open it, Hans, open it."

"You nosy bastard, you're as excited as I am."

Hans opened it tremulously and read it to Friedrich.

"It says, 'Yes, your darling Lily."

The two jumped up and down like school boys until their commanding officer entered whereupon they assumed a strict military demeanor.

4

Lily held on to her father's arm as she slowly walked down the aisle to the organist's performance of the Wedding March. She looked ahead towards the nave and saw Hans standing there tall and erect. Mercifully the joy that radiated from her was not shattered by hearing the complaints whispered by Hans' pioneer uncle. He had returned from Southwest Africa and remained in Germany for the wedding, after settling business affairs arising from the deaths of his two brothers. Only those immediately next to him could hear Joseph von Wallenstadt mutter,

"My God, he's the only man left in the family to continue the von Wallenstadt name, except Baby Paul. And who's he marrying? A Protestant, damn it, whose family was Jewish. It's a disgrace. Believe me, Emma, if you could give birth to a child I wouldn't even be here."

After the wedding Lily adapted to her new role quickly. She became a welcome addition to the social life of the community and her presence was highly sought. Lily continued performing, although less frequently, and Hans accompanied her to all the places where she performed. Hans' moodiness had practically disappeared, except for the times Lily was not with him.

This was a time of intense political change in Europe; there was much unrest. The Socialist movement in Germany was gaining strength. Dissent in Russia (prior to the October, 1918 revolution) was on the increase. In October, 1912, Bulgaria, Serbia, Greece, and Montenegro declared war on Turkey. During this period

German militancy reached its ascendance and its economy was at its peak.

These were good times for Solomon Mendelssohn-Bartholdy. New business opportunities beckoned in the United States. Solomon told Lily of an impending business trip to America. *Herr* Mendelssohn-Bartholdy was to leave in the spring of 1914, sailing on the Kronprinz Wilhelm from Hamburg, returning via England in late Spring of the following year.

Lily said to her husband several days later,

"Hans, father asked if we would like to accompany him to America. I'd love to, but I have to see *Herr* Schlessinger in Berlin to discuss plans for my next concert. It's something that I can't postpone, nor would I want to re-schedule the concert. I don't think that would be appropriate."

"When would you have to go to Berlin, my darling?" queried Hans.

"I thought it would be best if we could go after father sailed from Hamburg," she replied.

"I must stay in Konstanz, Lily; my attorney is coming to discuss financial matters. I'm sorry, dearest, but I too can't postpone this."

"Oh Hans, I don't like being without you."

"Don't worry, Lily. It'll just be a matter of a few days and you'll be in my arms before you realize that you've left."

"Oh, I don't think so, Hans, I'll miss you terribly."

"Lily, once you're involved with the piano, it takes over your entire mind. You probably won't even have time to miss me."

Lily smiled demurely, saying nothing. She knew that he was probably correct in his assessment, for as much as she loved him, nothing could consume her more than her music. She and Hans were mortal, but music was immortal.

5

Simon Mendelssohn was one of Lily's English cousins, of whom she was quite fond. Lily and Simon had spent many happy days together, when as children, her father would take her to London, or when Simon would visit with Lily in Germany. Simon was tall, lithe with dark, blonde hair and light, green eyes. He was the same age as Lily. As children they would play duets for four hands, the usual variety of indoor and outdoor games, and go for walks and talk with each other endlessly. Simon had been in Germany and he was going to surprise Lily by seeing her at the Hamburg pier when she and Hans came to see *Herr* Mendelssohn-Bartholdy sail. When Lily spotted him, she ran to him and exclaimed as she embraced him:

"You rascal, Simon. I didn't know you were going to be here."

"I thought I'd surprise you, and even visit with you for a bit before returning to England."

"Grand," said Lily. "I'm off to Berlin for a few days, but why don't you return to Konstanz with Hans. It would just be a short time and I'll be back before you know it."

"Excellent idea," replied Simon.

"Do you enjoy mountain climbing, Simon?" asked Hans. "I was planning on doing this while Lily was in Berlin."

"Rather!" said Simon "I'm quite good at sports, and I received honors at football."

"Really?" answered Hans. "You don't look the type that would be playing football."

"Ah yes," replied Simon, "but looks can be deceiving."

The assembled crowd boarded the ship for a reception in *Herr* Mendelssohn-Bartholdy's stateroom.

"This is so exciting, papa," said Lily, "to be going off to America. I wish I were going with you."

"I do too, Kitten, but as much as I'll miss you, your place is with your husband."

As the call for those going ashore sounded, Lily went to her father. He could not help noticing the tears in her eyes, that she had unsuccessfully attempted to conceal. *Herr* Mendelssohn-Bartholdy put his arms around his daughter and said:

"Time goes quickly. I'll miss you, Kitten, but I'll be back before you know it."

"I hope your business goes well, papa," replied Lily, as she tried to conceal her emotions.

"Now, no more tears, Kitten. Are you not the great performer, so well-controlled and able to conquer all?"

"That, papa," Lily replied, "is only when I'm at the piano."

"You'd best hurry, Kitten, or you'll be sailing with me to America. Doesn't your train for Berlin leave soon?"

"I have time, papa. Hans and Cousin Simon will see me to the station."

Twenty minutes later the vessel left the pier to sail north on the River Elbe, into the Baltic Sea and thence to the Atlantic and America. Lily waved to her father waving back at her, until the passengers seemed to meld with the deck of the ship, that ultimately disappeared into the horizon. As Lily watched she was burdened with an *angst* that she had never before experienced. Her father had gone, and events in her life seemed to be unsettling and disturbing. An amorphous sensation of unknown, impending change enveloped her.

She was, like her husband, a child of privilege. Lily was born into and accustomed to wealth. She had married into the aristocracy, that in turn led to greater privilege. The world she knew was one of art, beauty, and material well-being—surely not one of politics and deprivation. In Germany's well-ordered society and, in the Mendelssohn-Bartholdy's purview, threats to their values and life-style were so vague as to be non-existent. Yet it was as if a storm on the horizon was delaying a summer's outing, but all that could be seen were distant clouds that dissipated quickly, only to melt under the power of a bright sun, to return once more. She could not put her finger on what bothered her. She had no control over these feelings, and this seemed to fuel her anxieties further. Was it her father's departure, coupled with the events in Europe that made her uneasy? She felt sad and tearful, but she repressed her tears, and re-directed her affection towards her Cousin Simon as she turned to him and said:

"Simon, it was such a wonderful surprise to see you. I'm happy that you can stay with us a while."

"Yes, Simon," intoned Hans, "your visit will make it easier for me to tolerate Lily's absence more so than I would have otherwise. That's one of the reasons I planned to do some mountain climbing."

The trio adjourned to a restaurant where Lily toyed with her food as the men ate heartily.

"We'd best hurry, Lily. We don't have that much time before your train departs."

"Yes, dear," she replied dutifully.

The three left the restaurant and entered a waiting taxi that took them the short distance to the railway station. The station was busy. It was always filled with people, going, coming, seeing people off, waiting to greet arrivals.

"I always have a touch of anxiety when I travel," said Lily.

"How so, darling?" Hans inquired. "You've done it so often."

"I don't know, Hans. It's funny. When I'm about to perform at a concert I feel confident and much more secure, possibly since I'm in control of what I'm doing. At the station, with all the commotion, things are not at all within my control. Usually, once I've settled comfortably in my compartment the anxiety abates, but then I feel excited about leaving. Once the train leaves I feel more comfortable and secure. When I go to bed and snuggle under the blankets, the rhythmical sound of the train wheels on the tracks lulls me to sleep—but then I like to open the shade and look out of the window. I enjoy seeing the countryside going past, and when the train stops at a station I like to look outside to see what's going on."

"Lily," said Hans, "you are always the innocent, little girl, but your brilliance, talent and charm make you all the more appealing. I love you, my dearest."

Lily boarded the train as Simon kissed her good-bye and waited on the platform. Hans accompanied her to the compartment. They kissed each other tenderly and Hans left the train to join Simon. The trio waved as the chugging and hissing locomotive headed towards Berlin.

6

"Well, Simon, we have time for a coffee before our train departs," said Hans.

"Good idea, Hans," replied Simon.

The two men boarded the train for Konstanz. They were quartered in the rather small *wagon lits* sleeping space, but they managed to undress and get into their beds.

"Simon," asked Hans, "What was Lily like as a child?"

"She was like a dancing flower, Hans, always singing, happy, working on her piano."

"Even then?" Hans interrupted.

"Especially, then," continued Simon. "She was always serious about her piano playing, but her seriousness would give way to joy and great pleasure. She would start to play a piece, get immersed in what she was doing, and it would seem that she and what was being performed were as one. Lily seemed to rise above the mere physical aspect of the piece; one could see the contentment on her face, imagine what she felt inside. Uncle Solomon was a loving, caring, and giving father, but he was quite strict about Lily's education. She studied many languages, just as I had to do, and she's fluent in several. As you know, Lily speaks English as flawlessly as I would like to think I speak German."

"You do very well, Simon," Hans said, laughingly, "but I can tell that you're English."

The two continued talking late into the night, about Lily, the

Mendelssohn-Bartholdy family, England, Germany, Hans' sports achievements, and such.

Early the next morning they left the train at Konstanz where Hans' driver was awaiting their arrival.

"Good morning, sir," was the driver's greeting.

"Good morning, Keltmann," Hans replied.

"Shall I take you directly home?"

"Yes, Keltmann, if you please."

"Sir, a message was delivered for me to relay to you. Count Friedrich will not be able to go mountain climbing with you on Thursday."

"Pity," replied Hans, "Simon, I'm really glad you're here. I don't think I would ever attempt a climb by myself. It's far too dangerous. Have you ever climbed in the Alps before?"

"Heavens, no," Simon replied. "The highest mountain I ever climbed was in Wales."

"Well, if you're sure you're fit, we can tackle a smaller peak, just over the border in Austria. We have a few days before the climb, so we can use them to exercise and to increase our endurance. I can also give you a few pointers on climbing, if you have no objections."

"Why, thank you, Hans, I'd be most grateful for the help. I'm quite looking forward to it."

The two men arrived at the von Wallenstadt estate and its impressive surroundings.

"The air here is bracing," Simon commented, the clarity of the sun glistening against the golden buttons of his blue jacket. "Have you always lived here?"

"Almost always. I spent my early years here with my parents."

"I'm looking forward to meeting them," Simon said.

"Unfortunately they'll not be here to greet us; they died in an accident several weeks prior to my marriage."

"How tragic," Simon replied.

"Yes, it was," Hans continued. "They were in a coach with my uncle and aunt. My aunt had recently given birth to my Cousin

Paul and my parents had gone to fetch them. The horses were startled by several dogs, and they bolted. The driver couldn't control them, and the coach turned over. My parents, aunt and uncle were crushed to death, the driver was thrown clear of the coach, but died shortly thereafter."

"How ghastly," said Simon.

"You know, Simon, there are certain things most of us take for granted. Usually your parents are always a part of your life. Life is inconceivable without them, but it goes on, and you live. However the anguish of their death will take a long time to heal. I was deeply depressed, and I still carry the scars of this tragedy, but I married shortly after the funeral. It was Lily who really saved my life. I think I would have gone mad, if not for her."

"And your little cousin, what of him?"

"Paul survived, by some miracle. He is a bright, handsome child. Lily and I are rearing him. You'll see him shortly, that is if his nanny lets us. She's very protective of him and he follows a strict schedule."

"Wonderful, I shall look forward to it," Simon replied.

"Shall we have a game of soccer before lunch, Simon?"

"Splendid," he replied. "I'd like that."

The men left the coach. A servant ushered Simon to his quarters; Hans adjourned to his room. They met shortly thereafter and went out to the grounds to play their game.

"You're an excellent player, Simon. Where did you learn?" asked Hans.

"I was lead player in public school, but I didn't want to tell you that," Simon replied, after winning the game.

"Well, let's freshen up, have lunch, and later in the afternoon, we can work on the exercises that should help you in mountain climbing," said Hans.

The two men lunched and conversed incessantly. They had so much to tell each other. After lunch they took a stroll, sat in the garden chatting some more.

"Well, let's change again for the mountain climbing

exercises," Hans said.

"Fine, Hans, I'll be down in five minutes."

They worked at the exercises for about two hours. It was now late in the afternoon.

"I think you've done quite well," said Hans. "I'll see you in about an hour. We can have some sherry and then dinner. Do you play chess?"

"I do, but I must admit that I'm not as good at chess as I might be."

"Well, then maybe I can win at something," Hans retorted.

The two laughed and met shortly afterwards for sherry. The talk began again; they both were learned men who exulted in their knowledge. They would question and challenge each other on topics from religion to ancient history, each trying to entrap the other. After dinner the repartee continued until the chess game began; they became silent as each tried to outwit the other. As the clock struck midnight, the butler inquired whether he might bring them a hot cocoa.

"My," said Hans, "I've lost track of the time. I think we'll finish this game tomorrow, if it's all right with you, Simon."

"Yes, of course, but don't get up during the night to change any of the pawns, if you please."

Hans laughed, slapping Simon on the back. They went upstairs where, after all of the day's exercise, both physical and mental, they fell asleep promptly.

The next day consisted of more sports and conversation. The two were fast becoming good friends.

"Tomorrow we'll head for Hoher Freschen, across the border in Austria. It's a relatively easy climb. I want you to start off easy and then we'll gradually increase the intensity of the climbs before we attempt the more difficult peaks. I've arranged for us to use a cottage outside of Dornbirn, not too far from the mountain."

"I'm quite excited about all of this," Simon explained.

"It should be fun," agreed Hans.

7

The two left early the next morning, arriving at the Dornbirn cottage shortly before dusk. As they entered the cottage they encountered a short, stout woman in peasant dress.

"Good evening, sir," she said curtsying. "I have laid out the table for your supper. The larder is well-stocked. Please, sir, let me know if you require anything further. I shall come back tomorrow morning to bring fresh milk, and to see if you need anything else."

"We shall probably be out by then, *Frau* Mueller, but I shall leave a note for you if we do need anything further. Thank you for your help."

"Yes sir," she curtsied, "a good night to you," and as she left the cottage she said, "sir, we are all dreadfully sorry about your uncle's death."

"Thank you, *Frau* Mueller," Hans replied as the servant left.

"Did *Frau* Mueller know your uncle?" Simon inquired.

"Oh yes, quite well. He owned all of the land here, including this cottage and the farm."

Simon and Hans supped simply, on soup, dark bread and butter, cheese, sausage, and eggs. This was followed by steaming coffee and a *torte*, that *Frau* Mueller had baked. Immediately afterwards the chess board was placed on the table. The two sipped brandy and continued their never-ending chess game until the heaviness of the brandy and the hypnotic flames leaping at them from the hearth clouded their minds and reduced them to a languid stupor. They started to stumble to their beds on the opposite side of the room. Simon went first, Hans followed, falling over his suitcase.

"Here," said Simon, "let me place it on this ledge for you, so it'll be out of the way."

Simon reached for the adjacent, wooden chair, stepped on it and placed the suitcase on the ledge. That done, he turned around to step down, the chair collapsing in the process. Hans, following immediately behind, attempted to grab Simon in order to halt the fall. Simon fell into Hans' arms and, as Simon turned around, the two were face-to-face. Hans' eyes reflected themselves in Simon's. Hans looked at his face in the mirror of Simon's eyes and then he observed Simon's face with its jaunty boyishness. The men stood there first looking at each other, and then into each other; theirs was an unfulfilled longing, and they each waited for the other to give a signal that it was acceptable to proceed with its fulfillment. Hans could wait no longer and he placed his arms around Simon's body and slowly, but cautiously drew it towards him. Simon again gazed into Hans' eyes with a look that turned more serious, a look that invited Hans' to take the next step. The two men's lips came closer; slowly and deliberately they met. Hans' tongue left the confines of his mouth and explored Simon's lips and, sensing no reluctance on Simon's part, slowly moved his tongue further into Simon's welcoming mouth. The two tongues touched sensuously, exploring and tasting each other. The men's breathing became rapid, and increased in short gasps as their hands felt each other's bodies. They fell into the first available bed; Hans quickly removed Simon's clothing and then his own. The two naked bodies, laying side by side, touched each other. They each felt their bodies' ever-increasing warmth; their fingers went up and down each other's skin, excitement intensifying with each second. Hans mounted Simon as he lay in bed, Hans' hot body heaving gently with punctuated breaths emanating from his mouth. Simon groaned in delight, just lying there and enjoying the sensation of what was happening. Hans arched his body as his tongue worked its way upwards from Simon's feet. He concentrated on each spot of Simon's leg or pelvis, before continuing to the next. They moved in rhythmic unison, their lips, their minds, and ultimately their whole beings, sensing each movement in an undulating ballet. As their rhythms increased so did their desires; they emitted stifled moans of joy, until finally, their moans changed to muffled groans as their brains exploded with the delight of each other. They both lay side by side for several moments, arms around each other savoring the beauty of their experience, and, with its ebb a renewed passion and desire to repeat the feelings that they had just experienced. They both started to make love again, smothering each other in kisses, attempting to satisfy that once-denied craving that manifested itself with succeeding waves of physical and emotional delight as their continued activities kept on feeding their mutual desires. Finally, many hours later, Hans took the ultimate step as Simon screamed and grimaced in pain, but ultimately relaxed to enjoy the experience. They finally went to sleep in each other's arms.

As day's first light entered the window Simon awoke, and realizing what had occurred, an enormous sense of guilt swept over him. He looked at Hans' sleeping body. Tears filled Simon's eyes as he lay in bed staring at the ceiling. Hans moved slowly as he awakened, stretched out his limbs and yawned. He turned towards Simon glancing at his tear-stained face.

"What's the matter, Simon? Why are you crying?"

"Hans, I'm consumed with guilt over what we did last night. I love Lily dearly and I would never want to hurt her."

"Nonsense," said Hans, "I love her too. We are men, Simon. We can do what we wish, be it with ourselves or other men and women."

"But it's wrong," countered Simon.

"Did you enjoy it? Be honest, Simon."

Simon looked at Hans' handsome face, so handsome that Simon just kept on staring.

"More than anything I've ever experienced," Simon replied.

Simon leaned over and kissed Hans. Hans lay in bed lightly stroking Simon's back with his finger tips. The excitement slowly welled up in both of them; Simon becoming the aggressor as he began to make love to Hans. He turned Hans over on his stomach and kept on kissing Hans' body, leaving hardly an inch untouched. It was such a handsome, strong body, he thought. Simon gently bit the flesh around Hans' buttocks, his kisses moving around Hans' body. He finally brought his body's full weight on top of Hans, moved his arms underneath Hans' chest and gently nuzzled the pliant flesh of Hans' nipples as Hans moaned with pleasure. Hans rolled over as Simon took the erect nipples between his teeth and sucked them softly. He pushed Hans' legs up and over, and, before Hans realized what was happening Simon entered him. Hans yelled out quickly and became silent as he experienced the fullness of Simon's being. They achieved climax in each other's arms, and, afterwards, just lay in bed, high on the achievements of their experience. They continued reveling in each other's bodies, until a knock on the door disrupted their activity. Hans jumped up quickly.

"Quick," he said, with urgency in his voice. "It must be *Frau* Mueller. Go into the other bed." Simon did this quickly as Hans' voice of inquiry boomed,

"Yes? Who is it?"

"It's me, sir, *Frau* Mueller."

Hans opened the front door, further securing his dressing gown around his naked body.

"Is there anything else you need, sir?"

"No, *Frau* Mueller," Hans replied. "We're fine."

"Can I prepare your breakfast for you?"

"We're fine, *Frau* Mueller, thank you for looking in. I don't think you need to bother stopping by again. We'll walk to your house when we're ready to depart; possibly your husband can drive us to the railroad station."

"Of course, sir."

"Good-bye, *Frau* Mueller. Thank you again."

"My pleasure, sir. It is an excellent day for climbing. I do hope you enjoy it."

"Thank you, *Frau* Mueller," Hans echoed, and he then shut and bolted the door.

Simon left his bed, his lithe, nude body chilled by the crisp, morning air. Hans opened his robe slightly, walked towards Simon, and opened his robe more. Simon walked in front of him as Hans closed the robe around the two and heated their bodies with each other's warmth; this aroused them. They returned to bed and to the continued rejoicing of their pleasures. They made love and fell asleep. Hans re-lit the fire. After eating some cheese, dark bread and butter, downed with cups of hot coffee and milk, they sat and played chess and talked endlessly. They returned to bed to continue their mutual passion.

As the day wore on, and the sun shone high in the sky, Hans said:

"It's getting quite late, if we're going to do any hiking today. I think it's too late to attempt the mountain climb."

"Hans," replied Simon, "I feel that I just want to lie here in bed. I feel filled with the heavens, as if I'm no longer a part of this earth, but I am a bit tired. It's a hard thing to explain."

Hans laughed and said:

"Well, m' boy, we *have* engaged in quite a bit of physical activity."

Simon retorted with more laughter as he came towards Hans and cradled Hans' head in his hands. It wasn't long before they resumed their love-making. This continued with occasional breaks for food, a cup of tea, a game of chess, but sunset found them sipping brandy and hot cocoa, nude, except for their dressing gowns. They returned to bed, both exhausted from their activity, but they would awake and resume it, from time to time.

The next morning as they breakfasted on boiled eggs accompanied by bread, butter, and jam, Simon said:

"Hans, I've loved Lily like a sister, since we were both children. Neither of our parents had more than one child, so we've been particularly close to each other. I love Lily very much, and I have a deep, deep sense of guilt about what's happened. I think I'll have trouble facing her again. I don't know how I can act."

"Simon, I thought we went over this," replied Hans. "I told you that I love Lily. I love her more than I've ever loved anybody. I want to spend the rest of my life with her, and I want to give her everything I can, and I want her to have my children. We already have a head start with my Cousin Paul, but I want a son of my own. I'm not sorry about what you and I have done, Simon, or the feelings that we've experienced. It was, and is, very beautiful, but you must not feel guilty. I have absolutely no guilt. In our society it's standard and acceptable for men to have their *garçonierre* where they can entertain the woman of their choice. So, what if society bans what we have done? It's done by so many, married and single alike, but not mentioned in polite company. It exists, like so many other things in our lives. Also, why must we turn our backs on it? I accept it for what it is. No, Simon, I feel no guilt about what has happened."

Hans approached Simon and took him in his arms. Simon started to sob.

"Simon, Simon, what is the matter?"

"Hans, I can't help it. I'm overwhelmed with such guilt."

"What are your feelings, Simon? We're both men, both close. We have shared many happy hours together in mutual pursuits, both sexual and otherwise, that have given us great pleasure."

"How can you face Lily after what we've done, Hans?"

"I've told you, Simon. I love Lily, and when I'm with her I'll love her even the more."

"You would do this while I'm in your company, Hans?"

"Why not, Simon? Could you not do likewise if the situation was reversed?"

"I think I'd have a great deal of difficulty with this, Hans."

"But, Simon, why?"

"Because, Hans," Simon stammered, "because I've fallen in love with you," he blurted out quickly.

Hans, startled by Simon's revelation stepped back, threatened by what was said.

"I can see, Hans, that you do not share my feelings," said Simon dejectedly.

"I've said nothing," Hans muttered, "I don't think I can allow myself this luxury, even, if it exists . . . and if it exists I dare not recognize it, either to myself or anyone else."

"Why," replied Simon angrily, "after that pretty speech you just made?"

"Simon," replied Hans, "you don't understand, making love and being in love are two separate circumstances. I'm not saying that I don't care for you. I am saying that I cannot allow myself this luxury."

"But, why, why?" asked Simon. "Does it have to do with loving Lily? Do you mean that you say you love me, even though you love her? Can a man love more than one person, whether they be men or women?"

"Of course, dear Simon. One can love many different people in many different ways. You must realize that I have a duty to my wife, my country and myself. I can't let my emotions stand in the way of these duties. I know that my duties are my destiny. I don't think that the English, as much as I admire them, share this kind of feeling."

Simon started to sob uncontrollably.

"Hans, I don't think I can live without you."

Hans took Simon in his arms, as a father whose son had been injured, and said:

"Simon, Simon, Simon, my dear Simon. Of course I shall never forget what we have shared. You will see, though, that as time passes, your feelings will change, and you'll go more easy on yourself and find a companion or mate, regardless of gender, who will please you. Have you never loved before?"

"No, no, Hans, you are the first, and I think maybe the last."

"I think not," said Hans. "You are young and beautiful. You'll find somebody or somebody will find you, and the marvelous experiences and feelings that we have had will renew themselves within you, and they will renew themselves on an even higher and greater plane than we have experienced."

"I somehow doubt that. I don't see how my mind can be capable of any greater love than I have just experienced with you."

"You'll see, my darling Simon, you'll see," said Hans, as he placed his index finger on Simon's wet cheek. "Simon?"

"Yes, Hans."

"Simon..."

"Yes, Hans, tell me."

Hans stood opposite, staring at Simon. Hans had the look of a dejected child, but the libido of a mature adult. He might have minimized his affair with Simon, but he wanted more than just a passing fling.

"Tell me, tell me Hans, you want to tell me that you love me, but you can't find the words to tell me. Tell me."

Hans said nothing, but held Simon close to him and Simon could feel Hans' body quivering. He looked at Hans and saw that strong jaw and tough face wither with a feeling of sensitivity of which he thought Hans was incapable. Hans drew upon every strength in his body to control his emotions successfully.

"I love you, Hans, and I know that you love me, even though you can't get yourself to tell me."

"We had best return to Konstanz," said Hans, rapidly changing the conversation. "The Mueller farmhouse is just a few kilometers walk. *Herr* Mueller will fetch our baggage."

"I don't think I could step up to take it down," laughed Simon, feigning a display of humor, "not unless you were standing next to me to catch me if I fell. I feel like crying. Hans, I cannot return to Konstanz now, maybe never. Lily may have already returned from Berlin. I just can't face her or even be under the same roof with her while you're present. I'd like to return to England immediately. You can tell Lily I had to return on urgent business and ship the remainder of my clothes to me. I hope you understand, Hans."

"Of course," Hans replied sadly.

The two walked in silence to the Mueller farmhouse. *Herr* Mueller quickly hitched his horse, went back to the cottage, placed their luggage in the carriage. He drove the men to Bregenz, on the southeast side of the Bodensee, the lake whose crown is the city of Konstanz. The train to Zurich arrived where Simon would make connections for his return to England. *Herr* Mueller brought Simon's luggage to the train and placed it on the overhead rack. As Simon boarded the train he wanted to reach out to Hans to hug and to kiss him, but that would have been unseemly. Each man, a product of his own environment, deeply felt those feelings that he could not publicly express. It would have been acceptable for an Italian or a Russian, but they were neither, and so the depths of their feelings were constricted and externally buried. As the train slowly left the station Hans could see the tears in Simon's eyes. Simon continued to hang halfway out of the compartment window. Hans stood, immobile, his iron will resisting the sadness and its expression that he felt so deeply. Duty above all, he thought, but it does take its toll.

Hans' train arrived shortly thereafter. He boarded it, thanked *Herr* Mueller, and sat silently, deep within his thoughts until he heard the conductor's call:

"Konstanz, Konstanz."

Hans' driver, Keltmann, opened the coach door. Hans entered and sat silently during the ride home. The butler bowed as Hans walked though the heavy, oak doors of the von Wallenstadt home.

"Hans, Hans, darling," Lily called out as she glided down the regal staircase to embrace her husband. "I'm so happy you're home, dear. Did you all have a good time? Tell me all about it. Where's Simon?"

"Yes, yes, my darling, let me take off my coat first," he answered as he lifted her off her feet, whirled her around, placed her down, kissed her and laughed.

They walked into the adjacent room, laughing and talking excitedly as Lily closed the door behind them.

8

The Germans were challenging the world, wanting it to realize that their nation was its master. Hans and Friedrich, gentleman military officers, now spent much of their time in the chancellery. They worked closely with Helmuth von Moltke, Chief of the German General Staff.

On July 28, 1914, Austria-Hungary declared war against Serbia. On July 30, as Russia mobilized to come to Serbia's aid, Austria-Hungary ordered full mobilization. On July 31, the Kaiser's government reacted to the Russian preparation by advising them that it must be stopped within twelve hours. An ultimatum was then delivered to France, demanding that within eighteen hours she must let Germany know whether she would remain neutral if Germany attacked Russia. France was completely non-committal, but at four o'clock on the afternoon of August 1, the French mobilization began. Shortly thereafter Germany set its wheels in motion, and declared war against Russia. A German invasion of neutral Luxembourg began, followed by an invasion of Belgium; when that occurred, Belgium's King Albert appealed to France and Great Britain for help.

On August 4, the British Ambassador in Berlin, Sir Edward Goschen, advised the German government that Belgian neutrality must be respected; at 11:00 p.m., August 4, 1914, Britain declared war against Germany.

Thus began the most devastating war that history had ever known. It involved over 90% of the world's population and the deaths of over eight million people. Battles would take place in Europe, Africa, and Asia, on the land, on the seas, and for the first time—in the air. As news reached Lily Mendelssohn-Bartholdy von Wallenstadt, her once happy life was to change its course.

"Hans," Lily said to her husband, "how am I to go to England to visit with family, and what about dear Cousin Simon? What's to happen to all of us?"

"Lily, dear," countered Hans, "there's little to worry about. I'm sure the whole matter will be settled quickly, and life will resume its normal course."

"But Hans, what of papa? How will he get home? He was to stop in England first. Will my letters reach him in America, or in England if he's there? Will his letters reach me?"

"Darling, don't fret so," said Hans, "you're setting up situations that we may not have to be concerned about. I'm sure this entire thing will end quickly."

Shortly thereafter, Hans and Lily moved to Berlin as dictated by Hans' military duties. He spent many days and nights at the Chancellery. Lily was disturbed by his absence. The amounts of time he spent there did little to assuage her fears. As she and Hans lay in bed at night and Hans held and loved her with ever greater intensity, she felt cared for, wanted and needed. Yet, in spite of that, Lily sensed that Hans' daily involvement with the war occupied his mind, destroying the exclusivity that their relationship had once known. So Lily wrote long, loving letters to her father, played the piano and attended teas and social gatherings, while Hans busied himself with his military obligations and the camaraderie of his upper-class male companions. Hans was arranging the logistics of troop transport. It took a great deal of planning to move troops with the accompanying materiél and supplies to the front. As these procedures were set in place he next turned his talents to planning for troop offensives. Lily devoted much of her time to the war effort. Wounded troops started filtering back from the fronts and into local hospitals. Lily frequently gave concerts to these patients, but with a deep concern to be of greater use, she decided to become a nurse in order to help the wounded. They were honored to be attended by such a well-known figure.

Solomon Mendelssohn-Bartholdy was in New York when war began. He was ambivalent about the situation, but he was a true German. He supported the Fatherland; yet he was sympathetic to the British with whom he had such close family and business ties. He would play and re-play the scenario repeatedly in his mind. Germany was his country, and ultimately he must support the country in which he was born, reared and loved. He appreciated Germany's technical achievements, military might, and business leadership. It had, after all, granted him status and wealth. As with most German citizens, he was completely loyal to the country in which he lived. He, as most German males, subscribed to the *Übermensch* (Superman) theory, but in his view he was part of the class to which the *Übermenschen* belonged. He had embraced the faith of Martin Luther to belong more fully to the nation that he loved. *Herr* Mendelssohn-Bartholdy had no doubts in his mind that Germany would triumph in the conflict. He was concerned for his daughter's safety, but this was tempered by the knowledge that she was safe in Berlin, protected from all the horrors of war. On May 2, 1915, he sailed for Liverpool. He was advised by the British office in New York that, due to his British family and business connections, he could do this without any problem. He was sure the war would end quickly and he would be returning to Germany forthwith. On May 7, 1915, as his ship, heading towards Liverpool, was passing the Irish coast, German submarine torpedoes hit the vessel with a subsequent loss of over 1,000 lives. *Herr* Mendelssohn-Bartholdy was one of those passengers whose body still rests beneath the sea, along with the sunken ship, the ill-fated Lusitania.

Lily heard the news of *Herr* Mendelssohn-Bartholdy's death shortly thereafter. Stunned by the tragedy, she went into a period of deep mourning and depression. Hans had a Mass said for his father-in-law at the local parish church where he and Lily worshipped each Sunday. Family, friends, and parishioners were quite supportive. Lily, a pragmatist, continued with her life as before, but the knowledge that she would never be able to see her beloved father again left a void in her heart. She buried her sorrows in her piano playing and voluntary nursing duties as Hans continued his work at the Chancery.

The year 1915 slipped by without producing the anticipated German victory. Hans von Wallenstadt now reported to General Erich von Falkenhayn who replaced von Moltke as Chief of the German General Staff. Germany's battles with the Allies drained the country of all of its resources. All supplies were concentrated at the fronts—this resulted in massive civilian shortages of food, fuel, and consumer goods. The country was glum and depressed, since the popular thought that the war would end many months before was dashed. Berlin was bleak with sunless days and empty streets, except for an occasional smattering of women, children, and old men.

The British successfully blockaded Germany on the sea. Lily and her maid, Helga, would alternate standing in long lines for food, along with the rest of the civilian population. Dairy products were available as well as turnips, turnips, and more turnips. What was once poured into the cattle troughs was now served on German tables.

The battle that had begun in February lasted through December. In spite of all the deprivation, Lily and Hans were relatively happy during this period. Although war made its demands, they were able to share time together, a luxury that was denied to many. Hans' love for Lily, as well as Lily's love for Hans, ripened; spurred by the awareness that their mutual existence rested on a tether that might be yanked away from them without notice. The knowledge that their next separation might be their last was always present at the back of their minds, but they disregarded this and rose above it. The war had given them an undiscovered bravery that might never have bloomed during peace. Hans went back and forth from Berlin to the front;

from the front to Berlin. He traveled on the unending trains that brought supplies to the front and returned with the severely injured and the coffins of the dead.

Hans was to leave Berlin for the front in two days; the interlude of his private peace was ending. He and Lily spent their last two days together. He sat at her side as she played the piano. She would finish and he would kiss her hands, her face, her lips. They completely surrendered themselves to each other and the beauty and depth of their love-making was intense and tinged with an unspoken anxiety.

As the driver's knock on the door echoed throughout the cold house, Hans turned to say good-bye to Lily. He moved towards her, and for the first time since she had met him, she noticed his eyes filling with tears. Lily had donned a cloak; her face was filled with determination.

"Why have you put on your cloak, my darling? Are you cold?"

"I'm going with you to the train station," she replied.

"No," he said, "I want you to stay here."

"Hans," Lily said, grasping his hands, "I'm going with you. The small amount of time remaining is too precious to me to waste."

He had never seen such fire in her eyes.

"I love you too much to lose you, my darling," she continued.

"You must come back to me soon, you must," she pleaded.

Hans said good-bye to Helga as he and Lily entered the carriage. They sat down and held each other's hands. Hans could not look at Lily, for to do so would have meant an emotional outburst. Lily kept her gaze on him. He finally turned towards her and their eyes met. Lily's were filled with hope; Hans' were glazed. They sat, in silence, until they reached their destination.

The railroad station was buzzing with activity. The hissing locomotives threw their hot, steamy, white breath into the cold, winter air. Hans stopped in front of his compartment; they faced each other. Lily said nothing. Hans' lips moved slightly, but his words were soundless. He entered the coach without embracing

Lily. He kept looking at her standing on the platform. The train whistle blew, the locomotive chugged and Lily walked along the platform as if hypnotized. She stopped and watched Hans. He kept on looking at her from the window until their images of each other were but an unforgettable memory.

Lily walked back along the platform towards the waiting carriage. The day became damper and colder and more empty than ever before. She walked into the frigid house. Helga took her cloak as Lily went into the conservatory and sat at the piano. She played and played, her fingers gliding over the keys in a restless frenzy of determination and sadness. Finally her hands fell upon the cold ivory, producing the discord that she felt in her mind. She sobbed quietly and went to rest on the sofa where she drifted into the brief respite that sleep provided.

The next day, March 17, Hans left the train at Maubeuge and joined Ludendorff's staff. Almost a year later, in February of 1918, Hans was able to return to his wife.

"I knew you would return to me, my darling," said Lily, as they embraced at the doorway.

Lily noticed how exhausted he looked. She held her husband's arm tightly, as if to proclaim that he was hers and the army could not have him any longer. She took him into the music room where he sat on the sofa. She removed his boots and went to embrace him again, but he had fallen into a deep sleep. Lily covered him with a quilt and sat on a chair beside him, holding his hand. She offered a silent prayer of thanks for her husband's safe return, and fell asleep on the chair, still holding Hans' hand—her eyes moist with tears of gratitude.

They were together for most of the month of March, in between the time Hans spent at the *Reichstag*. Lily, busy as ever, was assisting as a nurse in the hospital and teaching piano to young, gifted students at the *Singakademie*. The war was a huge drain that siphoned the spirit and joy of this proud city, but the Prussian adherence to duty and obligation motivated most citizens to persevere.

9

At the end of March, 1918, Hans von Wallenstadt was assigned to work directly for General Eric Ludendorff who was preparing for the Spring offensive. The attack began at 4:40 that morning on March 21, as German artillery opened fire. Visibility was near zero as the German troops pushed through British lines, heading for the Somme River.

Hans, as Ludendorff's aide, was at the front for the first time. He followed about one-half mile behind the first rank. The fog enshrouded the entire landscape and Hans had no idea where he was. Each step he took seemed to echo and re-echo around him. As the fog lifted he found that he and his men were in a British encampment, both sides startled by this sudden realization. In the distance, advancing towards Hans, from the lifting fog, was a vaguely familiar face.

"Hans? Hans?" cried the British soldier.

Hans was shocked into immobility as Simon Mendelssohn came running towards him. They paused for a moment. Simon continued running towards Hans. They both wanted to hug and console each other, a drop of water in the bucket of hell. Suddenly, as their outstretched arms almost touched each other, a shot rang out, a bullet piercing Simon's neck. Simon's expression of joy changed to one of pain and horror. Friedrich running behind Hans had thought that Simon was going to attack and shot him. Hans knelt beside Simon and held his hand. It's all a nightmare; it's all untrue; this cannot be, he thought.

"Nurse, nurse," shouted Hans in English.

Simon tried to speak, but the blood spilling from his mouth was suffocating him. Simon looked into Hans' eyes, and with his last breath whispered:

"You were wrong, Hans, I've never loved anyone else," and his words trailed into unintelligibility, and vanished as he ebbed into unconsciousness and the peace of a soldier's death.

Hans looked at Simon's lifeless body with its vacant, green eyes staring upwards. He knelt down besides it. He touched Simon's face and his lips, coated with saliva. He felt Simon's warm blood dripping down his fingers. He stood up in dismay—too stunned for tears and wiped some of the ever-present dirt from his trousers, more from force of habit than concern. He stared silently at Simon; oddly he felt his penis getting hard. He turned towards the silent Friedrich, standing beside him.

"He was my wife's Cousin Simon, Friedrich, the one with whom I went mountain climbing when you couldn't come. I'll miss him dreadfully, Friedrich."

Hans' eyes filled with tears and he looked upwards towards a heaven that was not his to see. He could not continue speaking, his voice choked in his throat. There was carnage all around—the pervasive smell of spent cartridges and fires heavy in the air, the specter of death at every turn. German troops kept pouring into the area, quickly outnumbering and surrounding the British, shooting all those who resisted and taking the remainder as prisoners. British medics were treating English and Germans alike, without regard to nationality, saving and aiding whomever they could.

Hans and Friedrich walked further into the British encampment. They noticed that the British had supplies of chocolates, cigarettes and food stores that the German troops had not seen for years. The German leaders had convinced their troops that the French and British had less than they.

"Friedrich, I've lost my spirit, my determination. I'm sick of this damned war. I don't have the will to continue. We've grown up together, went to university together, lived almost our entire lives together, Friedrich. I feel the young person that I once was is gone. I used to have an innocence, or so I thought. I feel old, Friedrich, so old."

Hans' feelings towards Friedrich were ambivalent. He loved him as a friend, but hated him for killing Simon, even though he knew it was to save his life. He wished a shot would kill Simon and then himself. He was sick of war.

"Friedrich, I want to be by myself for a few minutes. I'm just going to rest behind that tree."

"I understand, Hans, I'll wait for you here."

Hans sat down at the base of the tree, staring into the fog, filled with anger, hopelessness and a deep yearning for Simon. He opened his fly, pulled out his penis and masturbated until he climaxed just as Friedrich appeared.

"Hans," Friedrich called out, "are you okay?"

Friedrich looked at Hans and knelt down next to him. He put his arm around Hans' shoulder and said:

"Hans, I know what I've done has hurt you, but you know my feelings for you. I was only trying to protect you."

"Of course, Friedrich, you've bailed me out of scrapes almost all my life, and I know what you've done was for my own good. How were you to know? The whole damned thing is so farfetched, so is everything—our lives here, the war, it's all so unreal. It's like watching a lousy play and acting in it at the same time. I'm tired of it all, so tired."

"Hans, we must do what we have to for Germany. It's not going to be forever, Hans. Try to pull yourself together."

Friedrich helped Hans to his feet, gave his shoulders a squeeze and they walked slowly towards the sound of the guns at the front.

The lack of supplies increased the desertion rate amongst German soldiers, but there were some fantastic advances in the fighting that continued. Ultimately the British and French held their ground, and for the first time—in June of 1918 at the Marne

River, the German troops encountered American soldiers. As the numbers of American troops arriving in France increased, the balance of strength shifted from the Germans to the Allies. On July 18, the first counter-offensive with Americans involved stopped the German advance. By August 3, the Germans were being pushed back. It was in mid-September that France's General Foch altered the rail lines that provided the Germans with supplies. In October, Ludendorff was close to a nervous breakdown and he returned to Berlin. Hans accompanied him on a train ride that seemed endless. He could not purge his mind of Simon's body that lay before him whenever he closed his eyes.

10

It was now December of 1918. Hans' carriage arrived at the house entrance. Helga, cleaning cloth in hand, had opened the door; her face filled with a look of sadness and tears. But, her expression brightened when she saw Hans. He entered the house and could hear Lily playing the piano in the conservatory. Hans opened the doors quietly and beamed with joy as he watched Lily play. He turned around to shut the doors and Lily, sensing a presence in the room, turned her head to see her husband once more.

"Oh Hans," she cried, "My darling, thank God you've returned to me again. Thank God! You've been back and forth to the front so many times, when will you be home for good?"

Tears of joy streamed down her cheeks as Hans, who had assumed a strong Teutonic demeanor, melted in her embrace.

"Oh Hans," Lily said, "I knew you would come back to me. We both seem to be reliving the same scene over again, but I'd gladly relive it a million times than face my life without you."

They were always tense when they first met after such a time span. Lily torn apart by the absence of her husband, Hans anticipating his return to Lily with his sexual ambivalence like that of a clock's pendulum whose ticking he never heard. The entire war was still unreal to them. They hated the war vehemently and longed to have the security of their previously comfortably ordered lives returned to them.

After a period of sitting and chatting, the reality of Hans' return had begun to sink in and the two were much more comfortable and relaxed. Hans filled with pride when Paul, his small cousin whom they were rearing, waddled into the room with Helga.

"He's gorgeous, Lily, and you've done such an excellent job with him," said Hans, as he lifted the smiling child into the air.

Hans played with the child for a while until Helga took him out of the room. The two continued to discuss the events of the time.

"Hans, it's awful, all of this devastation," said Lily.

"Yes, darling, the war stinks."

Hans took Lily's hand and his eyes brimmed over as he said:

"Lily, I am thankful you're safe here in Berlin, away from all the horrors of massive death and the war."

"Yes, dear," continued Lily, "I don't think any of us here at home can realize how awful the war at the front must be, but darling, I mean the devastation here in Berlin."

"In Berlin?" replied Hans with a semi-laugh.

"Yes, in Berlin," countered Lily with extreme seriousness. "Hundreds and hundreds are dying here every day. *Herr* Schmidt, the butcher, three of my students, *Frau* Kranz."

"But Lily, there's no fighting taking place in Berlin. What are you talking about?" Hans said quizzically.

"Hans, there's an epidemic of influenza. It's like the Plague. People are sick and dying all over the place. None of us leaves the house unless it is absolutely necessary."

"Oh," he said quietly, momentarily stunned.

He was absorbed with the war and his own survival. He did not concern himself with much of anything else and gave little thought to what was occurring elsewhere. Hans' aim was to do the best job he could and return home alive. Now the World War was accompanied by a world pestilence and people on all continents were fighting a more severe and more ruthless enemy.

"Lily," said Hans, as his mind returned to his own concern, "The Kaiser wants peace, the war cannot go on much longer."

"I'm glad, Hans. I'm tired, so tired of all of this. I want our lives to be normal, and . . ."

Suddenly her face brightened, reinforcing a look of pleasure and joy.

"What, darling, what?" said Hans with a touch of anticipation in his voice.

"Sweetheart, with all the excitement I didn't even mention it. We're going to have a baby."

"Oh Lily, Lily," Hans replied tenderly. Again, he was at a loss to say anything further.

He took Lily by the hand and they went to their bedroom. Lily barely showed her pregnancy. Hans was intrigued with the life inside her. He placed his ear on her stomach as he kissed it and caressed it.

"Lily, I'm so excited. Our child, our child. What shall we name him?"

"Well dear," she replied. "It might be a she."

Hans laughed and said:

"I think we're going to be the parents of a baby boy."

"Why, Hans, will you not love the child if it is a she?"

"My dearest," replied Hans, "it will be our child and I will love it regardless of its sex. How could you ask such a question?"

They both laughed. Hans looked at her lovingly. He put his arms around her petite frame, drew her close to him and kissed her tenderly. She felt the touch of his warm lips; those lips so denied her and so wanted. She became hot with desire.

"Our child, our child," he kept on repeating. "I want you, Lily. God how I want you. Is it okay?" he asked sheepishly.

"What do you mean, dear, is it okay?"

"Our baby, Lily, our baby, will making love affect it?"

"Now, darling, you're the innocent. You have nothing to worry about."

That said, he arose hurriedly, locked the door to the room, undressed himself and Lily and made love to her on the sofa. Hans always tried to acquit himself as a paragon of masculinity. At times he was uncomfortable making love to Lily. He felt he should do what was expected of him—no more, no less. He enjoyed his climaxes, but so often, his mind was not with Lily, but elsewhere.

Lily had never heard of the word "orgasm" nor had she ever experienced it. She loved Hans, to be sure, but she always felt that something was missing. They spent hours on the sofa before going upstairs to their bedroom. Helga had prepared a tray of sandwiches and tea. They ate the sandwiches and drank the tepid brew, laughing and talking until sleep came. They would sleep sporadically and fitfully, hold and love each other. It must have been about three o'clock in the morning when Lily said:

"Hans, dear."

"Yes, Lily," Hans answered as he roused himself.

"How long do I have you for, my darling? Do you have to go back?"

"Yes, I have to, Lily. I don't know how soon, but my stay will have to be short. This is just for your ears," Hans commented, "but our troops are deserting. We're running out of food and supplies at the front, and at this point our troops are outnumbered. It has to end soon."

"It won't be any too soon for me, Hans."

This period that Hans and Lily spent together was more intense than ever. Every moment was a treasured luxury; they could not bear to be away from each other. They would touch and hold each other, as if this were a hedge against Hans' departure.

11

Hans had survived yet another trip to the front and returned home once more. He was a broken man. How could he translate the war's mass slaughter, the mass killing of human beings? Even though he tried to conceal his feelings behind a stiff formality while at work, Hans could carry on no longer; often he thought death would be a welcome respite to the horrors he witnessed. He carried Simon's death on his shoulders as if he were an ass overloaded with its burden. The house was cold and barren. Autumn had brought an unexpected cold snap and there had been no fuel for heating; all the coal had been diverted to the war effort. Helga would collect what wood she could, but there was never enough.

Hans became ill with influenza in late October. There was little the doctor could do. Lily spent all of her time at his side. She said to him in her grief:

"Darling, you will never die. You will live in our child."

Lily spent her days and nights in the room with him. Hans exhaled his last breath as Lily looked at his still-flushed face. She said nothing, arose and rang for Helga to bring her a cup of tea. She sat next to Hans' lifeless body as she held the cup in her hands, more to warm them than anything else. She placed the cup on the saucer, set it on the bed table, held Hans' hand, stroked his forehead, and wept softly.

She had never felt so empty, her father Solomon's death now affecting her more than it had ever done before. Previously, it had been the realization of an act in which she did not participate.

Yet, the death of her father was still a more distant loss, not the loss of a spouse with whom she shared her everyday life, and who would be the father of her child. Lily was almost barren of emotion. She was now one of the German war widows who at war's end would number 533,000.

Hans was buried in Berlin the very next day. There were few visitors, the fear of illness kept them from coming. Friedrich visited daily.

"Friedrich, I'm grateful that you spend all of this time here, but I don't want to keep you from your duties."

"Lily," he replied, "I have the need to be here so we can mourn our loss together. I miss him so much, Lily."

"I know," she said, as she clasped her hands around his, "you were so very close throughout your lives."

Friedrich shook his head sadly.

"What are you going to do now, Friedrich?"

"I'm quitting this damn army, or what's left of it, as soon as the war ends; we can't go on much longer. We have to build a new Germany, Lily. I want to help do that, but first I've many things to take care of. The war has damaged us all on so many fronts. We have to heal ourselves somehow. Good-bye Lily, God bless you and Germany."

Lily resumed her teaching and volunteer nursing duties immediately, as a therapy to keep her mind occupied with things other than her grief. Few students would venture outdoors, but there was always a dedicated cadré who personified the staunchest traditions of Teutonic bravery. There were also those who would risk almost anything to take a lesson with Lily Mendelssohn-Bartholdy.

As Lily neared her term of pregnancy, she stopped teaching at the *Songakademie* and spent most of her time at home. She received friends, students, and well-wishers; even General Ludendorff had stopped by to pay his condolences. The awareness of never seeing Hans again was fully experienced; it hurt, and the loneliness was felt deeply.

Berlin was restive. Ludendorff resigned on October 27. He wanted the fighting to stop, but the Kaiser wanted to continue. The German Admiralty, out of defiance, decided to make one last stand. The day that Ludendorff resigned, the fleet was ordered to sea. A mutiny occurred, the sailors demanded the Kaiser's abdication, amnesty, and peace. Finally, the Kaiser left Berlin for Army headquarters at Spa.

Germany was always a pawn of its military, who felt that civilians should exist to support them, but now the tide had turned. There was now a complete breakdown of authority within the country. On November 8, riots erupted and a full scale revolution took place. Lily could hear the commotion in the distance. She and Helga huddled anxiously, shivering under blankets in the cold rooms. The curtains were drawn and the house was dark, cold and damp, a single candle burning in front of them. How much longer can we go on like this? thought Lily—but we will persevere, Hans must be proud of us.

Kaiser Wilhelm finally abdicated. He crossed the border into The Netherlands where he remained until his death in 1942, never again to set foot on German soil. Germany capitulated to the Allies on the morning of November 11. The armistice was signed in General Koch's railway carriage and took effect at 11:00 that morning. The war had ended.

In Berlin, at three o'clock that afternoon, Lily Mendelssohn-Bartholdy von Wallenstadt gave birth to a daughter whose features were a replica of her father's. The infant was christened several days later at the local parish church, Friedrich acting as Godfather. The newborn was named Hannah, in memory of the father whom she would never see.

Lily was a changed person, as were many in Germany. The war had depleted the morale of the citizens, Lily was no exception. She never had the need to involve herself in anything but culture; financial matters were always taken care of for her. Necessity now demanded Lily's intervention, she was beset with difficulty. Now widowed, she had to deal with finances, a subject as foreign to her as another galactic system. The following week she visited with Hans' attorney, *Herr* Blätten, who managed the von Wallenstadt funds. Lily discovered that Hans had left no will or stipulation for Lily's support.

"It is most likely, Countess," intoned the supercilious Blätten, "that the reason your husband had made no express provision for you was that he knew you came from a well-to-do family."

"Yes," countered Lily, "but my father conferred a sizable dowry to my husband upon my marriage, and I am rearing my husband's uncle's son. I think provision should have been made for the child."

"Countess," said Blätten, "the entire situation is academic since the von Wallenstadt funds were almost wiped out by the war. Also, the estate owes money that it does not have. Investments were made in companies that were quite reliable before the war, but are now bankrupt. There are no assets left, with one exception. The Count had remanded that, in the event he predeceased you, a trust fund from discrete moneys would be established for any of your issue, the interests to be paid, per capita, not per stirpes, with the principal to be so divided when these issue reach their majority."

Lily sat there ignorant and oblivious to all of the legal blather.

"What about the von Wallenstadt properties?" queried Lily.

"Countess, the family estate was in the hands of creditors before the Count's marriage to you. The family was not in good financial standing. We had hoped, through the investments made, that funds would be realized to offset this situation. As I said, the war destroyed those areas where, under normal circumstances, a profit might have been made. Since you have a daughter, Countess, the full amount of interest will be payable to you as her parent and guardian, until the age of her majority, at which time the principal will go to your daughter."

"And what is that sum, *Herr* Blätten?"

"It is close to 4,000 *marks* monthly; that should enable you to live in some degree of comfort. Have you investigated your father's holdings, Countess?"

"Yes, *Herr* Blätten, my father left me his entire estate, but the values on his German holdings have depreciated since the war. The British assets have been frozen; I don't know when they'll be released. I am hopeful that I'll be able to realize something from them when all of this war business is settled."

"As I said, Countess," replied Blätten, "I think you should be quite comfortable. Of course, if you concertize you should realize additional income over and above that which you shall be receiving. I can contact your uncle, Israel Mendelssohn, the banker, to handle these affairs; there will be the usual fee for these services."

"You know, *Herr* Blätten, you speak to me as if I were an idiot. My uncle has his own problems right now, and he doesn't need mine to add to them. I'll admit my financial affairs were always handled by my father and then my husband, but I am far from being a school girl. You talk to me this way because you feel I'm a woman and ignorant. You would deal with me differently if I were a man.

"I'm sick of the condescension to women in our society. I am not a *hausfrau*. I am a career pianist who has earned money and I am not dependent on men to carry on with my life. You men make me sick. You create wars, die and leave your women alone to find their own way. Well, I will find my way," she said with determination. "We should kick out you drones as the bees do. I'll be in tomorrow to sign the necessary papers. Thank you, *Herr* Blätten."

Herr Blätten sat there stunned and said nothing.

Lily left his office and burst into tears. Hans, she thought, I miss you so.

The peace treaty, signed at Versailles in the spring of 1919, was harsh on Germany. Vast tracts of land and colonies were lost. The indemnity to be paid was enormous. West and East Prussia were severed by a newly formed Polish corridor where the Baltic port of Danzig was to be located. Reparations to be paid by 1928 were one billion gold *reichmarks*. The Socialist government signing the peace treaty was vilified by the German citizens who felt it highly unjust. The switch was made from a monarchy to a democracy. Political chaos occurred throughout the government as the Weimar Republic was established. Violence and murder were endemic and lawlessness raged throughout the nation.

Several months after the signing of the peace treaty, Lily received a letter from her family in England.

London, S.W. 2
4 April, 1917

Dearest Lily,

I received your last letter, the first one since the end of this horrible war. We wish you could have been here in England with us. We were truly saddened to hear of your husband's death; tragedy seems to beget tragedy. I am sorry, my darling, to add yet another misfortune to your list. We had been notified that your Cousin Simon had been killed in France. There weren't many details about it, but he has been awarded a medal posthumously. I look at the piece of metal, an honor given by England to be sure; but it cannot replace the emptiness I feel at losing my dear son.

Simon married, Lily, just after the start of the war. We had sent you an invitation, but I doubt that you had ever received it. He has left a wife and a young son. I am enclosing a photograph of the three of them. I know that you loved each other as brother and sister. We have lost so much that cannot be replaced. I pray to the almighty

God that we shall find peace in our hearts, in spite of our losses.

Lily, dear, come to visit when you can, and plan to stay as long as you like. It might be best for you and the two children. Please give it serious consideration. Your Uncle Saul sends you his best wishes and begs you to come to England as soon as possible. He has not been well. I fear that the loss of your father, his brother Solomon, and then our son Simon, has only added to his incapacitation. We are getting old, child, and we do not have much family left. We want to hold on to the little that we have. We look forward to hearing from you.

With love and faith from your aunt,

Harriet Klar Mendelssohn

12

As the years went by it became clear that Hannah, although she had the von Wallenstadt looks, possessed the Mendelssohn-Bartholdy talent for artistry. In the true Mendelssohn-Bartholdy tradition, Lily and Hannah often performed together, usually pieces for four hands. Hannah loved music and would listen to her mother play for hours on end. Since Lily was Hannah's piano teacher it was not unusual that she could read music before she could read words.

Hannah was always neatly dressed in bright frocks, although Lily, like so many other German women, wore clothes whose dowdiness was only surpassed by the reflection of the time in which they lived. Clothes were expensive, and even those who could afford them would make do with what they had. The thriftiness experienced during the war became habitual.

After the assassination of Foreign Minister Walter Rathenau (a Jew who had many enemies), the political crisis caused economic chaos. The *mark* plummeted to worthlessness (4.2 *trillion marks* equaled US$1.00). All one heard in the streets was the disillusionment and loss of faith in the Weimar government.

Lily maintained a standard of living better than most of her peers. She had started to receive small sums of money, in pound sterling, that were sent to her from England. Lily's uncle, Israel Mendelssohn in the Berlin Mendelssohn bank was assisting, and an aunt of Lily's had died leaving a small bequest.

Lily was a patrician in her own right. Even during this difficult period she would entertain friends at tea, attend concerts and have guests attend her musicales. Life was difficult at best, but bearable. Her financial situation really started to improve when she accepted an invitation to play in London's Aeolian Hall. It meant additional income, in British pounds, a chance to see her father's family whom she had not seen since the war, and a change from the Berlin life of which she was so integral a part. She had a successful tour, and on returning to Berlin resumed her busy social life. At that time Lily moved to a small villa near Herr Strasse, in the fashionable Grunewald section.

It was at one of the receptions at the *Reich Musikkamer* that Lily was introduced to Christian Merth. She thought him plain, both in looks and demeanor. He had brown hair and eyes and a sallow face. The horn-rimmed glasses he wore added to his unattractive appearance.

"I have heard much about you, Countess," he said, making general conversation.

"Oh really, *Herr* Merth?" she replied in a cordial, but matter-of-fact tone of disinterest.

"Yes, madam, I have heard you play at many concerts and I have always been charmed by your talent, manner, and if I may say, good looks."

Lily found this last remark disconcerting, but she smiled demurely, thanked him, excused herself politely and went on to mix with some of the other guests. From time-to-time she would notice that he was staring at her. She would smile, exchange a polite nod and continue conversing with the others.

The following day a huge bouquet of roses was delivered. Helga brought them to Lily, who was seated at her pianoforte. This was a special instrument that she prized, since it was handed down from the Mendelssohn-Bartholdy family. The piano was given to Solomon Mendelssohn-Bartholdy's family by Felix's son, Paul. It was one that Felix and his sister Fanny had used. Lily looked up as Helga entered the room.

"Oh, Helga," she exclaimed, "what lovely roses. It's been

such a long time since we received flowers . . . and I haven't even given a performance."

Lily opened the envelope that accompanied the bouquet, pulled out the card and read:

> With all compliments,
>
> CM

CM . . . CM? Who is CM? She thought, and attributed it to one of her musical admirers. The following day another bouquet of roses was delivered, and the day after, and the day after that. Of course this piqued Lily's curiosity since she had no idea from whom they were. On the sixth day another delivery was made. Lily read the accompanying card:

> Countess, it would be my great pleasure to have you join me at dinner tomorrow evening. My car will pick you up at 7:00.
>
> CM

Who *is* this person? I cannot accept an invitation from someone I don't know, she mused. Nevertheless, by 6:30 the following evening, Lily was all dressed to dine; her curiosity intense.

The car arrived at 7:00 p.m. promptly. Helga was at the door as Lily was straightening the folds of her gown.

"Are you sure you don't know who this might be, Countess?" queried Helga.

"Well, I'll find out very soon, won't I?" said Lily.

"Good night, Countess," said Helga.

"Now don't wait up for me, Helga. Everything will be fine."

"Yes, madam," she replied as Lily stepped out into the cool night air.

It was beautifully clear and Lily was excited by the situation.

She was quite happy, and she wanted to stay that way. The driver presented her with another bouquet and escorted her into the waiting automobile.

The car stopped in front of the restaurant. Lily exited, holding the hem of her gown and properly balancing the floral bouquet. The restaurant Scala, a nightclub on Lutherstrasse in the Schöenberg district, was one of those avant garde cabarets that were so popular in Berlin at the time. Lily was escorted to a private room, elevated above the cabaret floor with a long, horizontal window facing the stage, but hidden from view on the main floor. The table was set for two with a small candle holder covered with a red shade; the illumination was quite dim.

From the shadows, at the far end of the room, Christian Merth emerged, impeccably dressed.

"Good evening, Countess. I am honored that you've accepted my invitation."

Lily remembered the face, but she could not place the name or where they had met. She smiled graciously as *Herr* Merth held her chair and gently pushed it towards the table until she was seated. He then went to his place at the opposite side.

"I have taken the liberty of ordering for us, Countess. I hope it pleases you."

"Of course," she said, discomforted by the sight of her admirer.

After the wine was poured the waiter asked,

"Shall I serve now, *Herr* Merth?"

Wonderful, Lily thought, now I know his name.

"Please," Merth replied and the waiter clicked his heels and exited.

Merth turned towards Lily and said:

"I have been looking forward to this moment ever since I met you at the *Reich Musikkamer.*"

Now it all fell into place for Lily and she sat back and started to relax.

She was tired of bearing the brunt of what, in her society, was a male responsibility. She wanted and needed male companionship and here, she thought, is the first man who has really paid attention to me since Hans died. She was softened by this and strove to overlook Merth's beady eyes peering through eyeglass lenses as he spoke. He's no Hollywood movie star, she thought, but it is a change of pace. I'll just enjoy dinner and that will be that.

Merth had an assertive personality, nonetheless Lily discerned a certain old-world softness and deference as he spoke—and speak he did for almost the entire evening. Lily was the perfect foil for his words. She would nod her head in response and found Merth convivial. She was quite mellowed by the time she and Merth finished coffee and after-dinner drinks. Shortly thereafter he arose, clicked his heels, came to Lily's side of the table, and took her hand in his. Lily rose as he bowed, kissed her hand and said:

"I must depart now, Countess. My driver will see you home."

"Thank you, *Herr* Merth, for a most enjoyable evening," Lily replied.

Merth exited quickly and as he did the driver entered and held the door open for Lily, escorted her to the waiting car and drove her home. Helga was at the door when Lily entered.

"Helga, why did you wait for me? You should have been sleeping by now."

Helga smiled, wished Lily a good night and went to her room. Lily went upstairs, undressed and collapsed into her bed; where she relived the evening in her thoughts. It was fun; she enjoyed the man's companionship. She went to sleep feeling better than she had in a long time. She hoped she would see *Herr* Merth again—and she was not disappointed.

The next day, promptly at noon, the bell rang and a delivery of flowers arrived. Lily read the card:

> Countess, it would give me great pleasure if you would join me at luncheon this Thursday at 12:30.
>
> CM

Lily was scheduled to teach that day. She asked the driver to wait and penned the following note.

> My dear *Herr* Merth:
>
> Thank you for your kind invitation to join you at luncheon this Thursday at 12:30. I regret that previous commitments preclude my acceptance.
>
> Cordially,
>
> Lily von Wallenstadt

The driver took the note, returning two hours later, at which time he presented Lily with the following:

> My dear Countess,
>
> May I ask you to join me at dinner, this Thursday evening at 8:00.
>
> CM

Lily indicated her acceptance to the driver.

Thursday evening the driver arrived at the appointed time, and the same procedure to the same restaurant was repeated. *Herr* Merth was seated at the table. He rose swiftly as Lily entered the room. He clicked his heels, kissed her hand and looked deeply into her eyes. The man's trying to make a pass, she thought. Flattering, but his looks are so plain. Hans was so handsome and this man is really ugly. Lily averted her gaze, but then returned his glance. It was a look of defiance. Merth brought his body directly in front of Lily, his face about an inch from hers and said:

"Countess, my days and nights have been filled with the anticipation of this meeting."

Lily felt his closeness, his warm breath on her lips and she was enveloped by the smell of his tobacco. She felt flattered, needed, wanted, and more secure than she had felt in a long time; without moving she replied, in a formal, but cool tone:

"It is my pleasure, *Herr* Merth. I am glad to see you again."

He escorted her to the table and they proceeded to dine. Few words were exchanged between them. *Herr* Merth would stare at her unabashedly, his eyes and every part of his body filled with desire for her. Lily felt his intentions, but feigned oblivion to the situation. *Herr* Merth said nothing; Lily said nothing. The two just sat there eating. *Herr* Merth looked at Lily with tenderness and longing. She returned his glance with a smile. The solitary candle on the table, the dimmed lights in the room, the headiness of the wine, all served to relax Lily. As the evening progressed, she found herself in an ethereal, hypnotic state. Midway through dinner, Merth rose, approached her, offered his hand and, without uttering a word took hers, indicating that she should rise and follow him. She liked the feel of her hand in his, it was strong, masculine, dominating. He placed himself directly in front of her and surrounded her petite frame with his arms, his face drew closer to hers and she was motionless as his lips pressed against hers. Merth's appearance became insignificant as Lily, sexually deprived for so long, responded to his advances. She felt heat rushing throughout her body as if she were being consumed by an inextinguishable fire. Slowly, her body started to tingle with a feeling of desire that she had never before known, her breath became more rapid; she began to turn limp. Merth placed his arm around her waist as he walked her into the adjoining room. How could this unattractive man elicit such feelings, she thought; but he did and she wanted more.

Lily barely noticed it in her ardor—a smallish, but adequate room with huge, heavy Viennese curtains and a small lamp burning on a table, surrounded by Belle Epoch furniture. There was a bed, headboard against the wall, adorned with smiling seraphim, who had undoubtedly witnessed many trysts, but whose perpetual smiles hid all of the assignations that they were prisoners to witness.

Herr Merth started to undo Lily's dress and she was powerless to resist. She wanted to feel his touch, to be consumed, dominated, and to explore this new and exciting experience.

"Countess," he said, "I have wanted you more than you could ever know, more than any woman I have ever met."

Her breath came in a series of ecstatic gasps, her power of speech was gone. She reached towards the lamp and turned the switch; its brazen click was the only noise she heard as she leaned back in bed. Merth placed his hot body next to hers, his breathing increasing with his desire for her. He started to kiss and caress her entire body, savoring its sweetness. Lily moaned in delight, emotionally excited, physically helpless. Merth's desire for Lily became rapacious. He wanted to devour her, to have her body become one with his. His appetite was insatiable; his breathing increased with pulsating rapidity, ultimately gasping as he became more and more aroused. Lily's body alternately tensed and relaxed between joyous moans and shrieks of delight. She felt that her body was disappearing and her mind was one of pure joy, an endless spongy reservoir absorbing every drop of pleasure provided. Lily's body and mind devoured it until ultimately, in a rush and unity of mind and body, she climaxed.

After tasting the fruits of which she had been so long denied, she wanted a further, a deeper taste. She was frenzied and felt as if she was going to explode. Merth's body was above hers as she spread her legs and felt him enter. He became wilder and wilder as their rhythm increased to match the tempo of their actions and the lust of their desires. Lily, always the performer, was now the accompanist, following his pace. She moaned with delight. She felt as if she had become a part of Merth, as if a monster had arisen from within her body in order to consume her and yet to escape from its confines—and from these depths, from her being, manifesting itself throughout her entire body, was a feeling of ecstatic liberation and a freedom that she had never known. She orgasmed repeatedly, feeling as if she were dying, only to be re-born and die again, yet to be re-reborn incarnate, changed from merely human to a goddess of the universe. She shrieked as the feelings imprisoned within her escaped in a mad rush of exhilaration. *Herr* Merth filled her mind and body with the living drama in which she was both a participant and a witness. He exhaled in climax as he held her and tenderly kissed her face and lips; his release left him exhausted, still gasping for air. Lily lay sprawled on the bed, her mind rising above the confines of her body.

She was astonished to have realized the depth of feeling she had experienced. It must always have been there, she thought—like flecks floating in the bright sunlight, always there, never observed, except in the brightness of the sun, just waiting to be seen, and waiting until the sun touched them, as she had now been touched.

As she wafted further into the transcendental, her mind drifted to her late husband. I never knew it could be like this with a man, she mused. As much as I loved Hans I never experienced anything like this. Hans' love was dutiful and perfunctory. Unlike Hans, who would turn his back to Lily after making love, Merth drew her body close to his as he cradled her head in his arms and whispered words that are only for lovers' ears; for were others to hear them, it would be a maudlin assault on their auditory sensibilities. Lily, always a free spirit, listened as Merth saturated her with words about feelings that he had never before felt. He wanted Lily as his love prisoner. Merth, realizing the timbre of his words, continued:

"Language cheats lovers, Lily. Words, if they can even attempt to express these depths, these pinnacles of emotion, are empty, for they're words and not emotions. I've never felt such euphoria."

Lily, still savoring the sensations of her multiple orgasms and her own first-time elation, placed her arms around Merth's neck and whispered words echoing similar expressions to those that had just been heaped upon her. She looked at Merth and said:

"We don't have to speak of what's happened. We've lived it and it's now a part of our lives, a part that's so personal and precious, that only the two of us have shared and, at the risk of those platitudes to which you so eloquently referred, a part that will last forever within us."

The words sounded hackneyed, like a poorly written play, but it was the best they could do to express themselves. They would have been better off to have remained silent than to have reduced their emotion to words, but they were human, and the heightened truth to their feeling of fleeting unreality spurred them to speak in order to alleviate the intensity of their experience. Merth had released a previously untapped eroticism in both of them. His emotions, so long wrapped up in the strict, unimpassioned, Teutonic element had been liberated by the woman whom he now desired. She was his Isolde and he her Tristan.

13

The year was 1924 and Lily, at 29 years of age, was just discovering a facet of life which she did not want denied to her. Events in Lily's life were on the upswing. She had an exciting lover who cared for and entertained her lavishly; her uncle, Israel Mendelssohn, the prominent Berlin banker, had invested her funds wisely and she was now a well-to-do woman financially.

In addition to her frequent evening meetings with *Herr* Merth, Lily would often meet him for five o'clock tea at the Aldon Hotel on Unter den Linden. She was never a person to buy clothes, but she wanted to be nicely outfitted for Merth. She started purchasing new outfits and became a frequent customer at Becker's, the haute couturier on Tiergartenstrasse.

In 1924, Foreign Minister Streams was able to secure increased foreign investment, much of which came from the United States. The higher inflation faced by Germany stimulated investment in the nation by other countries; this ultimately improved the economic climate. Along with the infusion of U.S. dollars came a German espousal of American culture: jazz, American dress, a quest for the more avant garde in German art and literature.

Lily's love affair with Merth continued at an intense pace against this increased vibrancy that marked Berlin during those heady, but superficial days of the Weimar Republic. It was a new and different life for Lily—an exciting whirlwind of existence. Berlin was a magnetic place. The First World War had ended and a new era of freedom and modernism had dawned in art, architecture and sexual freedom. The city was the home of the Modern movement in architecture and new buildings were appearing all over; many bore the hand of her father's cousin, Erich Mendelssohn, who was one of Berlin's leading architects. The German capital was filled with the liberalism of experimentation and the permissiveness to flirt with ideas heretofore untested. The richness of its culture was a wealth of individuals' successes and a credit to humanity's creativity—in science, in art, in music. Lily's circle of friends and acquaintances read like a list of the most prominent and gifted intellectuals to be found in the country. She was sought by many of these people, not for her talent alone, but also for her personality. These relationships included Albert Einstein, who at that time was the head of Berlin's *Kaiser* Wilhelm Institute for Physics. One of her favorites was B. W. Schlesinger (better known as Bruno Walter) who had been appointed conductor at the *Stadtische Oper*. Lily frequently visited with Max Liebermann, at his home on the Wannsee. Liebermann was the founder of the Berlin Secession, a popular, modern art movement. He was also President of the Academy of Arts, but most of all he was an old family friend.

Although Lily invited *Herr* Merth to these events, he hardly ever attended. On those rare occasions when he did appear, he would sometimes be accompanied by colleagues, and when he spoke to Lily it was quite formal. Merth's speech was swift, clipped and authoritative so as not to reveal any personal association with Lily, but when he would kiss her hand his tongue would gently caress it, as if to tell her that their relationship was for them alone.

One event that Lily enjoyed was the annual Artist's Ball, held at the School of Applied Arts on Prinz Albrechtstrasse. She was quite excited when *Herr* Merth accepted her invitation to accompany her. He appeared masked in a full dress army uniform. Lily attended in a white gown from Becker's. As they entered the ballroom Lily saw Friedrich approaching. She caught his attention and introduced him to Christian.

"Christian, this is Count Friedrich von Essen, who grew up with my husband."

Christian clicked his heels and said:

"It's a pleasure to meet you."

"How have you been, Friedrich?" inquired Lily. "I haven't seen you since Hannah's christening, and that's a long time ago."

"I'm sorry, Lily, and I do apologize. I've been so caught up with the Social Democratic party."

"I know, Friedrich," Lily replied. "I read that you were running for office. Congratulations."

"Thanks, Lily. I'll be in touch as soon as the elections are over. I expect to be at the Ullstein Press Ball. Will I see you there?"

"Yes, Friedrich. I'll look forward to it."

"Until then, Lily," as Friedrich kissed her hand.

He bowed slightly towards Christian, who returned the courtesy.

"Let's dance, my sweet," said Christian and they made their way to the dance floor. "My Lily, my Lily," he whispered into her ear, as they waltzed around, "you give the world your talent and beauty, and I am but a drone beside you."

"Oh darling," she laughed, "but what is a queen without her drone."

Then they both laughed as they danced, without pause, through most of the evening.

"Lily," he said, as they whirled around the floor, "I am reaching the point where I cannot bear to be without you. I am going to lock you up and make you my prisoner for life."

Lily smiled, held him tightly and assumed that he would propose marriage. Ultimately the two could not wait to leave and ended up in their usual room where they made love.

At one point Lily was so involved in her profession that she could not see Merth. Wilhelm Furtwängler had asked her to appear in concert with the Berlin Philharmonic, who, at that time, played at the hall on Berburger Strasse in the Kreuzberg district. She had accepted and told Merth that she would have to devote herself to the preparations for the concert. She was to perform new works by Arnold Schönberg, with tonalities that she had never before explored. Schönberg had moved from Vienna to teach at the Prussian Academy of Arts. The Philharmonic was to perform *Klavierstücke,* the second piece that had been arranged for orchestra by Busoni in 1909, while Lily was to perform several of Schönberg's piano works.

She had another motive with her involvement in the upcoming performance. She had hoped that this absence would prompt Merth to propose after the concert. On the evening of the performance, Lily noticed that Merth was not in his seat at the beginning of the concert, nor was he there at the end to meet with her afterwards. She left the post-concert reception saddened and disheartened. Upon her return to Grunewald she found a note from *Herr* Merth resting on top of a bouquet of roses:

> Lily, my dearest,
>
> I regret that urgent business has precluded my attendance at your performance tonight.
>
> CM

Lily had not heard from Merth in several days; she had been thinking of him constantly. As a distraction, she decided to go shopping, and left on the U-Bahn for the Karlstadt department store in Neukölin. As Lily was making her way from the U-Bahn, she noticed a woman staring at her. She assumed it was a concert admirer and smiled at the woman. The woman approached her and said:

"I beg your pardon, are you not Lily Mendelssohn, the Countess von Wallenstadt?"

"Yes," replied Lily.

"I have something of extreme importance to discuss with you,

Countess. Can you meet me at Café Uhlandeck tomorrow at 3:00? It's on the corner of Kurfürstendamm and Uhland Strasse."

"Yes, I am aware of it's location, but may I ask why?" queried Lily, with a touch of displeasure in her voice.

"I am *Frau* Merth, madam. I believe you know my husband."

Lily felt as if she had been struck by a locomotive. She bit her lip and tried to hold back her emotions as she hurriedly replied:

"I'll see you tomorrow at 3:00."

She exited from the U-Bahn station at Hermannplatz, hailed a taxi and went home. Helga noticed that something was amiss when Lily entered the house.

"Is everything all right, Countess?" she asked.

"Helga, I'm not feeling well. I'll be in my room."

When Hannah returned to the house Helga told her that her mother was not feeling well. Hannah could hear her mother sobbing softly through the closed bedroom door. She knocked hesitantly.

"Mother, mother?"

"Yes, dear," said Lily. "Come in."

"What's the matter, mother?"

"Nothing dear," Lily replied. "I'll be fine. I . . . I just need some rest."

She had never discussed *Herr* Merth with Hannah. After all, it was not the proper thing to discuss with one's nine year old daughter, and as far as Hannah assumed, Lily's absences were connected with her career or general social life.

Lily had left the Grunewald villa with plenty of time to keep her 3:00 appointment. She arrived at 2:50 and took a table under the fan-shaped ceiling where she could see the patrons entering and leaving. At 2:59 sharp, the woman whom she had seen the previous day entered the café. Lily observed her countenance and dress. She was without make-up and plain, but not unattractive. She wore a gray, woolen suit that, although not dowdy was quite serviceable and had witnessed several years of wear. The woman's eyes scanned the café and she spotted Lily. She had a serious look, and as she approached the table Lily seemed at a loss for words. A waiter took their orders.

Lily feeling somewhat guilty about the entire episode said:

"Please, I had no idea."

"Please, no guilt, Countess. This isn't the first time. Our meeting yesterday was by chance, but I knew who you were. I've been aware of this for some time. I truly feel sorry for you. I felt that you should be aware of the situation."

"Madam," said Lily, responding to what she perceived as genuine concern, "I have been a lonely widow since the war ended. Your husband was kind and attentive, and I ultimately responded to his overtures. I've now become deeply involved with him and I find it hard to conceive how life would be without him, but now that I know the circumstances I realize that I cannot continue the relationship."

They paused as the waiter placed the tea and pastries upon the immaculately white tablecloth, each for the moment alone in her own thoughts.

Lily, visibly shaken, continued, tremulously:

"Tell me, *Frau* Merth, do you have any children?"

There was a look of sadness on *Frau* Merth's face as she answered:

"I have one beautiful son, Helmut," she said pulling a photograph from her purse that revealed a handsome, blonde, blue-eyed child with a slightly befuddled appearance.

"Why, he's about the same age as my daughter, *Frau* Merth," Lily exclaimed.

"Unfortunately, Countess, Helmut is emotionally retarded and spends all his time at a children's school. I do see him as often as I can."

For a moment they were no longer two women in conflict over one man, but simply two mothers. Lily empathized with the woman realizing that this misfortune could happen to any mother.

"It must be difficult to cope, *Frau* Merth. Did you ever think of having any more children?" she asked.

"Countess, I have not been successful in that attempt. Further, my husband has nothing to do with his own son. It's as if Helmut had never been born; his very existence seems to be a source of embarrassment to my husband. Also, my dear," responded *Frau* Merth, "my relationship with my husband has been one in name only; we hardly speak to each other any more. But let me get to the point, I am not asking you to discontinue your association with him. I have been through this type of situation more than once and my interaction with my husband is better when he has a lover than when he doesn't. You must be good for him, because I've never seen him so happy. I must say this has been the longest affair I've known of. But I want you to be aware that he is not a free man. I know how others have been hurt and I don't want you to be hurt as they were. I thought this relationship would run its course, but it hasn't."

Identifying with *Frau* Merth's feelings, Lily wondered, are all men like this? She signaled the waiter for the bill.

"*Frau* Merth," she said, "I'm most grateful for your concern. At the moment I'm uncertain as to how I should deal with this deceit."

"That, my dear, is your option," was *Frau* Merth's response.

Rising from the chair, she nodded silently, then grasped and squeezed Lily's arm, turned around and left the café.

Lily remained at the table, her world asunder, pondering, what shall I do, what shall I do? After a few moments she paid the bill, left the café, and walked along the street impervious to the bustle of normal city life. Suddenly Lily became aware of intense commotion with police and people running all over the area.

"What's happening, officer?" she inquired.

"It's those damn, rowdy trouble-makers, lady," he replied. "600 Nazi brownshirts attacking 23 Communist party members. The Communists were peaceful, but as the brownshirt attackers left they molested and beat-up any passers-by who appeared to be Jewish."

"What a disgrace," said Lily.

"Madam, I suggest you leave the area immediately," advised the police officer.

She thought it wise to follow his advice and quickly hailed a taxi.

Several days later a messenger delivered the usual bouquet of flowers to the Grunewald villa with an accompanying note.

> My darling Lily,
>
> Please forgive my absence of communication. I have been involved with urgent business. I look forward, my dearest, to our next meeting, which I hope will be soon.
>
> With deepest affection,
>
> CM

She read the note, tore it into shreds and tossed it vehemently into the fire, the flowers following thereafter. The person I love is a liar and a cheat. I will not see him again, she decided. But then again, she vacillated, he wasn't really being dishonest by not revealing that he was already married. Looking at it from his point of view, she realized, we could never have formed such an association otherwise. And anyway he hardly has any dealings with his wife at all. She continued this way for a while, making up excuses for what he had done. There was no pat answer that would mollify her injured pride and nothing could prevent her from what she felt to be right. Oh, I am still in love with him, she admitted to herself, making separation all the more difficult. It will be so strange, as mourning the death of a person who might be walking down the street. Nevertheless, she silently repeated her decision: I will *not* see him again.

Repeated notes came from *Herr* Merth with no response on Lily's part, until one Saturday morning, Merth arrived at her doorstep. Helga answered looking somewhat surprised when she saw him at the doorway.

"Tell Countess von Wallenstadt that *Herr* Merth is here to see her," he commanded.

"One moment, sir," Helga replied dutifully.

It was 9:30 and Lily was taking her coffee in a sunny sitting room. She loved to be in the sun and she breathed in the early May air, glad that the strength of spring was melting the Berlin winter days.

"*Herr* Merth is here to see you, Countess," said Helga.

"He's *here*?" said Lily in an astonished voice. "Quickly, Helga, show him in. Is Hannah still at her music lesson?"

"Yes, Countess, but she should return shortly," said Helga

"Show him in quickly, I wouldn't want Hannah to see him."

"Yes, madam," Helga replied.

Lily's heart was pounding with excitement. What would she say? How would she handle the situation?

Herr Merth strode into the room, bursting with anger. He approached Lily who rose slowly and turned to greet her unexpected guest. He grabbed her body into his arms, holding her tightly and said:

"Lily, why have you not responded to my letters?" Not waiting for a response, he kissed her—confidently, firmly, passionately. Wrapped in the mantle of male ego, he was protected from experiencing any self-doubt. He could not possibly imagine that there might have been another man, nor could he conceive any other reason for her actions. As he pressed her body into his, her resolve began to weaken ever so slightly, ever so tentatively. This was signal enough for Merth. Her absence from his life over the past few weeks had fueled his passion for her all the more. He could not get enough of her and she could not withstand the onslaught of his passion. Her desire sparked his own, his lust kindled hers. He pushed her down upon the chaise and removed the minimum of clothing necessary for them to consummate the sexual act, bringing her, then himself, quickly, forcefully, to climax.

The quenching of his desire permitted him to experience more tender feelings of affection toward Lily that he expressed while carefully cradling her head onto his shoulder and softly caressing her body. But as for Lily—as the passion waned, the memory of his dishonesty came back to her. With a surging resentment stiffening her muscles as well as her mind she pushed herself from him, angrily exclaiming:

"Christian, why didn't you tell me you were married?"

"How did you know?" he asked.

Lily told him of the meeting at the Hermannplatz U-Bahn station at which he grimaced. She continued with the meeting at the café and recounted what had taken place there.

"Lily, my darling, I would never, ever want to hurt you, and I wanted you too much to tell you this. Please believe me. Also, you know the situation with my wife, and she has given you carte blanche to continue seeing me. Under those circumstances, why should we deprive each other of our love?"

Lily looked straight into his eyes that were filled with his own self-assurance, as well as the love he felt for her, as he continued:

"You know I've admired you from afar for many years before I met you, but I would never have been so impetuous as to have a liaison with you unless my marriage had deteriorated to the point where it is now."

With her desire for him pulling her back from her anger she replied obstinately:

"I understand, Christian, but to be involved with a married man is not how I had ever envisioned myself."

"Yes, Lily, but I might as well not be married, and I also have needs—to love and to be loved. Why should I go through life with unfulfilled longing?"

Lily's face mirrored the logic of what was just said. Merth held her stiffly by the shoulders and said, excitedly:

"Lily, this is 1927, times are changing and we are not bound by the same constraints that bound our parents," and, almost as an afterthought, Merth commanded: "And, keep away from Neukölln, it's not the best place to be."

"Neukölln, but why, Christian?" she asked, in confusion.

"You know what happened six weeks ago when the *SA* attacked those damned communists, and you also know how the Jews were beaten up. What if you were in that area, caught up in all of this, and injured?"

"Yes," she continued, "it was an awful incident, but I should think an isolated one, and those men were nothing but a bunch of rowdies." Then she added, "You know, Christian, my family became Protestant years ago, and I converted to Catholicism when I married my late husband."

"Yes, my dear," he replied, "but you are a Mendelssohn and regardless of what you say, or to what religion you have converted, the blood of Mendelssohn runs through your veins. You are too precious to me to see anything happen to you."

Lily said nothing. She smiled and then, with the awareness that she was in her own home late on a Saturday morning, went into the bath of the adjoining bedroom and hastily prepared herself for the day. When she emerged she was glowing, both outside and inside.

"Christian, Hannah will be home from her lesson soon." Sensing that she wanted him gone, he asked,

"Can I see you later today?"

"I'm teaching this afternoon, Christian, but I'm free this evening."

"It would please me greatly to spend the evening with you, but I have some business to which I must attend."

"What business is that, Christian?" Lily asked boldly, never having vented her curiosity about his life apart from her.

"Some professional business, my dear," he replied softly, kissing her on the forehead. "I love you, Lily, remember that."

He turned and briskly left the room. As he entered the street and walked north, Hannah turned the corner on her way home.

14

Hannah was a serious, quiet, mature eight year old, whose life was a busy one. She was immersed in her music and other studies, but most of all, in her religion. The parochial school that she attended was of the highest caliber, as was her education. She became interested in God at an early age and her piano performances were imbued with a spiritual feeling; her love of God was in her music and her love of music was an outlet to God. She was enamored of liturgical music—Gregorian chants, Bach, and the like.

Lily was a loving mother, not only to her daughter, but to Paul, Hans' cousin, whom she had continued to rear. Though a strict disciplinarian, she tempered her love with practicality and proper organization in the children's lives. They each had their own daily commitments and responsibilities. Hannah had her schooling, music lessons, and a variety of other activities that she pursued; Paul, several years Hannah's senior, was heavily involved with schooling and sports. He had no particular desire to play music and Lily did not force it on him. He was, however, surrounded by the sound of Lily's and Hannah's performances and he did enjoy listening to them—usually with a football in hand. He was tall, muscular and handsome; Hannah and he looked as if they were brother and sister. Paul, the male of the house, was very protective of his Cousin Hannah and his Aunt Lily. He loved them both, but he adored Hannah.

Lily had teaching, music, and various social and professional responsibilities. Although, in this sense, Lily and the children lived quite separate lives, they did spend time together. Meal times were especially welcomed since these were generally shared by mother and children as a family unit. At breakfast, plans and goals would be reviewed for the children's day; at dinner the day's accomplishments in school, music lessons, sports as well as the day's disappointments would be discussed.

One Saturday morning Lily received a letter from Josef von Wallenstadt. He was Hans' uncle whom Lily had met at her wedding. Josef had returned to Germany from Southwest Africa that Germany had lost in the war. He wanted Paul to live with him and his wife since, as he had stressed, his wife could have no children. Lily contacted her lawyer who advised that it would be for the best to let Josef have the boy. Lily did not want to hand him over to Josef until she had thoroughly investigated the type of home in which Paul was to live. She, Paul and Hannah went to Cologne to meet Josef. The important thing was that Josef and Paul took a ready liking to each other. The two were both sports enthusiasts and it wasn't long before they were playing football on the grounds surrounding Josef's home. Two weeks later, with Lily fighting back tears, and Hannah quite openly displaying them, Josef came to collect Paul.

"Aunt Lily, Hannah, I will miss you. I'll come to visit and I'll write to you both. I promise."

However neither promise was kept during the eight months that intervened until Lily's next visit to Cologne. He seemed happy and well which, as she convinced herself, was the most important consideration, and she felt better knowing that the child had a male to whom he could relate.

Lily's meetings with Merth continued, as their personal schedules permitted, but never less than two to three times weekly. She never queried *Herr* Merth again, as to his line of work or how he spent his time. She had assumed, whether correctly or not, that Merth was an officer in the military (probably the most respected level one could achieve in German society at that time).

Lily never had any concerns about her own lack of faith or of Hannah's zealous pursuit of it. Music was Lily's God, but it wasn't Hannah's. Hannah immersed herself in Catholicism until she became one with her faith; faith provided her with the redemption she felt she had to achieve in a world where so much was lacking. Lily was not surprised at Hannah's breakfast conversation on this particular morning.

"Mama," said Hannah, "God has answered my prayers and given me guidance."

"That's nice, dear," replied Lily. "And what answers have you been given?"

"I'm to follow God's ways and help those who are poor and ill. I want to be a nurse, a Daughter of Charity, mama, an order of St. Vincent de Paul. I realize that I'm too young now, but in a few years I'll be able to do this."

Lily was silent for a moment, thinking before she spoke, and then replied:

"Hannah, darling, you must follow the path that will give you the greatest happiness and enlightenment, but I have a selfish concern. I feel that in your quest for God and service you will be lost to me forever."

"No, mama, I will never be lost to you, but I feel it is something I must do. Weren't you a nurse during the war? Didn't you help people? Didn't you like doing that?"

"Of course dear, but . . ."

"But, mama," Hannah interrupted, "I'll be able to do this and follow the ways of the Lord also."

"You're still young, my darling," Lily replied. "You may yet change your mind."

"Maybe, mama, I will change my mind, but the way I feel now I don't think this would ever happen."

"Hannah, I would not stand in your way if you truly felt that this was your calling, but I want you to promise me you would finish with your schooling. Will you do this for me?"

"Yes, mama, of course," Hannah replied.

Lily knew her daughter's seriousness and determination, and she thought that perhaps it might be wise for Hannah to pursue this route. Thoughts ran through Lily's mind: I shall enjoy her company as long as I can. I have lost my husband, I have lost Paul, and now Hannah? Thank God, my music will not leave me. I'll always have that, something in which I can find solace, beauty, romance, creation…and joy.

15

In 1928, the Nazi Party was a small group that espoused National Socialism and abhorred Communism. The German public was fed up with the nation's dismal economic state and the people wanted a voice. Adolph Hitler, the head of the Nazi party, promised a Germany of growth and peace. Hitler played to the masses by promising to recapture the Germany that once was and more.

On Friday, October 25, 1929, the New York Stock Market crashed and a world-wide economic depression followed. It seemed that the clock had turned back six years, as foreign investment in Germany shriveled, unemployment soared, and incomes were reduced. Germany was still suffering from payment of World War I reparations and strict governmental financial policies worsened the economy. On September 14, 1930, the Nazi party was successful in the *Reichstag* elections and instigated a rampage of window-smashing of Jewish-owned businesses.

It was July 27, 1932. Lily watched, along with many other Berliners, as hordes of Brown shirts trooped past her windows on their way to Grunewald Stadium. Four days later the Nazi Party won 37.4% of the national vote, (they only got 28.6% in Berlin). The Party became the largest one in the *Reichstag*. The *SA's* (*Sturmabteilung*) militarism and promises for a resurgence of national pride appealed to many, but there were still a great deal of economic problems and lawlessness in the nation. The country needed a cohesive force to bring it together. Adolph Hitler appeared to answer this need. In 1932, Hitler competed against

Hindenburg for the presidency. This was the beginning of the end of the Democratic Weimar Republic. The *Reichstag* was burned down on February 27, 1933. The *SA* took over all the Berlin prisons and occupied the former police headquarters on Alexanderplatz. The first concentration camp, Oranienburg, was established the following month. On May 10, the infamous book-burning occurred in which writings of Jews, liberals, and socialists fueled the pyre upon which the light of freedom was being extinguished.

At Lily's next meeting with *Herr* Merth, that occurred two days later, she blurted:

"Christian, why can't anything be done about that awful book-burning by all of those rowdies—and the police stood by and did nothing. It was incomprehensible. The works of Moses Mendelssohn were destroyed, and my father's family are now held in contempt by this government. It's a disgrace, more than that, it's disgusting and lacking in law, order, propriety and a sense of what's right and wrong."

"But Lily, you shouldn't be concerned. Hitler *is* bringing law and order to our country. All will be fine in the end," replied *Herr* Merth.

"I hope you're right Christian, but all of this is frightening. It seems like something from the middle ages."

On June 30, 1933, Hitler seized power and during the following weeks over 100,000 people: Communists, Social Democrats, and all other Hitler opponents were arrested and/or killed. Friedrich was amongst those arrested. He was taken to *SA* headquarters and from there was sent to Tegel prison where, like so many others, he was mercilessly beaten. He died two days later. Ultimately, many people who didn't support the Nazis, with the inclusion of some Jews, welcomed the order that Hitler had imposed, since the chaos on the streets had finally ended. People just seemed to regard the brutal events that took place as a return to law and order.

In September of 1935, German Jews were denied citizenship and it was now illegal for Jews to marry outside their faith.

"Christian, what's happening to our country?" Lily asked.

"You worry too much, darling," was Merth's reply, as he took her hand and fondled it in his.

"Christian, Germany is one of the most advanced societies in the world, and these atrocities and restrictive laws are now part of this society. And you tell me not to worry? I do worry, Christian. So many of my family are Jewish. I am deeply concerned for them and this country's future."

Christian nodded in contemplation, but said nothing.

Lily continued with her life much as before, as well as concertizing frequently. This was in spite of Goebbels' September 22, 1937, ruling—as *Reichminister* for the People's Enlightenment and Propaganda. He had created the *Reich* Cultural Chamber that was divided into music, fine arts, theater, literature, radio, press, and movies. All active participants had to register. Lily had mentioned to Merth that she "would never condescend to visit with those thugs." The authorities had never questioned her and she continued to perform.

It was now November 11, 1938, two days after Crystal Night, when the store windows of Jewish business had been smashed.

"I don't feel comfortable in my own country anymore; too many horrors going on. I'm thinking of going to London until this madness ends," Lily said to *Herr* Merth.

"Lily, darling, it will all work out, just bear with it," replied Merth. "I'm here, I will always take care of you."

"Will you, Christian? But how can you, against a government that deals in such irrationalities?"

"I love you, Lily. You'll always be safe with me."

"That is not the point, Christian. What is a person's quality of life supposed to be under this government?"

"Has yours changed, darling?" Merth asked.

"No, it has not," Lily replied, "but—."

"But what dear?" Merth interrupted. "Your audiences are as big as they were before Hitler."

"Yes they are, but I'm surprised you're even aware of that. You attend so few of my concerts."

"Now, darling," Merth continued, "I have my job to do as you have yours, now stop all this fretting."

Several days later Lily received a telephone call from her uncle, Israel Mendelssohn, the Berlin banker.

"Lily, I'll be leaving for England tomorrow. Jews have been stopped from conducting banking services and all funds have been impounded by the government. The bank is to be 'aryanized.' I think it unwise to continue this conversation on the telephone, but I wanted to let you know that your Cousin Franz will stop by in an hour to say good-bye. I suggest you make arrangements to leave immediately."

He hung up quickly without giving Lily a chance to respond. She was perplexed since she had no Cousin Franz. It was now after midnight. She waited near the door, peering out of the window. She recognized Manfred Schwarzmann, one of the junior officers, darting to her entrance. She admitted him immediately and offered him a cup of coffee.

"Thank you, madam, but there is no time. *Herr* Mendelssohn feels that we are no longer safe in Germany. He asked me to give you this."

Herr Schwarzmann pulled out a large envelope and handed it to Lily.

"It contains £25,000 British sterling notes," he continued. "Your uncle advises that you make plans to leave the country immediately. He is leaving tomorrow and you can accompany him; otherwise he asks that you contact him at his London office upon your arrival. If you need help, contact Georg Somassen after your uncle departs.[1]

"Manfred," asked Lily, "is it that bad that my uncle is leaving so hastily?"

"Yes, madam," he replied. "Your uncle has heard that the I.G. Farben cartel and other industries are pushing Hitler to do many unspeakable acts. We don't know how true it is, but the situation is getting tougher for Jews in Germany. He does not see it improving, but worsening."

"Oh," is all Lily could say, frightened by what she had just heard.

"Good-bye madam, and good luck," replied Schwarzmann.

Schwarzmann grasped her hand and exited as quickly as he had entered. Lily, utterly unprepared for this, felt anxious, scared, and very much alone.

How can I just pick up and leave? She thought. She ran up the stairs to her daughter's bedroom, opened the door, and walked softly towards the sleeping child. She looked at Hannah's pink face, and sat on the chair by the bedside. Lily stayed there for quite sometime. She didn't know how long it was, thinking; not thinking, in a state of shock. Tears were in her eyes as she knelt and tenderly kissed her daughter on the forehead; after a while she left the room.

Once in her own bedroom she was seized with a fright she had never before known. She could not relate to her surroundings. She felt as if she were in another time and another place; she could not associate her mind to the present time or situation. It was worse than her father's death, her husband's death, the problems she faced after the war. This was different. She was able to overcome what had happened previously, but she kept on thinking, this is different. This is different. Finally she thought, get a hold of yourself, Lily. You managed to survive everything in the past and you *will* survive this. She calmed herself, got into bed, but sleep did not come until the comfort of dawn pushed out the cruelty of the night.

She awoke abruptly three hours later. Next to her on her night stand was the £25,000. She thought for a moment, went downstairs, entered the conservatory, and walked to her piano. She furtively placed the bills inside the piano; carefully, so as not to impede the action of the hammers on the strings. She left the room hurriedly.

Lily's course of action was inaction. She could not bring herself to leave the country so quickly. She had a daughter to care for, and she didn't want to leave Merth. She contrived multitudes of excuses not to leave; in truth she was too frightened to do anything. Her life did continue without change and she now seemed unaffected by the scare that her uncle had given her. She was glad she didn't do anything hastily. For the most part, except for the night of Israel Mendelssohn's telephone call and *Herr* Schwarzmann's visit, Lily continued to feel secure in her country. She loved it, she did not consider herself Jewish, and she, like so many others, was waiting for Hitler to disappear from government, and, after that all would return to what it had been previously.

In October of 1937, Jews were excluded from Arts and Letters. Lily decided on her own volition to reduce her performances but she continued, without official interruption, to teach in the *Hochschule für Musik*; her classes were well attended. Since she performed less often and her popularity with the public had never waned, her performances were always sold out.

On April 26, 1938, new laws were enacted requiring that all Jews report monetary holdings in excess of 5,000 *Reichmarks*. The following June, Jewish businesses were prohibited from operating. In July, Jewish physicians could no longer practice medicine.

Lily was aghast at these abuses, still viewing the government as only temporary, and one composed of rowdies. The worst blow of all came when she heard that the statue of Felix Mendelssohn-Bartholdy had been torn down in Leipzig. At this point Lily started to wonder whether her uncle was right.

In the summer of 1938, Lily kissed her daughter good-bye, as Hannah left the Grunewald villa for the Convent of the Daughters of Charity. She was saddened by her daughter's departure, but she was wise enough not to stand in the way of something that Hannah wanted so badly.

16

In 1939, women, who had not been part of the workforce previously (Hitler felt they should be raising families), were pressed into service in many factories. Shifts were usually twelve hours daily at minimum pay, with maximum deductions being earmarked for various government activities. Many Germans hated Hitler, and this enforced type of slavery exacerbated their feelings, while others toiled willingly for *Volk, Vaterland und Füehrer*. Jews (usually segregated) and Gentiles alike were conscripted into the labor force.

On September 1, 1939, 25 years to the day after Germany started the First World War, Hitler invaded Poland and the Second World War began.

In 1940, mass hysteria permeated the German Jews and there was an exodus of Jews from Germany. Lily, affected by all of this, finally came to the realization that she now had to leave the country. She went to the convent where Hannah, now Sister Ursula, resided. Lily explained the situation to the Mother Superior who gave her permission to meet Hannah and discuss her plans. Lily wanted to convince Hannah to join her in leaving Germany.

"But mama, how can I leave the convent? I'm safe here. I have such peace from my faith and my work. I'm doing nursing at both the Catholic and Charité hospitals. It's all so exciting and rewarding. Please don't worry about me, mama, I'll be fine. I will ask the Blessed Mother to watch over you and to ensure that you're safe."

"Hannah dear, all those miles, so far away. I don't want to leave you but I feel it unwise for me, or you, to stay in Germany any longer."

"Mama, you have always let me follow my own path, and it's been good for me. Now, you must follow your path, and I'm sure it will be good for you."

"I hope you're right, darling, but there are no guarantees."

Lisbon was about the only legal exit port and Lily was planning to make arrangements to leave from there. Since she could not leave for England she decided to go to the United States. She went to the American Consulate on Hermann Goering Strasse, waiting in line with the many who were also applying for visas. People would nod at her in recognition, some somberly, as if to say, you too? Lily registered her name and left the mayhem at the Consulate. As she stepped on to the crowded street she saw a familiar-looking face she could not quite place. It was heavy with grief. The two approached each other and recognition followed. It was *Frau* Merth who seemed relieved to see Lily.

"Countess," she said, "I am so happy to see you. How are you?"

"Life has been better, *Frau* Merth, but I'm fairly well, thank you."

The two women started to speak simultaneously, they both laughed, and *Frau* Merth said:

"Do you have time to have a cup of tea?"

"It would be a pleasure," Lily responded.

"I know a nice place on Leipzigerstrasse."

"Excellent," said Lily as they walked towards the café.

Frau Merth seemed fatigued, but she became animated as she and Lily walked together. They chatted amicably, about nothing in particular; once seated and more comfortable, they ordered tea and pastries.

Frau Merth forced a smile and suddenly burst into tears. Lily held her hand for emotional support. It was cold and clammy.

"What's the matter, *Frau* Merth?"

"Countess," she said as she began to cry uncontrollably, "my son Helmut is gone."

"What do you mean?" sighed Lily quizzically.

"He's just disappeared. I went to see him last week and he wasn't there. One of the school staff told me that many of the students had gone on a picnic that day, but they never returned. I spoke to another one of the mothers whose son attends the school. He had gone on the same picnic, and he, too, did not return. Nobody can give either of us any information. I am heartsick, Countess, heartsick."

"Can't Christian make some inquiries, *Frau* Merth?"

"He is useless, Countess. He left the house two weeks ago. He took all of his things. We've not spoken since; not only that, I don't think he's had any concern. I'm not sorry that Christian is gone, Countess. It's better to be by yourself than to live with a person without love. Maybe you can do something to help me?"

"I would like to, *Frau* Merth, but I think it appropriate that I be as unobtrusive as possible. Things are not going too well for Jews now, and I may be considered as such."

"I did not know you were Jewish, Countess."

"I'm not really, but I don't know what the *Reich* thinks. I was reared as a Protestant, but my social status is still *klärungfälle* (social status uncertain), but I do have Jewish family; most of them have left the country by now. It's possible that I may be classified Jewish. In any case, I am no longer comfortable living in Germany.

"The government encouraged Jews to leave and now they've stopped them from even taking their furniture. The thought of leaving without my piano—it is one used by Felix Mendelssohn-Bartholdy—has held me back. I guess there are other pianos, but this is so very special to me. I went to the American Embassy today to apply for a visa. There are thousands of Jews clamoring to leave. I was told I would have no trouble since I'm considered a 'prominent' person. I don't like to push another whose turn would have come to emigrate; they're just as good as I am, but we'll see. When my status is determined by the American Embassy I'll leave for Lisbon, and from there, on one of the American Export ships to America. *Frau* Merth, I'll certainly let you know if I have any information about your son. Can you continue to make inquiries about him?"

Frau Merth responded,

"Countess, it's very difficult. I'm now working in munitions at the Siemens Elmo plant. I work six days a week. I have Wednesdays off. I'm lucky. I work the day shift, twelve hours. It's hard work and I have little time for anything else."

"I'll do my best, *Frau* Merth," replied Lily sympathetically.

Both women rose from the table with tears in their eyes. They exchanged telephone numbers and left the café. As they started to leave each other, *Frau* Merth turned towards Lily and said:

"I'm glad to have you as a friend, Countess."

"Oh yes," replied Lily, "yes," intimating that she felt similarly toward *Frau* Merth.

Both women gave each other a strong, supportive hug and walked away, in opposite directions. A cold mist enshrouded the city. It was damp and Lily pulled her coat collar more tightly around her neck. Now we have another war, Lily thought. People working night and day to produce weapons and ammunition? Why must this occur? We lost so much in the last war. Lily started to think about Hans and then about *Frau* Merth's son. She had heard something about it being a patriotic duty to have any mentally deficient persons killed, and, unknown to Lily, some families in the *Reich* were cooperating. Such thoughts, however, were so alien to Lily that she could not consider them reality, but loose talk. Lily was to see Christian that night. She would talk to him about his son, Helmut.

When she met with *Herr* Merth in the restaurant's private quarters, he was in an imperious, self-possessed mood. Lily didn't notice this since she was preoccupied with what she was going to discuss with him and she lost no time in getting down to it.

"Christian, I'm deeply troubled about several things and I'd like to discuss them with you."

Unaccustomed to being put on guard in this way, particularly by a person of the opposite sex, Merth became defensive.

"Yes, Lily, what's the problem?" he replied, feigning interest.

"Christian, given the current state of affairs, I'm leaving Germany as soon as possible."

Merth seemed surprised, and then hurt.

"Why, Lily?" he queried, "no harm will come to you in this country."

"But Christian," she replied, "what if I am classified a Jew? It's not unlikely. Also we would be guilty of *rassenschande* (race-mixing) which is illegal. Under the law we'd be unable to continue our relationship and, quite honestly, I don't know if non-Jewish Germans would be safe either. Look at the lives people are leading—slaving in armament factories. Why? To get us killed in another war? To have more women lose their husbands and sons? Do you think it would be easy for me to leave you, Christian?"

Merth, in an intransigent state of denial regarding Lily's intention to leave, began to understand the enormity of Lily's words, and at this moment, so did she. Heretofore it had been talk, just talk, a desire, possibly, just at the point of manifesting itself, but beneath actual consciousness. It seemed so incredible for Lily to leave a life of luxury and privilege, of loving, and being loved. It wasn't just Merth, but about all those people whom she had known for years, and whose company she enjoyed. Now the realization came: the nation that she knew and loved might not love her in return. In fact it might do her harm; as this growing realization translated from intellect to emotion she was seized with fright and felt powerless. Lily had the devastating sensation of being in a strange land, and of being forced to be a stranger among her own. She started to cry.

"Christian, when I saw the pictures of the refugees in Poland and then Czechoslovakia, fleeing before all of the tragedy, leaving their homes, possibly dead loved ones, it was very upsetting. It saddened me, but I don't think people can have the knowledge of having to do this unless they're affected themselves. The thought of leaving you, my daughter, all the people I love, has finally caught up with me. I don't think it's safe for me to stay here, but the reality of actually leaving is depressing. Also Christian, I'll be leaving in luxury on an ocean liner, not walking down a road with thousands of other people carrying their few precious belongings with them. Oh, my darling, my dearest."

Merth took her in his arms, held her closely and said:

"You're talking nonsense, Lily, you do *not* have to leave. You'll be safe in this country. I've never loved a person in my life as I've loved you. Do you think I'd stop loving you if you were declared a Jew? And besides, even if you were, you're different from other Jews."

"What do you mean, Christian? I'm no different than anybody else."

"But you are. You're a talented star and you have so much to give."

"But Christian, what about Israel Mendelssohn, the banker; Erik Mendelssohn, the architect; Felix Mendelssohn-Bartholdy, the composer, whose music it's now illegal to perform in his native land—and not just my family, but all the other talented people who are here or who have left the country. They and I are no longer welcome in Germany. I think of Moses Mendelssohn, the philosopher, whose books were burned. Didn't these people give to their country and the world?"

"I don't know about them, Lily. All I know is you, that I love you and I want you, and I don't want to be without you. You'll be safe in Germany."

"Christian, even if I'm safe personally, what about all the other Jews who are being forced to leave? Will I be the only Jew in Germany if they declare me to be Jewish? Jews are not wanted here. I must tell you, my sweetheart, I've applied to the American Consulate for a visa. I plan to leave from Lisbon in November.

I'm praying that it's only for a short time before I can see you again, but I doubt that this will be up to me. I love you too, Christian. Do you think it's easy for me to leave you? Not only that, I'm leaving my daughter as well, my only child. I begged her to come with me, but she wouldn't. She feels her place is here. She's grown now from the little girl that she was when we first met. She has a mind of her own and feels her belief in God will be all she needs. I hope that's so, Christian. I'm giving up the two people I love the most. It's very hard for me. I've anguished over it for many days and nights. You must understand—but sweetheart, there is another option open to us."

"What's that?" said Merth.

"You can come with me. You can apply for a visa to leave the country."

"Lily, that's out of the question for me. It's not that I wouldn't want to be with you, but my work dictates that I remain in Germany. All I know is that without you my life will be empty. I don't want you to go. I guarantee you'll be safe with me."

"But, Christian," Lily said with a laugh, "how can you guarantee such a thing? Please understand my position."

They held on to each other for the rest of the night, and then they made love together. He, with a special intensity, with the fear of losing her; she, out of anxiety, and out of fear of losing the people she loved. Her face was wet with tears, Merth's one of somber contemplation at the thought of losing Lily.

Early in the morning, just before sunrise, Christian made love to her, as if for the last time. Afterwards he burst into sobs and held her tightly.

"Lily, don't leave me, please don't leave me."

Lily had never seen him like this. He was like a child. She held his head next to her breasts and caressed his face and hair. Merth quickly became guarded and said:

"I'm ashamed to have broken down like this. It's never happened before in my life."

"I'm glad, my darling," said Lily. "Don't be ashamed of expressing your feelings with me," she whispered.

"Christian," she continued, "I'm not due to leave Lisbon until November. We still have time to be with each other."

"Lily," he said, "I'll see you whenever I can."

"Yes, my darling, yes," she replied.

17

The next morning, Lily, completely exhausted, left the taxi and entered the Grunewald villa. Helga came to greet her, and, seeing Lily's distress said:

"Are you all right, Countess?"

"Helga," said Lily, "I must speak to you. Come sit down."

She told Helga of her plans to leave the country.

"Helga," she continued, "I would willingly take you with me if you wish to come."

"Oh, Countess, I was hoping you would ask me. I want to be with you and Hannah."

"Hannah has chosen to remain in Germany, Helga."

"How can we possibly leave her, Madame?"

"It won't be easy, but this is something about which I've deliberated for a long time. I think I must leave. I've been unsuccessful in convincing Hannah. She's devoted to her work, the convent, and most of all her feeling towards God. At this point, I've come to realize that Hannah is mature enough in her mind to know what she wants. I'm sure she'll be safe in the convent, and I'm hoping this situation will be temporary and we'll be able to return soon. Tomorrow, Helga, we'll go to the American Consulate."

Helga bowed her head slightly, took Lily's hand and kissed it. Lily squeezed Helga's hand gently, smiled and went upstairs to her room.

The sun was setting, it was not yet night and not quite day, with long shadows cast in the dimming light. Helga knocked at Lily's bedroom door. Lily had been resting in the chaise lounge, thinking of her life to be. The knock at the door jolted her into the present.

"Yes?" Lily asked.

"Countess, there's a telephone call for you. A lady, she would not leave her name. She said she must speak to you on an urgent matter."

Lily's curiosity was only slightly aroused. She was in a pensive, melancholy mood and she felt that her life was burdened enough. She wished for no additional complications. She rose slowly, put on her dressing gown and headed to the downstairs study. She walked softly, entered the room, closed the door behind her and looked at the empty library shelves. Helga had discarded many of the books that were declared degenerate. Lily had kept a few hidden in her upstairs bedroom; an eighteenth century copy of *The Phaedon*, by Moses Mendelssohn was amongst them. Lily sighed, sat down, picked up the receiver and said:

"This is Countess von Wallenstadt speaking."

"Countess, please forgive me for calling, but can you meet me tomorrow, at your convenience? I want to discuss a Beethoven manuscript with you."

Lily recognized the voice as that of *Frau* Merth. During those times people lived furtive lives, turning around to look over their shoulders, suspicious of everyone they didn't know, and some they did. Telephones were easily monitored by the authorities, and it was wise to be as non-committal about every aspect of life as possible.

"Is it convenient to meet where we last saw each other and at the same time?" *Frau* Merth continued.

"The place is fine," said Lily, "but could we meet for coffee at ten?"

"I shall look forward to seeing you, Countess."

"Fine, then," said Lily as she placed the telephone receiver upon its cradle.

It was now quite dark as Lily left the study. She started upstairs and the telephone rang again.

"Countess von Wallenstadt speaking," she said.

"Lily, it's Christian," he said. "I'll pick you up in an hour."

"I don't think I would make very good company. I'm not feeling quite up to par right now."

"I'll be by at 9:00," he said. "Be ready."

She went upstairs to bathe and dress. The hot water did little to ease the tension in her mind, but it did help to relax her stiff body. Lily looked at herself in the mirror as she applied her lipstick; she saw a haggard-looking woman projected back at her, one who had a heavy, tight look topping her diminutive countenance. Moisturizing creams did not alleviate the face's reflection of her thoughts, her concerns, her fears. Lily heard the door bell ring. She exhaled heavily and prepared to go downstairs.

Helga answered the door, told the driver to wait, as Lily descended the stairs.

"What's the matter, Lily?" said *Herr* Merth as he looked at her over the dinner table.

Lily toyed with the food on her plate.

"You've eaten next to nothing," Merth continued.

"Christian," she replied, "Can't you understand? I've gone over this with you time and time again. Must I always repeat myself? I'll tell you again, and listen to me carefully; try to understand what I'm saying this time. I'm very worried. I'm forced to flee the land that I love and the people whom I love. I must leave my daughter and I must say good-bye to you. These are circumstances that are not in my control. How many times must I tell you this?"

"Lily," replied Merth, forcefully. "You do *not* have to leave. I have told you repeatedly that you've nothing to fear."

"But, Christian," she answered, "I've told you as many times that I have no guarantee of this, and, even if this were so, look what's happening; the oppression gets worse and if I *am* classified Jewish it will be even worse yet. I looked at my face in the mirror this evening. I looked like an old woman. I always wanted to be beautiful for you, Christian, but these events are aging me fast. Christian, I cannot reconcile myself to what's happening in Germany. For me it's utterly unbelievable. It's like a time that's in-between something else, a time that has not yet gone, before something else is yet to come. It's like a momentary dream in a night of continuing sleep, that will only end when I either wake up or die."

"But, my little poetic darling," replied Christian. "All of life and its history are like that—times that are in-between. You always talk of the days of the past. Were they so good for Germany? People starving, other countries advancing at our expense? We were so proud once, and now we are proud again. You're always talking of the times that were. Were they that good?"

"Maybe not, Christian, but we had freedom to think, to create, to live."

"I don't think that has changed that much, Lily."

"Oh come now, Christian, how can you say that? This society is the epitome of repressiveness. And Christian, how can you criticize me for thinking of times that were better for me? Time can be magic, Christian. My life before all these changes was one of gracious living and respect for others, that seems to be the exception rather than the rule now."

"Oh, Lily, you sound like you were living in a fairy tale."

"Maybe the life that I had led was like one but, Christian, when I play a Mozart piece, is that not a return to a former time? And, tell me, why can't I play a piece by a Jewish composer? Christian, life has become too insecure and frightening. I remember as a child the times I would romp with my cousins, and be tended to by my aunts—those lovely summers in England with my family. I felt those people would always be there, that they would never leave my life. So many have become old and sick or died in the last war, or whatever. It's something that's out of my sphere, something that really isn't or never was. It's like a fantasy now, dreaming that when I awake I can stretch out between the cool, crisp linen sheets, but feel warm and protected, loved and wanted. My aunt's maid would come in with the tea tray, set it down and open the drapes. The cool English air, laden with the scent of summer flowers, would come into the room and assault my nostrils with the boldness of their fragrance."

"Lily, darling, there you go again. You're such a poetic dreamer; stop living so much in the past," Merth replied. "We all have our childhood memories that we cherish, but we have grown up. You must be more mature about these things, Lily."

"About what, Christian? Being persecuted, having my family flee Germany? Can I be blamed for living in the past when the future seems to hold so little in store?"

"But you have your music, Lily."

"What kind of an answer is that, Christian? You're not addressing the issue I'm discussing, and you never have. It's like saying that my hands have been severed from my body, but I still have that pair of lovely, doeskin gloves. You are right, I do have my music and my memories; I don't seem to have much more."

"Lily," interjected Merth, "you're becoming a sentimental child, but I think that's one of the reasons I find you so attractive. You're as strong-willed and assertive as you are naive and alluring."

Lily, lost in her own thoughts and concerns, was oblivious to Merth's comments. She broke into tears.

Christian arose from his seat, his stark demeanor belying the feelings within that he had for Lily. He was tired of hearing Lily rant on and on about the same topic. He went over to her seat and knelt next to her.

"Lily," he said softly, concealing the anger and impatience that he felt, "I have told you countless numbers of times that I personally would see that no harm would ever come to you."

"I know, Christian, but it's not just you, it's everything. Are you bigger than the *Gestapo*, Adolph Hitler?"

Christian did not answer, but silently directed her to the adjacent, private room as Lily continued,

"Christian, I really think it best that I go home this evening."

Merth looked like a child whose mother had stopped him from having a sweet. He stared at her feeling hurt, and said:

"Are you sure, my dearest?" hoping that she would recant.

He stroked her and kissed her attempting, unsuccessfully, to use his powers of sexual stimulation.

"Yes, dear," Lily replied, "not tonight. I'll try to be in better spirits next time. Please understand."

"Yes, my love. I never would have thought that any woman would hold the power over me that you do," he replied. "Whatever you want."

He held Lily and kissed her tenderly. Then he rang for the driver, turned his back and quickly exited. Lily was exasperated. She returned to Grunewald feeling empty, misunderstood, and deserted.

18

It was one of those beautiful autumn days when the sun brightens the earth with its immodest clarity. The air was rich and pure with its own pride of being, infusing its inhabitants with the joy of being alive. Lily stepped out of the villa absorbing this intoxication.

"Oh, Schmidt," she said to her driver. "It's truly a beautiful day."

"Yes, Countess, that it is. Where can I take you today?"

Lily thought for a moment, not wanting to reveal her actual destination, and said:

"To Charlottenberg Tiergarten Strasse, at the corner of Hardenberg Strasse." She decided to walk from there to the café to meet *Frau* Merth. As they drove she noticed that the driver's face was taut and sullen.

"What is the matter, Schmidt, are you not well?"

"I am madam, but things are not. My wife has been conscripted for work in one of the munitions plants. I hardly ever see her. Several chauffeurs from the limousine service have also been conscripted. I am an old man, madam, and one of the drivers was older than I."

Lily did not reply. She had heard this type of conversation so many times and most people learned not to speak about the government since an innocent comment could be misinterpreted. People had been arrested for less; children even told teachers what negative comments parents might make, much to the parents' harm. It seemed that none was safe.

As they reached the corner of Charlottenberg Tiergarten and Hardenberg, Lily said:

"Good-bye, Schmidt, I hope all goes well for you." There was no response.

"Schmidt?" Lily continued, her voice rising slightly.

"Yes, Madame?" as he turned around to respond.

"Thank you so much, I do not think I will need you again today."

Schmidt's eyes met Lily's. She felt like clasping his hand in order to ally herself with his plight, but that would have been out of keeping with their relationship. They both knew what did not have to be said; their eyes told each other that.

Lily walked briskly and entered the café. She spotted *Frau* Merth, and went over to greet her.

"Good day, *Frau* Merth," Lily said cheerfully.

Frau Merth looked up at Lily with eyes that were red and teary.

"Good day, Countess," she responded. "There is such a chill in the air today," she announced in an audible voice, more for consumption of the nearby patrons than anything else.

Coffee was ordered and as soon as the waiter left, *Frau* Merth's plastic expression of pleasantness melted.

"Countess, I'm very grateful to you for meeting me on such short notice. I received news of my son from the authorities. It was a letter telling me that he had a disease and died. Several other mothers received the same letter—a form letter, of all things, a form letter about our own children. He was a healthy child physically, nobody told me that he was ill. Not only that, I was told that his body was cremated so as not to endanger others. Here's the letter, Countess."

Lily started to read the letter:

> For purposes of avoiding the outbreak or the communication of an infectious disease the local police authorities as per §22....

Lily finished the letter and raised her head in disbelief. Could it be that all those mental illness stories that circulated from time to time were true?

"I've heard of no disease scare, *Frau* Merth, could it have been something at the school?"

At that point Lily realized that she had never really questioned Christian Merth about his son. She felt embarrassed about it. *Frau* Merth continued:

"I don't believe any of it, Countess, it's not true," *Frau* Merth whispered. "Something unusual has happened to my boy. I find it difficult to believe that the authorities would harm innocent children, but I cannot come to any other conclusion. I'm tired of being so worried. I went to the school and was told nothing. There are no more students there. The school has been appropriated for military use. Is it possible that all the students died from a disease? I went to the local police station, the *Gestapo* Headquarters; I've even contacted my husband for help. Nobody can tell me anything. What has the *Reich* done to my child?" and with this *Frau* Merth started to sob quietly.[2]

"Is everything all right, Madam?" inquired a male voice.

The two ladies turned to see a *Gestapo* officer at their side. Startled by this intrusion, and with full realization of the reality of the situation, *Frau* Merth composed herself.

"Yes, yes, it's fine," she exclaimed. "Thank you for asking."

The officer observed *Frau* Merth carefully and then turned to Lily. Lily had kept her face down and had said nothing.

"And what is your name, Madam?" he asked Lily.

Lily, realizing it would be folly to hide her face, turned and looked at the officer.

"Mademoiselle Mendelssohn," he said before Lily answered.

Lily nodded with a slight smile, the officer stood and looked at them for a few moments. Lily could hear him mutter "Jewish sow," underneath his breath. He clicked his heels, said:

"*Heil* Hitler," and left the table at which the ladies were seated.

Lily was uncomfortable at this point and she wanted to leave the café. She was anxious to get to the American Consulate where she was to meet Helga. *Frau* Merth, sensing Lily's discomfort said:

"Forgive me, Countess, I've kept you too long."

Lily thought of the *Gestapo* officer's expletive, the situation with *Frau* Merth's son, and the possibility of similar danger confronting her own daughter. She became quite distraught and her eyes filled with tears.

"*Frau* Merth," she said, "I'm extremely sorry about your son. I'm sure I wouldn't be as calm as you if something happened to my daughter. I'll call you soon. Good-bye, *Frau* Merth, good-bye," Lily uttered and she quickly left the café.

Lily was disconsolate. She walked outside and headed towards the corner to make her way to Hermann Göring Strasse and the American Consulate. She vaguely thought she heard a voice calling her name. Lily turned around to see a *Gestapo* officer calling to her in the distance. She became frightened and feigned not hearing him. She stood at the corner, anxiously waiting for the traffic to stop so that she could cross the street.

"Countess von Wallenstadt, Countess von Wallenstadt," then "*Fräulein* Mendelssohn, *Fräulein* Mendelssohn, wait, wait," he called.

Lily became even more alarmed. Several people turned their heads to see who was calling; Lily started to cross the street. The *Gestapo* officer called out again as Lily neared the center of the street. A military car, going much too fast, turned the corner. Lily heard a woman scream, turned around as onlookers' faces gasped and froze. The military car, with brakes screeching, tried to stop, but not before the car hit Lily. She fell to the pavement and sank into unconsciousness.

19

At first there was nothing but a white light, the purest of lights which Lily had ever experienced. It beckoned her and lifted her into a silence and serenity which she had never known to exist. There were no thoughts, just pure being, appreciation and wonderment. There were figures in the distance, unrecognizable, until Lily got closer to them. Lily recognized her father Solomon; she thought how wonderful it was to be able to see him again. There was a woman standing at Solomon's side, who just beamed at Lily with a love as pure as the first breath of life.

"Momma, momma, is that you?" Lily said, but no words emanated from the woman's lips, just thoughts.

Lily did not have to speak, her thoughts were readily transmitted the moment they entered her state of consciousness. She approached her father and was encompassed by the intensity of his warmth and affection. Suddenly it was very dark and Lily became apprehensive.

"Papa, papa," she called. "It's very dark in here and I'm afraid."

There was no response.

"Papa, papa."

"What is it, child?" said Giselle, the nursemaid.

"I'm frightened, *Fräulein* Giselle. I want my papa."

"He is sleeping, child. I don't think we should awaken him."

"Oh please, please, *Fräulein* Giselle."

Giselle rang for the maid to summon *Herr* Mendelssohn-Bartholdy who came into the room a few moments later.

"What is it, my daughter?" he inquired.

"Papa, papa, it's so dark and cold. I'm alone and afraid."

"Lily, my dearest," he said as he enfolded her in his arms. "There's nothing to fear; nothing here to bother you."

"There are monsters, papa, monsters, and they're all around."

"Monsters? Nonsense. You're a big girl now. You're going to be seven years old. There are no monsters here."

"But papa, there's this big man from the *Gestapo* and he's been chasing me."

"Don't worry, Lily. I'm with you now and I'll always be with you. Call me whenever you need me. I'll always be by your side and never leave you."

"Never, papa?"

"Never, Lily. You've just had a bad dream."

"No, papa. I'm up, I'm awake and I'm not dreaming."

"It's a feeling, my dear. It will go away. Life is sometimes like that, but it changes and we change with it. Go back to sleep."

"But, I'm afraid to sleep, papa, and my whole body is aching."

"Don't be afraid to sleep, dear. You'll get rest, rest and feel better. Now go to sleep."

Lily felt his moist lips on her forehead. It felt good and she was comforted. She was warm and secure.

"Papa, Papa," Lily said as she again felt lips on her forehead and her hands being clasped.

"Is that you, papa?"

"No, mama, it's me, Hannah, your daughter."

"Oh, Hannah," said Lily, slightly opening her eyes as if she had just been having a conversation with her daughter, "you've left the convent."

"Just to be with you, mama. I'll go back soon. I've asked the Holy Mother to intercede on your behalf. She will help you."

"But I have no mother here, Hannah. She is not of this earth."

"Yes, mama, you do. She is the mother of us all, and I have prayed to her and to her son, Jesus, for your survival."

"Who?"

"Jesus, mama, our Father, he is always with us.

"My father is Solomon, Solomon, dear, and he said he is always with me."

"Rest, mama, rest. You've had a terrifying ordeal."

"Yes dear, my father said I shall find peace in rest."

Lily opened her eyes further and as the haze cleared she saw Hannah standing next to her.

"Oh, Hannah, dear, what happened?" said Lily weakly.

Hanna took Lily's hands in hers and said:

"Oh, mama, praise be to God who has answered my prayers. You were in an automobile accident, mama, and you were brought here."

"Where am I, dear?"

"The Jewish Hospital, mama, at Schulstrasse 79."

"But you don't work here, do you?"

"That's right mama, but I have permission to spend time here and nurse you."

Lily smiled and laughed a bit.

"Why are you laughing, mama?"

"Well," replied Lily, "I'm just thinking of the Jewish patients, particularly the *Ostjüden* (religious Jews from Eastern Europe) seeing a nursing nun in her habit."

A gentleman in a white coat walked into the room.

"Mama, this is Dr. Lustig, who has been looking after you."

"Hello, *Herr* doctor," said Lily. "Thank you for helping me."

"You're quite welcome, madam, but according to the government I cannot be called a doctor anymore. The government has decreed that Jewish doctors are to be called 'treaters.'"

"A rose by any other name, doctor, oops . . . treater. And am I the treatee?"

Dr. Lustig laughed.

"I'm glad that you're alert, madam. We did not know what your condition might be. How do you feel?"

"Tired, doctor, very tired, with a bad headache. When do I get to go home?"

Lustig laughed again and replied:

"It will be a while. You've been unconscious for over almost ten days, with multiple lacerations, some broken bones, and a concussion. We'll have to take each day at a time."

Suddenly, Lily said:

"Helga, I was supposed to meet Helga."

"Momma," Hannah replied, "she has left the house. Jews are forbidden to employ non-Jews. She's been conscripted and is now working in a munitions factory. The doctor feels it best that you remain in the hospital until you can care for yourself since it might be difficult to get nursing care and domestic help for you. I hope it won't be too long, mama, but it's the best option for the moment."

"Hannah?"

"Yes, mama."

"I have been classified Jewish?"

"Yes, mama, and you cannot be addressed as Countess or use 'von' in your name any longer."

"No problem for me, dear. Most people still call me Mendelssohn, anyway, and I'm proud to bear that name and use it. What's your classification, dear?"

"*Mischling* (mixed race), momma; that was decided after you were classified. They kept on telling me what a fine family my father came from."

"And what did they say about your mother's?"

"They were impressed, mother. Regardless of how they complain about the Jews, your name is very much respected; many people seem to be embarrassed about this entire situation."

"Well, I'm glad there are a few decent people left in Germany. Ohhhh," Lily murmured.

"What is it, mother?"

"I have pains in my left leg, and my chest hurts each time I take a deep breath."

"Thank God, you're alive, mother. You've suffered several broken ribs and the bones in your left leg were shattered. Mama, I have to leave now to go to Charité Hospital."

"Do you work long hours, Hannah?"

"Yes, mama, but I do the Lord's work. I'm grateful that I've been chosen to do this."

The next day Lily was upright in bed, in a sort of semi-sleep. She gradually discerned the colors of a uniform and opened her eyes to see a *Gestapo* officer standing in front of her.

"Good morning," said the voice in the uniform.

Lily raised her head slowly, fighting back dizziness and a throbbing headache. She stared at the face without expression.

"Are you feeling better?" the voice continued.

How could I be better if I'm here, she thought, but realized this was merely a pro forma expression of courtesy. There was something familiar about the man's face. She had seen so many faces through her concert performances and social occasions; Lily could not place this one. She continued to discuss pleasantries and nothing much in particular. Lily felt it best to say as little as possible; she waited to find out what the officer wanted from her. As he kept on talking she realized that the face behind the voice was that of the person who had called after her as she had left the café on the day of the accident. The officer continued to chat amicably and Lily realized, from his conversation, that he had visited her many times before on the hospital premises. At that moment Hannah entered the room.

"Paul," she said, "how kind of you to be visiting momma again."

Hannah's smile was warm and genuine. Lily looked on, somewhat perplexed.

"I must go now, I shall be back to visit with you soon," Paul said.

He clicked his heels, with the usual: "*Heil* Hitler," and left.

"Hannah, who is that?" Lily inquired.

"Oh, mama, don't you remember? That's Cousin Paul von Wallenstadt, father's brother's son, your cousin by marriage. You had raised him as a child, mama. Don't you remember? He had seen you the day you had the accident and was calling after you when it took place. He had just arrived in Berlin and he was on his way to visit you."

"Hannah, that's Paul, little Paul?"

"Well, mama, as you can see he's not little anymore. It was so good to see him again. He had asked me your race classification and he was genuinely sorry you were classified a Jew."

"Sorry, dear, for whom? Because I have been classified as being Jewish? What is all this ridiculous classification business? Sorry for the Jews and their trials that this regime has thrown on Jewish shoulders? Do not fall into this popular Nazi trap, my daughter. You may have a nun's cloak and an Aryan father, but half of the blood that courses through your veins is mine, and all those who preceded me; underneath your beautiful Aryan face and blonde hair runs the blood of Abraham, Isaac, and Jacob, as it does through so many of these so-called "Aryans." As for me, dear, my cycle must now be complete. I was reared a Protestant, albeit many of my father's family were Jewish, converted to Catholicism when I married your papa, but yet the Third *Reich* says I'm Jewish. It's no shame to me, as it has been to so many German Jews. They were so condescending to the *Ostjüden*. Now these imperious, German Jews realize that this government makes no distinction amongst Jews. Do not forget those renowned personages from my family. They will once again be revered in this land, as much as they are now seemingly despised. This oppressiveness is inhuman; this entire government is based on deceit. It's a government headed by a maniac and the tragedy, dear, is that so many of the people have been caught up in pageantry, conquest, and bravado, while personal liberties and culture are surpressed. How can the minds of the citizens grow and expand if they are told what to do and how to think? This will be the ultimate undoing of this government. And who is this Hitler anyway, but a lower class Austrian, a Linzer tart. This is my country, Hannah, for I'm a German as much as anyone else in Germany. I have the right to be here and I have the right not to be molested and not to be a party to supercilious sneers and curses, whether I'm a Protestant, Catholic or Jewish. Your father was an excellent military man, Hannah, but I strongly doubt that he would ever have become a *Gestapo* member, but of course with a Jewish wife it would have been impossible. And then what of these so called "honorary Aryans," who are not Aryan by the Government's definition, but made "honorary," to suit the convenience of the government. It's all hypocrisy, hypocrisy and duplicity confusing the minds of the citizens, and ultimately pure lies . . . and that's what the people buy. Wake up, dear, and never lose sight of this."

Hannah, used to her mother's soap box oratory, was somewhat taken aback at her mother's anger. She leaned over to kiss the tear that ran down Lily's cheek.

"I love you, mama" said Hannah. "I didn't mean to sound stand-offish."

"I know, dear, I know, but I'm just so angry at what's happening."

"Forgive me, mama, I'm on duty at the hospital tonight. I must leave or I'll be late."

"You work such long hours, dear."

"Good night, mama, I'll see you in the morning."

"Yes, dear, forgive me for prating on so but you do understand."

"I understand, mama."

20

"Good morning, Sister Ursula," said the heavily-accented voice of the gentleman in the white doctor's coat.

"Good morning, doctor," replied Hannah as she made some entries on records at the nurse's station.

Juan Ellabo had come from his native Peru in the mid-1930s to attend medical school at the University of Heidelberg. After graduation he interned at Charité Hospital and, unable to leave Germany, his immediate future dictated that he remain there. He and Hannah usually worked in tandem. Ellabo had always been attracted to her tall, statuesque figure. She was an able nurse whose diagnostic skills far surpassed the training which she had received. Ellabo would frequently commend Hannah on her conclusions, which she often reached before he could form his own.

"Well, Dr. Ellabo," she would occasionally reply, "the Lord endows me with this ability so I can better serve Him."

Ellabo's comment, said with a smile, would usually be, "Yes, Sister."

Ursula's consummate skill continued to impress Ellabo. One day she looked up and caught him staring at her. She smiled at him in return, but for the first time she realized the significance behind the stare. She saw him doing this many times, and when she did she would avert her eyes from his glance and continue with her tasks. In spite of her skills in her field, her interaction with men on a social level had been so limited that she did not know how to react.

Upon returning to the convent, Sister Ursula requested an audience with Mother Superior. It was granted and scheduled for the next morning after matins and before Hannah left for the hospital.

"Good morning, Mother," Ursula said, as she glanced at the round face behind the large, plain, oak desk.

"Good morning, my child," she responded.

Mother Superior sat there waiting for Ursula to continue, but Ursula sat in contemplative silence. Mother Superior said nothing, but waited. Finally she looked up at Ursula and said:

"What is it, child? Are you troubled?"

"Mother," responded Sister Ursula slowly. "I have reason to believe that one of the physicians with whom I work is attracted to me."

"Well," replied Mother with a worldliness that extended far beyond the cloistered walls, "I am not surprised that men would find you attractive. The problem lies not with the men, my dear, but with your perception and ultimate reaction to their attentions."

"Mother, my love and devotion have always been to Jesus; that has never changed."

"Then what bothers you, child? Are you attracted to the doctor?"

"I admire him, Mother, as a physician, but I've never thought of him in any other context. The reason I've asked for this audience is because this is the first time I've become aware of this sort of situation and I'm ignorant of these ways. I don't want to hurt the man, and I do enjoy working with him. I would like to continue doing so."

"My child," replied Mother Superior, "it is mainly what the Lord wants that you should consider. Be contrite, pray, and in your prayers be guided by the counsel of the Blessed Mother. She will guide you on what to do and how you should do it. Be respectful to the doctor and bear in mind that you have chosen to serve the Lord by caring for the sick."

"Thank you, mother," said Sister Ursula as she rose.

"Sit down, child, I have another topic to discuss with you."

"Yes, Mother?" queried Sister Ursula, somewhat surprised.

"When is Countess von Wallenstadt due to leave the hospital?"

"I'm unsure, Mother, but the doctor suggested that she stay there as long as possible. She's been classified a Jew by the authorities. It will be difficult, if not impossible, to get nursing help when she returns home."

"My child," replied mother, "please tell her she is welcome to convalesce here until she has the strength to continue on her own. We will try our best to be of comfort to her."

"Thank you, mother, that's very kind and I'm grateful. I shall certainly extend the invitation."

Hannah lost no time in reiterating Mother Superior's invitation to Lily.

"I'm most appreciative of Mother Superior's offer, dear," said Lily, "but what am I to do all day and in the evenings? Will I be able to practice on the piano?"

"Yes, mama, I am sure it can be arranged during certain hours. We do have a piano which Sister Margarete plays. You can rest, read the balance of the time, and even help in the garden when you get stronger."

"It sounds quite feasible, dear," replied Lily, " let me think about it. I'll discuss it with Dr. Lustig."

"An excellent idea, *Fräulein* Mendelssohn," said Dr. Lustig. "I recommend it most highly. I think you'll be ready to leave by next week."

As Dr. Lustig left the room Paul von Wallenstadt entered. Lily looked up at Paul, happy to see the child she had reared from infancy, but uneasy to see him in the uniform which he wore.

"Good morning, dear aunt," he said.

"Good morning, Paul," she replied. "How kind of you to visit me."

"How are you feeling?" he asked.

"Much stronger, thank you," she replied.

"And Cousin Hannah, how is she?"

"Quite well, thank you," responded Lily.

"Will she be here soon?"

Aha! thought Lily, Hannah is the object of Paul's attention. Paul waited a while for Hannah, who arrived shortly after his departure. Lily did not mention Paul's visit to her daughter.

Paul continued to visit Lily daily, and more often than not would meet Hannah as well. In time, Hannah could sense Paul's attraction to her, but she followed Mother Superior's advice concerning Dr. Ellabo, and applied it to the situation with Paul.

Hannah's prayers for guidance seemed to be answered by the Virgin Mother. Hannah no longer felt that uncomfortable among men, and she could comport herself appropriately. Unwittingly, Hannah's beauty and new sense of emotional accomplishment made her appear even more desirable to her male admirers.

Lily was discharged from the hospital on June 22, 1940. Schmidt, her driver, greeted her with flowers as he held the car door for Lily and Hannah. They were going to the Grunewald villa, prior to proceeding to the convent. Upon arrival at Grunewald, they saw a sign posted on the door saying:

ATTENTION!

THIS PROPERTY HAS BEEN CONFISCATED
FOR GOVERNMENTAL USE.

"What is this?" shouted Lily angrily. "My home is gone?"

A young guard stood outside.

"What *is* happening?" asked Lily. "This is my home."

"Mademoiselle Mendelssohn?" the guard asked.

"Yes, I am she," replied Lily.

"The *Gestapo* have appropriated this building."

"Oh, they have," Lily responded wryly. "And just where am I supposed to go? I do have things inside you know."

"You may claim your clothes and personal effects, madam, but works of art are to be left as is."

The guard unlocked the outer doors. He handed Lily a letter with the ever prominent insignia of the Third *Reich*.

"What is it, mama? What does the letter say?" queried Hannah."

"The *Reich* has told me that I may remain in the house until further notice, but I must now pay rent. I'm instructed to go to the *Gestapo* Headquarters on Prinz Albrecht Strasse."

"Hannah," Lily said, with an urgency in her voice that her daughter had rarely heard, "you see why I must leave the country? My house is taken from me and I have to pay rent to live in it."

"Yes, mama, I do understand."

"Hannah," Lily repeated, "I do wish you would reconsider and come with me."

"Yes, mama," responded Hannah, in a way that Lily knew there was no change of heart.

A *Gestapo* car pulled up in front of the house and a tall, blond officer exited and strode up the stairs. It was Paul von Wallenstadt.

"Do forgive this, Aunt Lily," said Paul apologetically and visibly embarrassed. "I just found out about it."

"Can I go get some things, Paul?"

"Of course, Aunt Lily, take what you want."

"Must I go to Prinz Albrecht Strasse?" asked Lily as she handed Paul the letter.

"Let me see if there is anything I can do, Aunt Lily."

Lily and Hannah walked upstairs to the bedrooms where they packed a bag for the convent. As Lily left, she walked into the music room, towards her piano. She caressed it, as if she were leaving an old friend. She thought of playing something on it, but her feelings drained her of physical strength.

"Come, Hannah," she called, "I'm sure the house will be here long after we're not."

It was a sorrowful time and Lily felt she had no one to turn to for solace. The emptiness of the house heightened Lily's feelings. She missed Christian. She thought of him often, but she had not heard from him since her accident. Hannah was not the best confidante for Lily. When Lily would discuss things with Hannah, Hannah would relate them to God and prayer. At this juncture, Lily did not want to hear Hannah's musings. As Lily and Hannah exited, Paul, who was waiting outside, clicked his heels, saluted them, and said, "*Heil* Hitler."

"May I drive you someplace, Aunt Lily?" inquired Paul.

"No, Paul," replied Lily imperiously, not wishing to get into a *Gestapo* auto. "I do not wish to ride in the lap of those who've helped themselves to something that's not theirs. Schmidt, my driver will take me."

"Yes, ma'am," Paul replied. "Sister Ursula?" Paul continued, indicating both the offer of a ride and his hope of its acceptance.

"Thank you, Paul, but I'll accompany mama."

A telephone call was placed to the limousine service, and Schmidt drove by a few moments after that. Once settled in the car, Lily said to Hannah:

"Paul manages to see you a lot, doesn't he, Hannah?"

"Yes, mama, he does. It's nice to have a family member around."

"Of course, dear," replied Lily, concealing her doubts and concerns about Paul's intentions.

21

The convent in which Hannah served was one of those places that would typically fit the description of its function. Thick, stone walls holding back the world on the other side in order to surround those who followed their monastic pursuits within.

Lily's cell was cold and dank. An electric heater was supplied with some additional accoutrements that were not normally provided to the convent's inhabitants. This raised the level of comfort in the cell close to that of some sub-standard hotel room which might cater to those whose circumstances forced them to be more concerned with utility than luxury. The room was small with a bed, one electric light, a chair with a separate reading lamp, and a sink. A small window rose high above Lily's head—too high for her to open. At times Lily thought that the outside air might be warmer than that within her room. The lack of amenities was more than compensated for by the care given to Lily. Dr. Lustig had organized a program for her, in addition to his thrice weekly visits. Lily had an hour of physical therapy each morning and afternoon. The meals, spartan, but nutritious were taken in a room separate from that of the convent's other residents. Mornings and evenings were spent reading. Lily was able to play the piano in the afternoons. The piano was installed for her use in a separate cottage on the convent grounds. The marked, external sterility, inculcated in Lily a deep internal peace—much more than she had for months. The setting removed her from the brutal treatment inflicted by the Nazi government.

Hannah continued her work, which was, at this point, exclusively in Charité Hospital. As such, she worked more closely with Dr. Ellabo. She also had frequent visitations from Paul, who would, usually inconspicuously, manage to drop by and talk to her while she was on duty.

"Paul," she would always say, "I'm really not permitted to talk to you, even though you're my cousin. It's against the rules and you know that."

Talk to him she did, however, usually uttering similar comments.

Hannah rarely saw her mother as often as she had previously. She had returned to her regular schedule, secure in the feeling that her mother was in good hands. Dr. Ellabo continued to "court" Hannah, but she was able to rise above the situation with tact and good humor.

One day, as Hannah was leaving the hospital, a woman approached her.

"Pardon, Sister, but are you Sister Ursula?"

"Why, yes," Hannah replied, "but I'm sorry, I don't seem to recognize you. Do I know you?"

"No, you don't, Sister, but I know your mother; would you be kind enough to deliver a message to her for me?"

"Yes," replied Hannah, with some degree of hesitation.

The woman, sensing Hannah's discomfort, quickly said:

"I prefer not to place anything in the post."

"I understand," replied Hannah, realizing that items in the post might be censored.

Hannah took the envelope, and when she returned to the convent, she gave it to another nun who delivered it to Lily. Lily did not open it immediately, but she paused to consider what it might contain and who might be sending it to her. She rather suspected it was from Christian—who had called at the Grunewald villa and had been informed of her whereabouts—but the handwriting was not Christian's. She had received hundreds of letters from well-wishers, but she sensed this was different. Well, here goes, she thought, as she opened the missive.

The quality of the paper was poor, all resources channeled into a war machine, personal stationery not being one of the government's highest priorities. Mundane things like this always had an effect on Lily. She was used to writing on high quality vellum and handling the cheap, paper stock offended her sensibilities. After a few moments she read the note.

31 July, 1940

Dear Countess,

I was quite upset to hear of your accident. I was not even aware of it until sometime later. We had left the café heading in different directions and the newspapers had made no mention of it.

I look forward to seeing you, at the usual place, when you are feeling better.

Cordially,

Dorothea Merth

22

In August of 1940, President Roosevelt halted Jewish immigration from Germany. Certain countries were open to German emigration and prominent persons could still avail themselves of U.S. visas at the American Embassy. Lily's original visa had expired. It was good for four months minus one day.

It was December, 1940, four months after Roosevelt's order, when Lily was ready to leave the convent. In a farewell meeting with Mother Superior, Lily said:

"Mother, it's not without fear that I'm returning to the world outside of these walls. My visit here has been a time of peace, contemplation, and inspiration for which I shall be ever indebted."

"What do you plan to do, child?" inquired Mother.

"I've spoken to my husband's cousin, Paul."

"The *Gestapo* officer who visited with you last week?" interrupted Mother curiously.

"Yes, Mother, I know what you're thinking, but I want you to know that I reared the lad, even after my husband's death. My late husband's uncle returned from Africa and took the boy. It was quite traumatic for us both. But, Mother, I love him still and he tells me that he loves me, which I truly believe. It hurts me to see the uniform he now wears. I doubt that he would have been a *Gestapo* officer had I continued to care for him, but then again, one never knows. He was always strong-willed and had a mind of his own. You know, Mother, I sometimes wonder what my former husband's situation would have been under these circumstances.

He was a good soldier, devoted to his country, from a prominent "Aryan" family. I think he would have been proud to have served his country, but I don't know what his reaction would have been in this type of situation. I know that he loved me, but I think that most German men put duty before love. What would I have done then? Well, it's a bridge that I don't have to cross. I'm sure there will be many other bridges, however. But, in answer to your question, I plan to go back to my home in the Grunewald. My cousin has made inquiries and arranged for this. The building has been sequestered by the authorities, but I've been told that I could return. I'm to be charged a rental for living in my own home. I'm concerned, Mother, since I was told that I must stop at *Gestapo* Headquarters before I can re-enter the house, but I guess that's one of the other bridges to be crossed."

"Thank you again, Mother, for everything."

Mother Superior rose from her chair to approach Lily. Lily took her hand and kissed it.

"My child," said Mother, "you have brought a great deal of beauty to many people in your lifetime, and you have left us with much. I wish you the best of luck. Our doors will always be open to you; may God bless you."

23

Using a cane for support, Lily entered the *Gestapo* Headquarters, the building on Prinz Albrecht Strasse, the interior so familiar to her. It had formerly housed the School of Applied Arts, and it was here that Lily had waltzed through the evening with Christian Merth, seven years before. Lily looked up at the grand staircase, and then down again, where at its base was a reception desk manned by a young soldier who greeted her cordially.

"May I help you, Madam?"

"I am here to see Paul von Wallenstadt," Lily answered.

"Your name, please?"

"Lily von Wallenstadt," she answered.

The young man, assuming it was Paul's mother, rose quickly from his chair, gave her a sharp salute and directed her to Paul's office.

"Aunt Lily," Paul exclaimed, when she was ushered in. "How are you?"

"On the mend, Paul, on the mend."

Paul helped her into a chair.

"All the papers are here for you to sign, Aunt Lily. I'm sorry, but your rental can be revoked at any time and no items except your personal effects can be removed from the house."

The situation continued to irritate Lily, but she said nothing. Lily read and signed the papers placed before her.

"There is one more detail, Aunt Lily. Reinhard Heydrich would like to meet with you. One moment, please."

Lily became startled, anxious and concerned. Heydrich was the Chief of the *Gestapo* and a person who was virulently anti-Semitic, reputedly sadistic, worse than Himmler, and feared by both friend and foe. Paul placed a call, held the telephone away from his ear and said:

"He will meet with you tomorrow evening, Aunt Lily. A car will fetch you at 6:00. This will give you time to rest and dress before the evening."

"Dress?" replied Lily in astonishment.

"Yes, you're being invited to cocktails and dinner."

Lily was flabbergasted. She could not fathom why a person like Heydrich would have an interest in her, particularly since she had been classified as Jewish.

"Paul," said Lily, "I'm really upset about this. Why does Heydrich want to see me?"

"I don't know, Aunt Lily, but I understand that he's looking forward to meeting you."

"He is?" she replied. "Well, that makes me even more upset."

They'll probably hand me a bill to pay for my own dinner, she thought.

"But Paul, I just don't understand. I'm classified Jewish and this man regards Jews as sub-human."

"Aunt Lily," Paul said, in complete innocence, "we in the *Gestapo* are all taught these things about Jews—and to despise them—but I don't feel any differently towards you. I love you as I always have ."

"Well, thank you, Paul," Lily replied sarcastically. "What about other Jews?"

"I don't know, Aunt Lily." All I know is my affection for you is genuine, and I don't care what anyone says about this in relationship to you. I do what I'm told to do."

"I understand, Paul," Lily replied, with resignation.

Lily returned to the Grunewald villa. It was wonderful to be home. After a nap and some rest, Lily went to see her beloved piano. There it stood. She could not wait to touch its keys, which, under her fingers, were a creation of sonorous beauty. This was the moment for which she had been waiting. Lily sat down to do her warm-up exercises and as she continued there was a dull thud and no response from several of the keys. She lifted the piano lid to see several English pound sterling notes which had been wedged under the keys, where she had hidden them when the Banker Mendelssohn gave them to her several years earlier. She smiled, replaced them securely on the side, and resumed her practice without incident.

Lily was planning to dine out, since there was little food in the house. Suddenly she was startled by a knock at the door. She made no move to respond. Lily heard a key turning in the latch and she could feel her heart beating against her chest. The door opened and there, framed in its portal, was Helga. Tears flowed readily as the two women embraced.

"Helga, I'm so happy to see you. How are you?"

"I'm working hard at the munitions plant, twelve hours a night, but my heart is here with you, Countess. I'm off today and I've come to straighten the house for you."

"But Helga, that is *rassenshande* and you could get into trouble. Also, you work hard; it seems that all the German civilians must be working at these factories."

"I think you're right, Countess. And, as far as my coming here, pffft!! Who'll know? I thought the laws for Jews employing domestics were that they had to be over 35 years old. Well, I doubt that I'll see that age again."

The two women laughed heartily.

"Countess," continued Helga, "you're in no condition to do anything yourself; I want to do this."

Lily protested, not wanting Helga to get into trouble, but she welcomed the assistance. Helga stayed about two hours and before she left said:

"I'll be back in a few days or so, Countess."

24

Lily was ready to see Heydrich by 6:00 p.m. the following evening. She was well rested, had visited a beautician, and was adorned in a dazzling, white, evening gown. The door bell rang promptly at 6:00 p.m. Lily placed a fur wrap over her shoulders, put on her gloves and opened the door. The driver bowed and escorted her down the stairs into the waiting car. This reminded Lily of her first meeting with Christian. She was overcome with nostalgia and a deep loneliness for him. She was sure that he was out of her life forever.

It was a few minutes drive to their destination, 56-58 Am Grossen Wannsee, also located in the Grunewald. This was one of Lily's favorite streets. It was but a short distance to 42 Am Grossen Wannsee, where Lily had attended the receptions hosted by Max Liebermann, when he was the President of the Berlin Academy of the Arts. *Herr* Liebermann had died in 1935.

Lily entered the *Gestapo* mansion slowly, using the cane for support. An orderly met her at the door and escorted her to the room where the famed and feared Heydrich was waiting. There was no illumination in the room, save for that provided by the logs burning in the fireplace. She walked slowly and deliberately, as if an actress playing the role of a queen, more so out of need rather than the intent to impress. Lily guided herself, commandeering all her inner strength. Here she was to see the man who received his orders from Goering, the man who made Nazis and non-Nazis alike shudder at the mention of his name. Heydrich could and did dispose of people with the ease of one who extinguished a cigarette. He rose as she entered, bowed, clicked his heels and with outstretched arm said:

"Heil Hitler."

Did this terror of Germany expect her to reply in kind? Lily curtsied slightly, feeling the pain in her leg as she did so, and with a smile, infinite charm, femininity, and finesse, as if bowing before the Kaiser, said:

"*Mein Herr*, it is an occasion to meet a personage of such importance."

"Be seated, madam," he replied. "Would you care for a drink?"

"An *aperitif* would be fine, thank you, *Herr Obergruppenführer.*"

Lily projected breeding and title, old world personage that she was, but her demonstration of deep respect barely managed to conceal the utter emptiness and contempt which she felt in meeting Heydrich. As she smiled, she observed this man who evoked fear in all who met him—a blond, blue-eyed man of steel looks and personality. Lily felt it best not to speak until spoken to. She did not; he did not. They both sat in silence. Heydrich would look at and through Lily as if she was a creature in a test tube. Lily readily recognized his disdain, would not concede to him nor to her own discomfort, and ignored it. She sat quietly, under his observation, her white gown sparkling from the reflected light, which shone upon an adjoining silver urn and bounced back again. The entire effect gave Lily an ethereal appearance, as if she might disappear altogether if the light were diminished. An orderly arrived with an *aperitif* and hors d'oeuvres. Lily accepted the drink from the silver tray, feigned a sip, and placed the glass on the adjacent table.

Finally Heydrich spoke:

"My family knew your husband's family quite well," Heydrich said condescendingly.

He employed a clipped, icy Prussian military voice. Lily nodded.

"A fine Aryan family," he continued. "You have an attractive daughter, too, madam."

Lily blanched internally, retaining her external composure. Nothing escapes these pigs, she thought.

Silence again descended upon the room. Heydrich observed Lily in his detached manner. She would occasionally bring her glass to her lips and replace it on the table. Heydrich continued to stare at her. Lily would match his gaze with a gentle countenance, glance at Heydrich and then direct her eyes elsewhere. As she did, she noticed a piano near the far wall and her eyes rested on the instrument. Heydrich, noting her every move, reacted to this as if Lily were a fish who bit the hook.

"Does the piano interest you, madam?" he asked.

At that moment an orderly entered the room announcing that dinner was about to be served. Heydrich rose and looked at Lily, indicating that she was to rise. He watched as Lily struggled to extricate herself from the deep folds of the chair, but the chair seemed to hold on to her, as if she were a morsel in the mouth of a lion, who was struggling to retain its prey. Lily finally rose to her feet, adjusted her gown and her mind set. She glanced at Heydrich who said, in an imperious, deprecating tone:

"The dining room is to the left, madam."

Lily departed from the room slowly, Heydrich accompanying her at the same pace. Once in the foyer, however, he quickened his pace and left Lily behind. Lily noted scores of *Gestapo* officers entering the dining room ahead of her, then all was quiet. She continued to walk down the empty hall, finally arriving at the portals of the dining room. Primping herself slightly, she entered the room and stopped. She glanced around the room and noticed about a dozen officers all seated, with Heydrich at the head of the table, the seat opposite him, empty, awaiting her presence. Lily, acting somewhat as the ingenue, remained in the doorway immobile. None at the table moved until Heydrich motioned to Lily, indicating that she should be seated. At this point Lily had to grapple with pulling the chair away from the table, holding on to her cane, sitting down, and pulling the chair back underneath the table. All assembled waited and watched. It was a clumsy situation and Lily tried to make the best of it. This being done she was physically exhausted. As soon as this was accomplished Heydrich gave the nod to one of the waiters and the dining room became a flurry of activity as the room filled with additional servers.

None of the *Gestapo* officers spoke to Lily. It was possible that they might have been afraid of Heydrich, who all the time was coldly staring at Lily. No matter, Lily played her role as the ultimate guest—gracious and smiling.

"Shall we adjourn for *digestives*," announced Heydrich, his clipped tones cutting through the room.

The assembled officers rose *en masse* and adjourned to an adjacent room. Lily remained seated.

"Will you not join us?" Heydrich said to Lily, without expression.

Lily nodded in assent. The officers departed as Lily worked to disengage herself from the chair. Heydrich lingered behind for a moment to watch Lily's attempts, and then he left as well. A steward approached Lily saying:

"May I assist?"

"Please," replied Lily.

Upon standing, she straightened her dress, fluffed her hair and started for the adjacent room. A mirror over a sideboard served as a means for her to freshen her makeup before she proceeded further. She entered the room as members of the gathering observed her every move. Heydrich was not in attendance.

A small podium with a piano and a music stand a short distance away did not escape Lily's glance. It suddenly occurred to her that she might be asked to play. She bristled at the thought of these thugs bringing a person of her stature to perform, but secretly she longed to have her fingers touch the keyboard.

Suddenly Heydrich strode into the room with a violin under his arm. He approached Lily and said, loudly enough, for all assembled to hear:

"Would you care to accompany me on the piano while I play the violin, madam?"

Accompany him? she thought. It's like holding the trash bin for the sweeper.

"It would be my pleasure," she replied sweetly.

"I thought we might do the Bach *Sonata for Viola da Gamba and Harpsichord*."

Lily looked at the violin and said nothing.

"I have transcribed the piece for violin. Do you know it?"

Lily paused and hesitatingly replied:

"I will be happy to try."

Of course she knew the piece; she had been playing a great deal of Bach at the convent. Lily surmised that Heydrich undoubtedly assumed she was quite stiff and had no time for practice or warm up.

"Bach is one of my favorites," Heydrich said, "Would you like the sheet music?"

"Thank you," Lily replied.

Well, she thought, his aim is probably to make a fool of me.

Heydrich sat stiffly in his chair. Lily assumed her position at the piano bench, but it was too far from the piano. She turned to Heydrich and said, in the fine, formal German that she usually used.

"*Mein Herr*, would you be so kind as to assist me with the piano bench. It must be moved closer to the piano."

Heydrich looked at her, rose from his seat, helped Lily to rise and move slightly forward, as an aide rushed to move the bench closer to the piano.

"Thank you kindly," she said as she nodded her head regally.

She was at the piano now, and she had assumed the demeanor and proportions of the concert star that she was. The officers looked at the scene unflinchingly as Heydrich took his seat, not readily realizing that by assisting Lily he had broken the tone which he had set heretofore. Lily looked at Heydrich who had re-assumed his air of superciliousness, as he nodded to begin.

Lily started to play the unfamiliar piano and she felt that it had a tightness to it, one to which she was not accustomed. As she continued it seemed to loosen itself and she, in turn, became looser. Heydrich started to move the bow across the strings, strong and secure in his knowledge and feeling of the music. The duo became more and more hypnotic, as if a maypole were at the center of the room and the instruments were two streamers wrapping themselves around it. The music became more tense and the rhythm increasingly frenzied, as if the instruments, in tandem, were making love to each other.

The audience, mesmerized by the performance, became wild participants in the love-making between the two instruments, and, unknowingly they released themselves to the eroticism. They became the objects of the giving by the performers and the adulation of the audience fed the performers, who absorbed it quickly and gave out more to their audience who in turn digested it rapaciously. It was as if the very life of each one depended on the existence of the other.

The officers were becoming transformed from passive observers into active and passionate participants in the twistedly erotic confrontation between the two musicians. Gradually they yielded themselves to the seductiveness of the music. They became the objects of the music, the carnality of Lily and Heydrich—each unit in this bizarre *ménage-à-trois* was ravenously absorbing the adulation of the other two and, in turn, returned the feeling with even greater passion.

As the slow movement started, there was a hiatus in this escalation of emotional intensity. Lily was able to look at Heydrich, the "iceberg" whose body and soul exulted in the living fear of the hell on earth which he, and those of his ilk had created; those who felt that Jews were vermin, to be stepped on like insects, and here was Lily, a Jewess, performing like a monkey on a string for the *übermenschen*. They, who used Lily for their entertainment as if she were but a *papier maché* marionette so easily manipulated by those who controlled the strings. Lily felt as if she were compelled to dance inches above the fires of the hell they had created, but yet in reality playing the piano was her passion, and she was able to indulge herself in that which she most enjoyed. She felt hate for her oppressors and hate for herself—that she could be so hoodwinked into this—but yet, did she really have a choice? Suddenly the hatred she felt was transmitted physically into her performance, which became a tool for sadistic oppression. This received an immediate in-kind response from the violin, but the violin, instead of being on a par with the piano, became subservient to it—and so it continued, with the violin playing wildly, trying to overtake the piano, struggling to conquer the unconquerable *untermensch*, but it was useless. Lily was unconquerable. Clearly she was the master; no longer on the previous equal footing, the violin seemed to plead for its very existence—which Lily allowed—but she would attack and re-attack as relentlessly as she herself had been put upon. Each succeeding measure produced more gradations of intense contrapuntal anger. He, alternatively caressing and begging, she unrelentingly hammering the keys that were but vassals to her fingers, hammering and hammering, as if with each chord she was suffocating Heydrich. The culmination of the performance was a climax of simultaneous pain and beauty, with Lily being the sadist, as she inflicted the agony of loss and defeat upon Heydrich.

The performance ended. Lily slowly turned towards Heydrich. He was glaring at Lily who appeared serene and triumphant. Heydrich was angered that he had permitted this woman, a Jewess, to have the upper hand. He was breathless, panting from sheer exhaustion, the perspiration glistening on his forehead. Lily appeared composed and smiled humbly. She bowed her head towards Heydrich with grace and dignity as if nothing had happened, but they both knew that something had. They looked at each other, just for a moment, neither of them revealing any emotion to the other. Then they turned to the audience and bowed.

This incident was indelibly etched into Heydrich's memory and further fueled his hatred towards Jews and women. Although

Heydrich never acknowledged it to himself, but he had actually enjoyed the musical whipping. From that evening onward he would have similar sexual fantasies with Lily playing the dominant role, which were to continue for the remainder of his days, until his death at the hands of an exiled Czech paratrooper on May 27, 1942.

The officers in the audience were wildly appreciative of both Heydrich and Lily. Heydrich rose, bowing to Lily and, with bowed head, glared at her and said:

"A glowing performance, madam. I will look forward to further sessions. I hope you will honor me by playing with a chamber group in which I participate."

Oh no, thought Lily angrily, as she smiled and bowed her head in return.

"There is a car outside to take you home," continued Heydrich.

Lily returned to the Grunewald villa somewhat despondent. She had no desire to interact with Heydrich and her head was filled with these thoughts as she finally fell asleep.

The next day a young officer rang the bell and presented Lily with a sealed envelope with the Swastika logo on the flap. Lily opened it and read:

> Mademoiselle Mendelssohn,
>
> We would appreciate the pleasure of your company next Tuesday, at dinner. Afterwards we look forward to hearing you play a piano selection of your choice. A car will arrive for you at 6:30 p.m.

What bondage, Lily thought. I must now be at his beck and call.

The following Tuesday, the car arrived—exactly on schedule of course. Lily was attired in a bright, blue gown whose color served to brighten her sagging spirits; it made her look much younger than her years—a look she wanted to project for that evening. Lily was ushered into the dining room and the steward assisted her in getting settled. This evening there was a much larger assemblage at the table, about 30 guests, both men and women, and they were all quite animated. Lily was silent, but this time the guests seated near her spoke. She replied, graciously and cordially, offering no conversation unless addressed directly. Every one was charming and behaved quite properly, but Lily felt as if she were in a cage full of wild beasts.

After dinner all adjourned to a ballroom with a podium in the front, and rows of chairs accommodating close to 200 people. There were many, in addition to the dinner guests, who were now assembled. Lily was escorted to a chair in the front row where she was seated. Heydrich and three other persons—one in civilian dress—went to the podium, bowed to the audience and began to play a Beethoven string quartet. Lily watched Heydrich and wondered how such a master of hate could be so sensitive in his playing. She observed each movement he made. She watched his stiffness melt with the music that he was creating.

During a pause he raised his head and caught Lily's gaze before she could look away. Without revealing any of her emotions, she held his eyes. He gazed back with a piercing stare, but it was no longer one of detestation. It was a look with a malevolent question behind it, analyzing—as if Heydrich were wondering what harm to inflict next. After the performance ended, the audience—including Lily—applauded. An announcement was made that there would be a fifteen minute interval, after which Lily was to perform. The crowd seemed animated and expectant.

Lily was having coffee when Heydrich approached her.

"Did you enjoy the performance, Mademoiselle?" he queried.

"I did, *Herr Obergruppenführer*," she replied.

As the overhead lights were flicked, Lily was advised that she was to perform next. The audience was seated and she walked to the podium with her cane and placid dignity. She was in great pain when it came time to step on to the podium, but she was assisted and ushered to the piano bench. She had chosen to play Johann Sebastian Bach. Lily bowed to the audience and began her performance. It was one of complete mastery and exceptional control. The repetitive rhythm of the piece seemed to lull the audience into a sense of transcendent appreciation, far removed from the realities of their daily lives. Lily played measure after measure, the audience waiting expectantly for each measure that followed, the piece ultimately exploding with disharmonious counterpoint fusing into a coda of harmonious beauty. The audience, Heydrich included, applauded in appreciation and shouted:

"Encore, encore."

Lily did not rise from the bench, but stretched her legs as she bowed her head to the audience. The encore was Mozart's Turkish Rondo that was performed with a lilting vivacity and humor. The audience was completely captivated and cheered wildly after the performance. Heydrich approached Lily and said:

"Thank you for the performance. Your selection was excellent. Bach is such a favorite of mine."

"That is surely one thing we have in common, *Herr Obergruppenführer*," Lily replied. "I have always been grateful that Felix Mendelssohn-Bartholdy resurrected Bach to the world, where he so rightfully belongs," she said, displaying an audaciousness that had been previously surpressed. As soon as the words left her lips she began to regret her action.

The response was met with a cold glare followed by the comment:

"Your car is outside, madame," whereupon he turned his back on Lily and stormed angrily from the room.

Lily, exiting to the waiting car, was greeted by the smiles and adulation of her audience.

25

Hannah continued with her work at Charité. Dr. Ellabo had become increasingly attentive and Hannah found it was becoming easier for her to adjust to his Latin temperament. It was so spontaneous and open, quite unlike that of the Germans who, for the most part, were much less expressive of their emotions.

A week after Lily's performance Paul spoke to Hannah, his mood quite serious.

"Heavens, Paul, what is it? You look so pre-occupied."

"Hannah, dearest Hannah," he replied. "I don't quite know how to continue. My Commanding Officer called me into his office yesterday. He had received orders directly from Heydrich. It seems that Heydrich has concocted this wild scheme . . ." Paul paused and could not continue.

"What is it, Paul?" asked Lily apprehensively.

"It's about your mother," he replied.

"What *is* it, Paul?"

"Hannah, harm may come to your mother if I do not carry out my orders."

"What orders, Paul?" asked Lily

"I have been told to sire a child."

"Yes, Paul. I don't understand. Who are you to marry and what has that to do with mother?"

"Hannah, you are to be its mother."

Hannah's reaction to this pronouncement was a laugh, but then her face became colorless.

"What are you saying, Paul, I don't understand. What are you saying? I'm a nun and I'm married to Jesus. How can I do such a thing?"

Hannah's eyes filled with tears, but she remained controlled; then she became angry and blurted:

"And why must this be done, and why with me, your cousin? What is the reason for this? Also, what would happen to the child? What will happen to my mother? What will happen to me? I've never slept with a man. Paul, I'm leaving now. I find this entire situation incredible and I cannot deal with it, and I'll not do it."

Hannah turned around and walked away from Paul. She returned to her post on the hospital floor, but she was too upset to function. She was able to obtain a replacement, and left the hospital to return to the convent. She requested an emergency audience with Mother Superior and then went to the chapel to pray.

About 20 minutes later Hannah heard the door squeaking followed by footsteps that echoed and re-echoed throughout the chapel.

"Sister," intoned a soft voice.

Hannah looked up to see the unfamiliar face that matched the voice. It was a person whom she had not seen previously, dressed in novitiate garb. She thought this highly unusual, but dismissed it and said nothing.

"Sister," the voice repeated, "Mother Superior will see you now."

"Thank you," replied Hannah.

Mother Superior was at her desk as Hannah entered her office. Hannah sat down, tried to compose herself, but burst into tears as she reiterated Paul's discussion and how she was unable to prevent their meetings. Mother Superior was stunned and silent.

"I have been praying for guidance, Mother, but I have had no response. What shall I do?"

"Prayers are not always answered immediately, my child," Mother answered.

Hannah continued:

"I love my mother. I would do anything to protect her, but I don't know why this is happening."

"Continue your prayers, child. Return to my office after morning chapel."

The next morning Hannah met Mother Superior again.

"Mother, I do not know if my prayers have been heard."

"The Lord hears all prayers, child. Sometimes we must accept inner calmness, and in this quiet time, with the Lord close by, make our own decision. Have you had any thoughts about this?"

"Yes, mother," Hannah replied with calmness and serenity. "I've been quite fulfilled in my present roles as nun and nurse. I want nothing more than to be permitted to continue this. Is God putting me to a severe test? I cannot really answer that."

"We are tested throughout our lives," Mother replied. "The Lord poses us with many challenges. The way we handle these challenges is the criterion of our growth and maturity in the eyes of the Lord."

"I have decided, Mother, that I must do what I can to help my mother. I know the Lord will understand. I realize I'll have to leave the order, but this may be my test."

"Do you wish to leave the order?"

"Oh no, Mother, that's the last thing I want to do."

"Do you wish to follow through with the proposal made to you?" Mother asked. "What did you tell the young man?"

"I told him I wouldn't do it, Mother. I can't imagine having sex with him. My God! We were raised as brother and sister. How could he even ask me? I had to speak to you and to the Virgin Mother."

"Let this stream run its course," Mother replied. "Meet with him again. See if you can get some additional information regarding the threat against your mother and this proposal that has been made to you. I suggest you go to the hospital and continue your life, as usual, as best as you can."

Two days passed and Paul appeared at the hospital.

"Can we talk at lunch, in about an hour, Sister Ursula?" he queried.

Hannah looked at him coldly.

"Please, Sister, please. This is not my fault," he pleaded. He was deeply embarrassed and acutely aware of how much he had hurt her, but even he could not begin to comprehend her shock, her outrage, her feeling of betrayal—for she had not been cloistered from the radical changes in the world outside and, sensing danger managed to conceal the turmoil within, behind a facade of calmness and rationality.

"Yes, Paul, I shall meet with you for lunch, but you know I must always eat in the nun's dining room and you can't eat there."

"I'll arrange for a private room, Sister. No one will know we're eating together."

"And alone, Paul, it's really out of order."

Hannah entered the private dining room an hour later. Paul was already seated. Hannah sat down and said:

"Paul, you cannot expect me to give up my life on the basis of this ridiculous proposal. What's behind all of this?"

"Sister, you do not know Heydrich. He is a fiend. It is said that even the *Führer* calls him 'the man with an iron heart.' Heydrich is a person who derives pleasure from inflicting pain and cruelty. He knows your mother and obviously wants to punish her by doing this."

"But Paul," inquired Hannah, "who is to say that something will not happen to mother if I don't go though with this? And if I do, it is also possible that something, or nothing can happen to my mother. I don't want to get married. I have absolutely no intention of having sex with you. I don't wish to be involved with this; Paul, you'll have to find someone else with whom you can perform this disgusting scenario."

"All I can tell you, Sister, is that I know of Heydrich's reputation and I wouldn't knowingly go against him. As far as marriage is concerned, you need not worry, that was never even discussed. It's the child they're after. I have been chosen to be the father, and you, not any other person, have been chosen to be the mother. Possibly the father could have been a stranger, but I'm pure Aryan and you're 50% Aryan, and we are both blonde and blue-eyed with Nordic features. The *Reich* wants more Aryan children."

"What are you thinking about, Paul? What are your feelings with respect to all of this?"

"Well, I'm very fond of you, Sister. You were truly a sister to me, but I'd not want you to be upset."

The callousness of this hypocritical solicitude galled her, but the absurdity of the situation intrigued her even more.

"No, Paul, that's not what I mean. What do you think of this entire idea?"

"I really don't know, but I have heard of *Lebensborn*, although it is something the government wants to keep quiet."

"*Lebensborn*? What's that?"

"It's something that's best not discussed," Paul replied.

"Best not discussed?" Hannah shot back. "You must tell me what's involved and everything you know about this."

Paul replied hesitantly:

"Sister, the *Reich* has a program where Aryan men father the children of Aryan women. The children are reared in beautiful surroundings and the mothers can stay with their children if they choose and work at the site. It seems that many of the women are nurses. The children, Sister, are actually the property of the *Reich* in order that the nation be peopled with Aryans."

"Paul," replied Hannah, with her anger increasing, "that is an obscenity, a defilement of a human being, and a sin against God. It is hardly an aggrandizement of a race. Besides in order to be an Aryan your blood line has to be traced back to 1750. My mother has been classified a Jew which means my child will only be 75% Aryan."

"I have been told that credentials will be provided substantiating that you are 100% Aryan. Besides, with our features, the child will be a credit to the *Reich*," Paul responded.

"Paul, how do you feel about using me to father this child?"

"Hannah . . . pardon, Sister . . . as I said, I've always liked you, yes, and I'll be honest, attracted to you. You're a beautiful woman with a marvelous character. I've liked you ever since we were children, but when I first saw you in the hospital my attraction to you increased. I would never presume to discuss a joint relationship with you, since I know your circumstances. You must realize it's a duty for me, and one which I must follow. If it is to be done, I'd rather be the person to father the child than some stranger."

"Paul, I'm stunned that this type of situation can occur in a supposedly civilized nation. It's a national curse."

"Sister, I must know of your decision. I report to my commandant when I return. It's better to have two lives . . . a child for the *Reich* and one for your mother."

"Do you mean my mother might be killed?"

"It's a possibility that cannot be overlooked, Sister."

Paul became intensely serious and looked straight at Hannah and said:

"Will you do it?"

Hannah did not respond, but she returned Paul's intense stare. She, too, had cared for him, but in a non-sexual way; she had a higher calling, and this type of liaison had never entered her mind. She wondered: did she trust him, is this my test? If so, there will be two lives besides our own that are involved. Would I be doing this because I really do want to sleep with Paul? She dismissed this immediately; it was her mother she was concerned about. What, my Jesus, what is to happen? She sat there for a few moments, as if in a stupor, bereft in mind and body, as if she didn't exist at all. Suddenly she felt a cool breeze across her flushed face, yet no windows were open. She felt as if there was another person next to her and she became more frightened than ever. After a few moments the feeling dissipated as she was overwhelmed with an enormous calm. Hannah had regained her equanimity, the frustration and anxiety had melted. She was enlightened and imbued with her faith and the existence of her

Lord. And it was, in these moments that her prayers for guidance were answered.

She took her hand, placed it on top of Paul's and replied in an eerily calm voice,

"Yes, Paul, yes. My mother gave me life, and I shall not only give her life, but one to the *Reich* as well."

Paul did not answer. He sat there in stunned silence, awestruck by the peace and beauty that emanated from Hannah as she spoke.

26

The clock was ticking rapidly for Jewish lives in the *Reich*. The war hardly seemed to touch the lives of many of the non-Jews in Berlin. The cafés were full and people in the streets seemed happy. In June of 1941, Jewish emigration was halted and shortly thereafter *Reichführer* Himmler ordered Friedrich Jeckeln to implement the plan of evacuation of Jews to the East.

On September 16, 1941, the yellow *Judenstern* had to be clearly displayed on the clothing of all Jews.

In October of 1941, Jews began to report to collection centers. One of the larger ones was the liberal synagogue at Levetzowstrasse 8-9. This became a center for deportees to the East. Jews would be loaded into furniture vans and whisked away before sunrise to waiting trains, where, for the most part, they were herded like animals into freight cars for their journey.

Hannah had returned to the convent. She told Mother Superior of her decision to bear Paul's child as well as the circumstances that led her to make that decision:

"The Lord told me what to do, Mother."

"My child," replied Mother Superior, "God is faith; human beings form the rules about religion. I know how you have agonized over this. We are living in different times, where the established rules have been replaced by new edicts, edicts that fly in the face of God. Under normal circumstances you would have to leave the order, but, as I said, these are not such times. I thought it might be Satan who is guiding you, but I truly do not believe this. This would not normally be a decision that I could make. I would have to discuss it with my superiors, but I too have prayed and pondered about the situation and the unquestionable lack of morality which it poses. The Lord in His infinite wisdom has guided you in your decision as He has guided me in mine. My recollection of our discussions concerning this matter, as well as yours in discussing them with me, will vanish once you leave this office. You will continue with your duties at the hospital and convent. Do nothing that will arouse any suspicion. When you are with child you will come to see me. I will arrange for an emergency leave. When you have done what the Lord has directed, you will return here and resume your duties to Him. You are a chosen person to be able to carry out God's mandate."

27

The infamous January 20, 1942 conference at Wannsee, which implemented the Final Solution of mass Jewish extermination, had come and gone. Lily's life was quite proscribed. She would practice for her weekly concerts at Am Grossen Wannsee where she would perform with Heydrich, who fiddled while Jews burned. How was Lily to know of this decision that was reached barely one hundred feet from where she performed?

She had received a *Gestapo* order advising that her home, previously claimed by the government for wartime use, was now to be used as bachelor officers' quarters. She was told she could remain in the villa if she wished. There was little choice since there was no other place for her to go. Lily was to have much less space—an apartment consisting of four rooms, which included the music room, a small sitting room and a smaller bedroom with adjoining bath.

Lily was busy with her music and involved with her frustrations. The reduction in the space available to her in her own home was the last indignation she believed she could tolerate. She was now, in effect, a prisoner of the *Gestapo*. She decided to leave Germany in any way possible and, since the borders were now closed to Jews, her departure would have to be an illegal one.

Lily met *Frau* Merth at their usual meeting place that Wednesday. The two had become good friends and would meet often. Lily had been telling her of Heydrich's emotional torture, and how she feared that each time she entered the Grunewald villa she might never leave it. She then told *Frau* Merth that she wanted to leave the country.

"Do you really wish to leave Germany?" *Frau* Merth queried.

"Desperately! Christian seems to have disappeared, and he's now out of my life. I don't even know if he's alive. My daughter is gone, completely vanished without a trace. I don't know if she's alive, either. I went to the convent to inquire and I saw—."

Lily stopped short. The person whom Lily saw was the novitiate that Hannah noticed while praying in the chapel. Lily had recognized the girl and she knew the girl's parents, Solomon and Doris Goldmann; Jews who had been evacuated to the East. The convent was housing the girl for her own protection. She felt it was best not to tell *Frau* Merth, both for the security of the convent and *Frau* Merth's own safety. The less one knew the better.

"You saw what?" *Frau* Merth asked.

"I saw how heavy the hearts of the Sisters were. It was quite sad."

"Countess, meet me here next Wednesday," commented *Frau* Merth.

"Of course," responded Lily.

Lily left the café and walked quickly through the streets. She no longer took public transportation as she once did. Jews were forbidden to use it and to appear with the *Judenstern* was usually to be marked a pariah. Some Berliners would turn away in embarrassment, ashamed to have this situation exist, but others were less passive. Transportation was not difficult for Lily. The *Gestapo* bachelors who now occupied Lily's home would often transport her in one of their automobiles. There were now maids in the house who cleaned the officers' rooms and Lily's as well. Lily did not take regular meals with the officers, but they would invite her to dinner occasionally. She was, after all, a famous personality, and rather than persecute a middle-aged Jewess, they were courtly and respectful. Lily would reward them with an occasional musical piece after dinner. She played for her supper, as she would remark. She would even find herself being cast in a motherly role. The officers were young and inexperienced to the sophisticated life of Berlin. They were all from other parts of Germany, and their hearts rested in their homes, not the *Reich* capital.

So it was on this Wednesday that one of the men was being driven to *Gestapo* Headquarters and Lily, as always, was offered a ride.

"Thank you so much for the lift," she said sincerely as she left the car, which was about two blocks from the café.

She preferred not to have the officers know where she was going. Lily's gait had improved, but she still used the cane to walk. Although it was always supposed to be in full view, her *Judenstern* was covered with a muffler. There were times she left Grunewald without it, and she was never questioned. Lily was easily recognized as a celebrity and occasionally she would wear the *Judenstern* as a mark of pride, to remind people that she was a Mendelssohn. She realized that people knew who she was. For the most part, Lily was honored, respected and warmly greeted in public places in spite of her racial classification.

Frau Merth greeted Lily cordially, they chatted superficially, and after coffee was served there was a silence.

"Countess," said *Frau* Merth in hushed tones, "Did you mean what you said about wanting to leave Germany?"

"If only I could, *Frau* Merth. It's still difficult for me to walk and I don't think I'm up to crawling through the grass to reach the Swiss border."

Frau Merth didn't smile at Lily's attempt at humor, but continued:

"Arrangements have been made for you to leave Germany, Countess."

Lily's eyes opened wide with astonishment.

"There is a Jewish organization known as Baum. They will get you out of Germany to safety. I can only provide you with minimum details. I think they might get you to Hungary (still unoccupied at the time), Sweden or possibly Switzerland. At this point I can only tell you how to proceed."

Lily did not know how to react. She was filled with

ambivalence—joy at the thought of leaving the oppression that she faced, yet fear at the prospect of doing it. It took but a second when she asked:

"Is it safe?"

"Of course there can be no guarantees, Countess, but if you follow specific instructions the danger is minimized. Many before you have left Germany without a problem."

"Forgive me, *Frau* Merth, for asking that question, but I was caught off-guard. Yes, I must leave Germany. How do I proceed?"

"Tomorrow afternoon take the 2:02 train from Fredrichstrasse Station to the Charlottenberg stop. The train will arrive there at 2:05. Remain in the rear carriage. At Charlottenberg, leave the train and walk towards the ticketing area. You will be greeted by a woman who will approach you as if you were an old friend. Of course you will not wear the *Judenstern*. The woman will ask how you are. Act animated, happy to see her. She will then invite you to join her for a cup of tea. Walk with her to the station exit, smiling and chatting. She will lead you to an automobile and you will both get in."

"What happens after that?" asked Lily.

"I can tell you nothing more, Countess. Leave everything in their hands. The less you know, the better. Take no luggage with you. It would be as if you were just going out for the day. You are a well-known person, Countess. Under the circumstances the more inconspicuous you are, the better."

"God bless you, *Frau* Merth. I am so grateful," replied Lily.

She was curious about this contact and she wanted to question *Frau* Merth further, but she knew it was unwise. *Frau* Merth arose from her chair, as did Lily. The two women embraced, both exited quickly and, as always, in different directions.

The next day was cold and raw. Heavy, dark clouds blanketed the city as Lily was ready to leave the house.

"Are you going out, madam?" asked Uwe, one of the officers.

"Yes, Uwe," she replied.

"I too. Can I drop you someplace?"

Lily thought quickly. A *Gestapo* car would add legitimacy to her escape.

"Yes, thank you. Leipziger Strasse near Unter den Linden would be fine."

Uwe bowed, clicked his heels, following it with the customary "Heil, Hitler."

He helped Lily down the steps and sat next to her as the driver closed the door of the waiting car.

"I understand you are performing next Tuesday at the *Kulturbund*," he said.

The *Kulturbund* was a Jewish orchestra that performed in Berlin at that time (most other *Kulturbund* orchestras had been disbanded by September of 1941). Lily was scheduled to make her debut there. She was forbidden to play with the Berlin Philharmonic in Beethoven Hall since she was Jewish; even *Reichminister* Albert Speer's petition to Goebbels could not get an exemption for her to perform there. Nonetheless her upcoming performance was a big event to which many in Berlin were looking forward. I have never missed a performance, Lily thought, but I must take this chance to leave Germany.

"Yes, Uwe," she replied, "I'm looking forward to it."

"So are we," responded Uwe, taking pride in Lily's upcoming concert.

She left the car, removed her loosely attached *Judenstern* and headed for Freidrichstrasse Station where, at 1:55 p.m., she settled herself into a seat in the rear car. The train left promptly at 2:02 p.m. She was alone in the compartment. Well Lily, you've been a good actress and now you'll have to be a great one, she thought. Three minutes later, as the train pulled into Charlottenberg Station, Lily heard gun shots. She looked out of the window to see police running along the platform. The train and the gunfire had stopped. As Lily arose to leave the train her compartment door opened quickly and a man in an *SS* uniform entered. The man sat in the seat opposite her. Lily gasped silently and tried to steady herself emotionally. She sat frozen in her seat. The officer opposite raised his head, looked at her and blurted:

"Lily, Lily, what are you doing here?"

"Christian, my God, Christian, it's you? You never told me you were in the *Gestapo*."

"No time to talk, Lily. The train has stopped and the police are questioning all passengers."

"What's happening?" asked Lily.

"The *Gestapo*'s rounding up members of a subversive group."

"A subversive group?" asked Lily.

The shaky tone of Lily's inquiry gave her away. Christian knew her all too well. He grabbed her hand and pulled her into the corridor. My God, he's going to arrest me, she thought; another German officer doing his duty. Christian grasped her wrist so tightly it hurt. He pulled her towards the nearest exit door and they left the train on the opposite side where there were fewer policemen, and less confusion.

"You'll be safe with me, my darling," Christian said protectively. "I'll see you home."

He and Lily left the station into Christian's waiting car. Once in the car they settled themselves and Christian asked:

"Lily, did you ever hear of a group called Baum?"

"Are they a string quartet?" she asked innocently.

"Never mind, where were you going on the train?" and noticing her coat warned, "you may get yourself in trouble without wearing the *Judenstern*."

"Christian, how do you know that I was classified a Jew and not a Protestant? Where have you been all this time? What have you been doing?" Lily asked as her anger increased.

Christian held her hand and replied:

"I've not been in Berlin, Lily," and Lily without thinking said:

"Is there somebody else, Christian?"

"Lily," he replied. "I've seen no one since I last saw you. How could you even think of asking a question like that," Christian said, blanching at what he took to be an insensitivity on Lily's part.

Merth continued to hold her hand and she melted in his grasp, completely oblivious of the uniform he wore. As the car neared the house she quickly came back to reality and withdrew her hand.

"Lily," he said, indignantly, obviously offended by her action.

"Christian," she replied with a perceptible degree of sarcasm, "I do not want you to be accused of *Judenbegünstigung* (favoritism towards Jews, which was a crime) by being in my company."

"Don't be so damned stupid," he growled at her.

"Please do not get out, Christian," Lily said sharply, as the car arrived at the Grunewald villa.

Lily exited from the car, closed the door, and walked up the steps towards the doorway. She turned around to see Christian staring at her. Tears filled her eyes; she smiled at Christian and, looking around to ensure no one was watching blew a kiss to him. Christian's hard face softened as he looked at Lily in the way he used to, with love and desire. He knocked at the window separating him from the driver and the car sped off.

"Did you have a nice afternoon, madam?" asked Uwe as he helped Lily take off her coat.

"Oh, it was just like any other," Lily answered, as she smiled and went to her room.

28

Although Hitler's popularity was never overwhelming amongst Berliners, it had been at an all-time high after France's surrender to Hitler on June 21, 1940. Now, the mood of Berlin had changed. The city faced continual air raids; Berliners were vulnerable to what their nation had been so ruthlessly inflicting on others. Bombs notwithstanding, the concerts continued playing to packed houses. Lily's thoughts were not involved in the war, but with what she shared in common with so many of the Berlin population—their love of music.

The day arrived for Lily's performance at the *Kulturbund*. She was a bit concerned since she had little time for rehearsal with the orchestra, nor had she appeared with one in quite some time. Lily was backstage as members of the audience made their way to their seats. The auditorium was filled to capacity. The majority of seats was occupied by every description of Nazi service personnel; even Richard Strauss, the top man of the *Reich* Music Chamber, was in the audience. Oddly enough, one of the charges of the *Reich* Music Chamber was to ensure that Jewish musicians and "subversive" music were banned from the concert halls. It seems, though, that the desire to hear Lily perform with the orchestra overrode all other considerations.

The conductor appeared on the podium, and the orchestra, many of whom had previously performed with The Berlin Philharmonic, opened with Mozart's "Overture to The Magic Flute." There was an intermission, then the audience returned and the members of the orchestra resumed their places. Lily stepped out on to the stage. There was a moment of silence followed by heavy applause. The auditorium hushed as Lily sat down at the piano and nodded to the conductor to begin. She was going to perform the Schumann *A minor Piano Concerto*. There was not a sound heard as Lily began her performance. The audience was enrapt in her interpretation of the piece. They knew that Lily was a direct descendant of Felix Mendelssohn, and they knew that he and Schumann had been close friends. Lily was imbued with Schumann's music, not only by its intrinsic beauty, but for the very same historical reason as in the minds of the audience. Many were mindful of this alliance and considered her possibly the next best person to the composer himself performing the work.

During the pause between the first and second movements Lily lifted her head to glance at her audience. She saw the forward rows occupied by Nazi officers with somber, rather sad expressions; many had tears in their eyes, evoked by the music. What could they be thinking? Lily wondered. Many, no doubt, had been thinking of Germany's victorious days, but now the tides of war were turning against the Fatherland. Life had changed for the "Aryan" masters and most rational thinking people realized it would be only a matter of time before Germany would lose the war (although many still had unswerving faith in Hitler and his power to triumph). The melancholy of the music seemed to have been intensified in the faces of the once-triumphant.

Lily began the second movement. She played it slowly and deliberately with a smooth, melodic tone that further intensified the sadness of the audience. The music acted as a magnet, unceasingly drawing the feelings of the listeners to it. For so many it was a *weltschmerz* of Romanticism, of a time that had come and gone, a time of civility and respect for people, when their rights were not subjected to the vagaries of the State. Lily was a steadfast part of this past, a representative of the age of civility and liberalism, of a culture free to explore new paths, nurturing creativity and enriching the lives of the people.

From its start, the sad sonority of the third movement gripped the already primed audience; with each passing measure they became more deeply and more ardently involved. Lily, now firmly ensconced in her *milieu,* was no longer living with the oppression of the Third *Reich*. She was doing what she had always done best—playing the piano. Repeatedly, the sadness of the strings and the passion of her performance continued until the piece came to a finale of electric brilliance. There was total silence as Lily finished. The audience, many in tears, had been transported to another place in another time; to interrupt this feeling with something so mundane as the physical movement of their hands would have robbed them of their heightened emotions. Lily sat at the piano, head bowed, with tears streaming down her cheeks. She had become one with the audience and reflected on all of her difficulties, as they had on theirs.

It was a chain reaction—the first person started to applaud and the momentum slowly increased as the audience's awareness returned to the present moment. They became infected with a desire to show their appreciation for the beauty that Lily had given them. The sad mood turned into a joyous frenzy of love and admiration. Lily rose from the bench and bowed humbly. She left the stage as the applause continued unceasingly. After three curtain calls Lily returned to the piano. She sat down for her encore as the audience became silent. It was to be a Beethoven *étude*. This piece, however, did not emanate from either her thoughts or her fingers—she chose instead the music of Mendelssohn. She began playing the last movement of his *E Minor Piano Concerto*. Audible gasps came from the audience and even the orchestra. Lily was doing the unforgivable, playing the degenerate music of a subversive composer. The orchestra sat silent as Lily performed without accompaniment. Slowly, members of the orchestra picked up the tempo and orchestration. The audience did not move. Now it was they who soaked in the fruits of the forbidden harvest. The air was exciting, even ecstatic. A few *Gestapo* officers could be seen with a look of imperious disdain at what they were hearing, but underneath the façade of propriety was the desire to hear the piece to its conclusion; not one single person left the room.

Lily played as she had never played before; her entire body and soul expressed what was so long restricted to her. The artistic repression created an opposite force and, like a spring pushed down to its limit with the dynamism released twenty fold, Lily expressed her reason for being through the piece. As the cadenza was reaching a climax the audience was filled with the beauty that the music had elicited, and then the piece came to an end.

The applause became uncontrollable: *Wehrmacht* and *Luftwaffe* men in the audience were applauding wildly, even a few *SS* officers joined in, forgetting for the moment that they were legitimizing the forbidden. At this point, several of the senior *Gestapo* officers rose and left the hall in a huff, as if their ears had suddenly been assaulted by what they had been enjoying all afternoon. Lily bowed to her audience, realizing what she had done.

Lily would not have flagrantly played the forbidden, "degenerate" music, but she *had* played it and she smiled secretly inside, not being sorry for what she had done. She left the concert stage hurriedly, towards her waiting car. Uwe was there to greet her. He ceremoniously clicked his heels and went through the standard greeting. He bowed to Lily, helped her into the car and they sped off to the Grunewald villa.

"Madam," Uwe said with a degree of innocence and genuine amazement, "I have never heard such a brilliant piano performance in my life. You are all the things they have said about you and more. I am honored to be in your home and, indeed in your esteemed presence. I feel so humbled and ordinary by comparison."

"Why, Uwe," Lily replied, sweetly, "if there were no people like you, there would be fewer people like me. You know, I think God created human beings so that He might have them to love. So it is with we who perform. If you were not there to love us, we could not do as well as we might aspire. It is nice to be loved, Uwe, and speaking of that I'm going to ask you a question.

"Why yes, madam," Uwe replied, "what is it?"

Lily quickly responded, "What does the *Gestapo* teach you about Jews?"

"We are taught to despise them."

"Do you know that I'm Jewish?"

"Yes, of course."

"But do you not despise me?"

"Madame Mendelssohn, I never think about you as being a Jew. I think about you as being a wonderful artist, a kind woman, and to me, a good friend."

"But how do you reconcile this with what you are taught?"

"I don't. I do what I have to do and I don't give it much thought."

"Thank you, Uwe," Lily replied. "You are an honest, sensitive young man."

"You are very kind, madam," he replied.

The Grunewald villa awaited them. It appeared that it was all aglow with light. As Lily entered, the men who lived in the house were there to greet her, as well as many of the other *Gestapo* officers and wives whom she recognized from her Wannsee performances. Streamers hung from the ceilings. Lily knew many of those present, but there were none of her Jewish friends. Stewards served champagne and hors d'oeuvres. It was a wonderful, festive evening quite like the old days when Lily received and was received. The guests began to depart about seven o'clock in order to reach their destinations before the evening air raids.

"I haven't spent an evening like this in many years," Lily commented to Uwe.

He was beaming.

"It was a wonderful evening," he replied. "If you will permit me, madam, I will have a special breakfast prepared for you in the morning."

"How exciting, Uwe. Thank you for all you have done."

"My pleasure, madam. It is an honor."

She went to her and room and prepared for bed. The air raid sirens sounded at 9:00 p.m. Lily was so happy with the day's events that she chose not to go to the shelter in the cellar. She fell asleep while the distant sound of British bombs seemed to be coming from another planet, surely not the one on which she lived.

It was 3:00 a.m. All was still in the house, the occasional sounds of fire engines were heard in the distance. There was a knock at Lily's bedroom door. She arose from a deep, dream-like sleep, donned a dressing gown and went to the door.

"Who is it?" she asked.

"*SS*," came the answer.

She opened the door to see two uniformed *Gestapo* agents.

"Yes?" she inquired.

"Mademoiselle Mendelssohn, please get dressed and come with us."

"Why?" she asked.

"Don't ask any questions. You have five minutes to get ready. You can pack an overnight bag if you like."

The anxiety rose from Lily's stomach and settled as a big lump in her throat. She dressed quickly and the *SS* officers escorted her to their automobile. They drove in silence to their destination, Moabit Prison. Lily was escorted to an empty room where the door was locked behind her. She sat there in silence. Every sound in the building was magnified beyond proportion, her anxiety and inner panic increasing with each relentless tick of the clock that hung on the wall. About two hours later, the door opened and a *Gestapo* officer entered the room.

"Mademoiselle Mendelssohn," he said politely, "may I offer you a cigarette?"

"No, thank you," she replied.

The officer sat observing her for a few moments and said:

"Did you not know that the music of Felix Mendelssohn-Bartholdy is banned from performance in the *Reich*?"

"Yes, I did," she replied.

"And, knowing this, you purposely played this music?"

"Oh no, I didn't purposely play it. It was something that I was used to doing and it happened automatically."

"Are you trying to say that you are not responsible for your actions?"

"Sir, you may not understand, but many times a performer's mind gets transported to another plane, and the thought process is quite different than it might be otherwise. I can assure you I meant no disrespect."

"Then why did you play the music?"

"I have explained that."

"Your explanation is not acceptable, Mademoiselle."

To the authorities it was bad enough to have a person classified as a Jew perform, but to perform "subversive" music, music that the audience enjoyed, was more of an embarrassment than could be tolerated.

The officer left the room and Lily remained there for the rest of the day and into the evening. She had never encountered a situation like this before. She kept on thinking of the English royalty who were beheaded, and their last hours leading up to their execution. In a sense, I think my situation is worse than theirs, she told herself. At least they knew their fate; I really don't know mine. Lily sat there listening, worrying and fretting until four o'clock the following morning. She heard a sound outside the door, a key being inserted into the lock, and it seemed a lifetime, until the tumblers turned and an *SS* officer entered the room.

"Follow me, please," he indicated.

Lily rose and followed him silently. It was mid-August, 1942, and the first light of summer's dawn was barely creeping over the eastern horizon. She was then escorted into a car outside the headquarters. Shortly thereafter the car sped off, Lily peering out of the window as if she had been a captured animal who was going to be thrown into a sack and tossed into a river. She passed the liberal synagogue at Levetzowstrasse. She could see people being ordered into trucks, which, when they were filled, had covers on all sides to disguise their human cargo. A while later, Lily realized they were nearing the Grunewald and she breathed a sigh of relief, thinking she was being driven home. She was, however, brought to the Grunewald freight station where people were boarding railway coaches. Lily was escorted into the rear car, in which several enlisted men were sitting; she was the only civilian present. The train left the station about 25 minutes later. It was going to the East.

29

Lily sat in the corner of the railway car, saying nothing, thinking everything. She felt she had been treated poorly. However, in comparison to the remainder of the train's passengers, she was treated much better than those who had spent many more days and nights with a minimum, if any, of food and water. Days and nights on basement floors of hard cement, before being loaded into freight cars for their trip to the East.

After what seemed like endless hours the train pulled into a station with the sign TREBLINKA clearly placed near the roof of the building. Lily looked at the quaint railway station. She noted that the clock indicated 2:50. She watched through the windows as the other passengers disembarked, herded, by Jewish men called the "Blue Commando." The *Goldjuden*, Jews who collected the passengers' jewelry and money were at work in the crowd, the gold in the new arrivals' mouths to be extracted at a later time, a time when Jewish technicians performed this additional act, without sanctity, from those whose soul no longer inhabited the house of the living. The Nazis, so meticulous in their planning, had organized humanity into a robotic mass of detail and seemingly effortless mechanization. The passengers, bereft of their precious possessions, were escorted directly into areas marked "factory" and "hospital." Those who went to "hospital" were immediately gassed.

Lily knew nothing about the camp. She sat in the railway car, a lone soldier at the far end. By this time all the train's cargo had been belched out, into a hell or death. Lily, getting a bit restless, checked the station clock. It had not changed time since she first looked at it. Why, she suddenly realized, it's just painted on the building! Ten minutes later two soldiers boarded the train, brusquely indicating that Lily was to come with them. They were Ukrainian guards, prevalent in the camp, and as mean, or meaner, than their German equivalents. Lily was taken to a small house away from the camp proper and was escorted into the kitchen. The guards spoke Ukrainian to the women in the house. The women were maids (the Nazi plan had indicated that Slavs were to be the slaves of the Nazis and they were used extensively in this manner). Lily did not even have time to go to the bathroom when one of the women thrust a mop at her and indicated that she was to wash the floor.

"I am not a maid, madam," she replied haughtily to the woman.

The woman was about to roll up her sleeves and beat Lily. Lily stepped back, incredulous at this display of manners so foreign to her.

"Mademoiselle Mendelssohn," said a deep German voice.

Lily turned to see a handsome, blonde German officer facing her.

"My name is Kurt Franz and I'm in charge of operations here. We are pleased to have you with us and we hope to be honored with a recital in the near future. Arthur Gold is in the camp as well; perhaps you can collaborate with him."

Lily had met Mr. Gold previously, a renowned Polish violinist and composer. She stood in front of Franz and said nothing. So, she thought, I'm to be kept prisoner for the entertainment of these beasts as I was for Heydrich. Franz turned around and left the room.

It was quite late now and the women were going to bed. Lily was escorted, down the back stairs adjacent to the kitchen, to a place in the cellar that was to be her bunk. It was next to the poison that was kept to kill the rats that inhabited the diseased camp. Lily was so tired that she just lay down on the straw-strewn floor and immediately fell asleep.

The next day one of the women came to her, indicating pleasantly in German, that she was to clean the upstairs quarters. Lily, realizing it was folly to resist, left the kitchen with rags and cleaning equipment in hand. She walked through the dining room and entered the living room. She gasped and stopped. There facing her was her piano.

"My piano, how did it get here?" she said aloud.

She approached it, dropped her cleaning materials, sat down on the bench and without hesitation, launched into a Weber *Conzertstück*. The music wafted out of the house and many in the camp, Jews, guards, officers heard the music coming to them softly, ethereally. It was as if an angel had come from heaven, not the Angel of Death, who was in permanent residence at the camp, but an angel of mercy, love and warmth. She played and played for hours, tears dripping down her cheeks. She was not bothered by anyone until Franz appeared in the room. Lily stopped, realizing that she had not done any cleaning.

"Your music is beautiful, Mademoiselle Mendelssohn. We shall look forward to frequent concerts."

Lily looked towards Franz, bowed her head without a smile, saying nothing.

Three days passed with Lily playing at different times throughout the day. The maids kept to themselves and Lily was quite isolated. On the morning of the fourth day one of the maids came to summon Lily, indicating that she was to go upstairs to one of the rooms with towels. Lily went to the room indicated, knocked on the door, and hearing no response, entered. She could hear the sound of bath water running and realized that someone was inside. What now, she thought, and she became apprehensive thinking that she might be abused.

"Is anyone there?" boomed a voice from the bathroom, barely audible over the sound of the running water.

Suddenly a man appeared at the door with a smile of joyous expectation.

"Lily, Lily, dearest."

Lily steadied herself against the wall. She was so shocked she could not respond.

"Christian, what are you doing here?" Lily shouted at him.

Merth went over to Lily to embrace her. She pushed him away and shouted vehemently :

"Christian, I want an explanation. I have been through Hell, but it seems to be Heaven in comparison to the other people in this place. What is this? Why are you here? Who are you really?"

Lily was unlikely to burst into tears. She was strong, defiant and resentful; not about to be mollified by Merth's mere presence and overtures of affection.

Merth looked at her, somewhat embarrassed with the situation. Lily sat in a chair staring at him, waiting for a response.

"Lily," he replied, standing upright and proclaiming proudly, "I am *SS-Sturmbahnführer*, Inspector of the Sobibor, Belzec and Treblinka camps."

"You? You? Christian. I cannot comprehend this; I find it difficult to believe. I've loved you, and you have loved me, knowing of my Jewish background, but yet you are in charge of exterminating people . Why have you done this? Why am I here, Christian?"

"I've done this because it's my destiny to serve my country. As for you being here, Heydrich became displeased with you. He thought he would be able to have you in a submissive state, like a concubine woman, ready to play for his amusement. Something happened that changed his mind. He then wanted you out of the way, and after your performance of degenerate music it was a good excuse to have you sent to the East, where you would be interned in a concentration camp. You were to be available to perform. The aim was to have you suffer, but not killed. Don't worry, Lily, he was killed in Czechoslovakia in June, but he had issued orders regarding your disposition. These were part of his orders."

"Christian, I'm to be available to perform? To perform here? I don't want to be here. This place is a cemetery, for those who are living and for those who are not yet dead—even the living seem dead, and I don't mean just the prisoners. All of the people here are like robots without souls; it frightens me to look at them. And I'm to be available to perform here? Why, it's like playing Mozart in a mausoleum. I am an artist, Christian, an artist, not a robot like the rest of the people here.

"Did Heydrich know about our relationship, Christian?"

"I cannot say, Lily. I think the *Gestapo* knows about everything."

"And you, Christian, what has led you to be involved in all of this?"

"I've worked extensively on euthanasia for years, Lily. It's one of my specialties. I was formerly assigned to the *SS* Criminal Police and I supervised the construction of the first Nazi Gas Chamber. I've risen from a person of relatively low rank to one where I am a highly respected officer and an integral part of military society."

"But why are you killing all these people, innocent people who have done nothing to harm you or their country?"

"Lily, it's being done for the racial purity of Germany. The Jews were running and ruining the country and Jewish intellectualism and liberalism were rampant. Something had to be done."

"And will you kill me too, Christian?"

Merth, shocked at Lily's statement, stepped back.

"Lily, that remark hurts me deeply. I have told you many times of the love I have had for you. It hasn't waned."

"But Christian, I don't understand. You want to rid the country of all Jews and yet you profess your love for me?"

"Lily, if I could, I would have wished you were classified as other than a Jew, but you weren't and I cannot help that, but I love you, and I want you."

"You want me? But Christian, you're a common murderer. How can I love a person who extinguishes life under such flimsy pretenses. There's no need for this. Christian, I've always loved you, but when I hear of your involvement in these unspeakable acts I'm repulsed to the point of hate. I've never felt that emotion before, until I met Heydrich. It's worse now. I feel betrayed, raped, Christian. I think death would have been easier than facing this moment. Not only that, I'm ordered about as if I were a servant. How could you?"

"Jews are not servants in the eyes of the *Reich*; they are considered unfit for this service."

"Really, Christian, just fit to die."

"You don't understand, they are considered far too brilliant for this, but their brilliance has always been misguided."

"Misguided? And what about Catholicism and Protestantism? Are they not offshoots of Judaism? Was not Christ a Jew?"

"Lily, the *Reich* differentiates between the Jews of the Bible and the Jews of today. Today's Jews have strayed too far from their chosen path."

"In whose eyes, Christian? In the end when the judgment of man and God is passed upon you and your kind, you will be found guilty of inhuman brutality. How can you, who call yourself a Superman, inflict such bestial acts on any living creature? It is you who are the sub-humans, not the Jews and all the other classes which you consider to be such. In the end, you and your kind will be judged. Germany will have a collective guilt for what it is doing now; a guilt that will haunt until it is a nation no longer, without means of expiation. Maybe one day, long after we are gone, you and your kind might be forgiven. I will say this, Christian, in all fairness, the guilt is not Germany's alone, but it belongs to every human who knew of this evil and who did little or nothing to stop it; these people are not exempt. It matters little that I'm persecuted as a Jew. No person or race should be persecuted unfairly. I would sooner live amongst a colony of ants then be considered a member of the human race—if this is what's called human."

Merth looked at Lily, who had spoken with a vehemence of which he never thought she was capable.

"Lily," he stammered, "you don't understand. What we are doing *is* for the good of the human race."

"I don't understand, Christian? Possibly it is you and those of your ilk who do not understand. This is ridiculous, I cannot talk to you. And me, what am I to do in this hellhole?"

"You need do nothing you don't want to, Lily. Orders have been left that you are here solely for music purposes. You can read the books in the house, practice on the piano, perform in concerts. Remember, that will benefit the people in the camp. I must leave tomorrow. I returned expressly to see you, but I will be back soon."

"Fine, let me return to my dungeon for some sleep."

"That's hardly necessary. You'll sleep in my bed."

"Sleep in your bed? The dungeon's floor is softer and more welcome than the hardness and cruelty of your mattress. And besides, aren't you afraid of what others will say?"

"To hell with them. Nobody says anything. They know what would happen to them."

"Exactly, Christian, you're proving the points I've made. I'm going to the basement now."

"No, you'll stay here."

"I'm leaving this room, Christian."

"You are to stay here, Lily; that's final."

Lily turned around and started to leave the room. Christian came after her, held her shoulders and turned her around. He placed his body and lips next to hers. Lily stood immobile, without feeling. She took her arms and pushed Merth away, but he pulled her closer to him. At that point, her weak leg started to give way, and she could resist no more. He took her to his bed and lay her down on the mattress. He started to undress her as Lily fought fruitlessly to keep him away. Merth had managed to let his pants drop and wiggle from his uniform. He mounted Lily and said:

"Lily, you're more exciting than ever. I never knew you had such passion and could elicit such desire within me. I love you all the more. I've realized my dream after all these years. I've always had the fantasy that I wanted you locked up, all to myself.

Now this is a fantasy no longer. You're here, Lily and you're mine, I don't have to share you with anyone."

It is said that there is a thin line between love and hate. Lily had crossed that line as much as Christian had, going towards the opposite direction. Christian felt he was making love. Lily felt she was being raped.

And as she lay there sobbing, tired and helpless, Merth kissed her repeatedly and the salty taste of Lily's tears was but an aphrodisiac to his sex-starved mind. As Lily felt him enter her body, her face contorted in anguish; she found peace in losing consciousness as her body relaxed and her mind went dim.

When she awoke the following morning she was alone in the bed. She felt unclean in both body and mind, her mouth was dry and foul. She went into the adjacent bathroom and drew a steaming bath. She kept on scrubbing herself, but she felt dirty. There were several fresh maids' uniforms, apparently laid out for her. She changed into one of them, left the bathroom and went towards the kitchen. The other maids were deferential, apparently aware of what had occurred during the previous evening. Lily poached an egg and sat down to eat it. She became nauseous with the first bite and returned to the upstairs bedroom where she had slept for most of the day. She awoke later in the afternoon, the waning, weakened beams of sunlight shining through the bedroom windows. She took another bath and returned to the kitchen, where she had a few bites of bread and some tea.

Lily then went to the large room. It was brightly lit with windows on the north and south sides and a pair of French doors adjacent to the piano. She sat down at the piano and opened the top to see the £25,000 in notes, untouched, tightly lodged on the side. She started to play and play and play, late into the night, the music again wafting throughout the quiet of the camp, with all experiencing its beauty. She finally returned to the upstairs bedroom, physically and emotionally drained. The sheets had been changed and freshly laundered again, and ironed maids' uniforms were laid out. Lily placed them in one of the bureau drawers, returned to bed and fell asleep quickly. Thus, her daily routine was established. Franz never approached her to concertize. The daily concerts obviously had satisfied the need for musical enrichment. He did show up one day with enormous amounts of sheet music that he presented to Lily in a most grandiose manner. She took them and graciously thanked him. Lily's former spark and zest for life were gone; her body became gnarled, the pain in her leg worsened, but her hands were firm and strong, and her musical mind clear and brimming with the desire to play. One day she started to play Mendelssohn. None came to stop her or complain; she was free, evidently, to play what she wanted, and all of the inhabitants in the camp absorbed whatever music she gave them, as if they were gasping for a breath of air where none existed. The music changed the dreary routine of the living and made it a little less intolerable.

Lily was prohibited from leaving the compound in which the house was situated. She would venture outside the house, occasionally, retreating to its confines almost immediately. The sight of the camp guards frightened her, and the knowledge of what occurred on the premises filled her with revulsion and sickness. Unlike the Jews who were involved in their tasks, wondering if the next day would be their last, Lily did not share the same feelings nor the proximity to the prisoners; this gave her a different and more objective perspective on life and death. A perspective that gnawed at her being each day and emotionally shot at her mind, as surely as if bullets were being pumped into her body. The difference is that Lily lived, whereas so many did not.

On Merth's occasional visits he would have sex with Lily. She was as oblivious and unfeeling about this as the walking, mechanical men who worked in the camp. Each assault left her weaker and more emotionally and physically perforated. Merth never seemed to notice, or if he did he never indicated that he had. He would always tell Lily that he loved her. He would sit in the large room for hours, like a pet dog sitting beside his mistress, listening to her music. This relaxed him, but also excited him sexually and his short visits were marked with an increase of sexual activity.

Lily's thoughts of Hannah, at first frequent, became less and less until they finally ceased. She withdrew into herself and her life continued in this limbo. Now Lily's prison was not the house, but her own mind, which had finally crumbled under the pressures that it could no longer tolerate. Lily's hip and leg became progressively worse, the pain more intense with each passing day. When she walked it was as if she were an extremely old woman, completely contorted in physique, the sparkle in her eyes now replaced by a vacant stare. She played the piano by rote, as if she had put a roll of music into the player piano, flipped the switch and pushed the pedals. Even then her music was filled with excitement and irresistible magnetism.

It was Monday, August 2, 1943, almost a year since Lily's internment. She sat, like a ghost, sipping coffee and eating unbuttered bread. She was given to mumbling to herself. She hardly spoke to anyone. The maids avoided her, the house had few visitors. Merth was really her only contact and she hardly ever spoke to him. He had left a few days earlier, but at this point it made no difference to Lily. She seemed oblivious to all but her music that she played faithfully each day.

Lily was entering the main room when a stranger came in. He was a young, *SS* officer whom she had never seen before.

"Bring me some coffee," he brusquely commanded.

Lily, deep within herself, did not respond.

"Did you hear me? Bring me some coffee," he yelled. "Why do they keep you here if you don't follow orders? You're worthless."

Lily started to laugh at the officer.

"You pig," he shouted and took his walking stick and brought it down on Lily's hand. "Now bring me some coffee and that's the last time I'll tell you."

Lily whimpered and looked at her hand. She could not move it, those treasured hands that were the instruments of her interpretations of the composers whom she brought to life. She went into the kitchen sobbing, filled with pain. The little sanity that she still possessed returned with an intense, vitriolic feeling. Lily took a coffee cup and descended the basement stairs to the place where she had first slept when she arrived at Treblinka. She walked slowly, but with purpose and each creak of the steps was like the strings of an orchestra to her ears. She no longer had any feeling of the pain in her leg. She felt a sensation of triumph welling up within her. Lily put a generous portion of rat poison into the cup, and went upstairs quickly, the slower creaks that echoed her descent, now shouting forth in staccato. Once upstairs, she took the cup to the pantry where she added sugar, coffee and topped it all with hot milk. She placed it on a tray, a pastry and napkin adjacent, and she hobbled into the large room where the officer sat, tapping his walking stick, waiting impatiently. Lily placed the tray on the table next to the chair.

It was now late in the afternoon, the air fetid with the heat. The atmosphere had been eaten by the sun and what was left was the exhaust of its belch. By this afternoon, however, the prisoners of Treblinka had accumulated enough weapons to carry through with a carefully planned revolt.

Lily watched as the officer's hand went towards the coffee cup. He looked at her, placed the cup back on the table and growled:

"Get me some jam for this pastry. Move, you lazy sow, move."

Lily stood there, thinking of who she had been, listening to these orders from a person who had no right to give them.

"Move, I said," he growled.

He took his walking stick and with full force brought it down on her back. Lily's body screamed with pain and she bent over, trying to catch her breath. The cane came down again and again with equal force as she stumbled towards the piano bench. The officer took the cup of coffee in his hand and said:

"And I want fresh, hot coffee."

He then took a large gulp of the poisonous liquid and grabbed his fiery throat as he gasped.

There were sounds of grenades and firearms in the distance—the prisoners' revolt had begun. Treblinka was now in flames, within a short time thereafter the house started to burn. Lily heard the screams of the Ukrainian maids as they ran from the house. The officer lay on the floor, writhing in agony. Lily was completely oblivious to the commotion outside. She sat down at the piano exultantly, and started to play the last movement of Beethoven's *Emperor Piano Concerto*. The entire spectacle amused her and she cackled at its absurdity. The large room started to fill with flames and smoke. The officer, still alive, lay on the floor screaming as his legs started to burn, and then slowly, with magnificent torture, extracting every bit of excruciating agony from his body, the flames enveloped him. Lily rose from the piano bench and hobbled to the French doors. She shut them and turned to the officer, who was barely alive, a triumphant smile on her face. She looked down at his fear-contorted face and proclaimed:

"I've won, sir. I've given my life and my music to my country. To me, my life and music are the same. My country doesn't want them or deserve them any more. So, dear, wretched man, for me my life is over. I'm glad to leave it, for it no longer holds any meaning for me. But I leave it happily knowing what I've given to Germany. May God forgive you, and all those like you, who have taken my beautiful country from me."

By this time the officer's immolation was complete. Lily sat at the piano, playing and laughing as the flames encircled her. She was in the spotlight once more, but instead of an audience she was surrounded by the heat of death. She felt nothing but the intense heat as her stage became smaller and smaller. The playing continued, the final laughter turning into screams as she became fodder for the fire and ultimately a victim of its fury.

Almost the entire camp was in flames, and even when the fires finally died down, an orange glow rose above the camp, punctuating the surrounding forests like a large exclamation mark. On that August 2nd, the Treblinka experiment came to an end.

Twenty-one days later, the British bombed Berlin with the most intensive air raid that the capital had experienced, causing wide-spread death and destruction.

During the following year, 1944, Christian Merth was killed while on patrol duty, in Istria, on the north coast of Yugoslavia.

30

Although the Allied bombings of the city were frequent they never seemed to interfere with Hannah's daily life. She had halted her nursing duties and now spent her time entirely at the convent. The moment had come for her to leave in order to prepare for the birth of her child. Hannah knew nothing of her mother's death that August 2, 1943. She looked forward to giving birth to her child, feeling it was her role in the implementation of God's plan. Hannah assumed she would return to the convent to continue her life as a nun and a nurse, but giving birth to the child was her destiny.

In December of 1943, Hannah was shocked to hear that seven regional Protestant churches had declared that Jews, were incapable of being saved by baptism and that they were the "born enemies of the world and Germany." They proclaimed that the "severest measures against the Jews be adopted." This was my mother's religion, Hannah thought, how could her church do this?

Hannah was now ready to depart from the secure life to which she had been so accustomed. She went to see Mother Superior who looked at Hannah with love and concern as she said:

"We shall look forward to your return after the birth of the child. I shall regard it as if nothing has happened, and your life here will resume as before."

The audience ended abruptly. Hannah bowed her head in tears as Mother Superior approached her and said:

"You are a brave girl, Sister Ursula, my prayers will be with you. May God bless you."

She kissed the ring on Mother's hand and exited.

Hannah could no longer fit into the clothes she had when she entered the convent. She was fitted with a white blouse, and a plain, gray skirt. It was odd for her to wear street clothes again. She was no longer a part of the Church's discrete sector, but one of the many. The heavy convent doors opened and Hannah walked into the sunlight and passed the gates of the wall that had been her home for so many years. God will come with me, she thought. I am not alone.

Hannah left the convent and reported to a *Gestapo* office on Burgstrasse. Supposedly, only Hannah and Mother Superior knew of Hannah's pregnancy; even Paul had no knowledge of this. Paul had left Berlin to go to the Eastern Front. During this period Hannah had been under the care of a Jewish physician who had since been imprisoned. He was not to be heard from again.

Hannah boarded a train for a *Lebensborn* facility that afternoon She was going to the Steinhoring Maternity Center in Upper Bavaria. Hannah looked out of the train window, watching the countryside pass, and with it she felt her life as a nun was passing as well.

Upon arrival, Hannah, and several other women who were on the same train, boarded a bus to the beautifully maintained facility. In a sense it was not unlike the convent from which Hannah came; it was surrounded by high walls to shield itself from the outside world. Hannah was assigned a bright room overlooking the forests beyond. She was expected to assist with nursing duties, which she did gladly.

There were many pregnant women who were also nurses and a feeling of camaraderie amongst the women developed easily. Many young girls—too young to bear children, Hannah thought—were also in evidence. As Hannah would soon discover, some of the girls' parents were unaware of their daughters' situation. Hannah enjoyed working and that kept her occupied. There was no mention of her background on any records, and nursing was listed as her profession.

One day, Hannah was stricken with severe pain in her abdomen. She was approaching her eighth month.

"What is it, Hannah?" asked Lotte, one of the nurses on the floor.

"Lotte, I don't know, I feel weak and sick. I'd best see the doctor."

"Well, Hannah," Dr. Hausmann said, "you will soon be providing the *Reich* with another child. Don't worry, it looks as if everything will be fine, but as a precaution I'm recommending that you do no further work and be confined to bed. You may get up to go to the bathroom, but you will take your meals in bed."

"Doctor," said Hannah, "Am I in danger of losing the child?"

"There is always that possibility, Hannah, but I don't see it happening right now. It will be best to follow instructions and do as I say."

"Yes, sir," Hannah replied.

Hannah returned to her room immediately and from then on she spent all of her time in bed. Meals were served there, she had many visits by some of the other women, and she tired quickly of confinement. She read a great deal of the Nazi-prescribed literature but unknown to her hosts most of her time was spent in prayer. The task in front of her was eased, for she was in the hands of the Lord.

Hannah continued to feel that the whole experience of having a child, in her circumstances as a nun, was a dictate of God. She was happy just to be serving the Lord, for she knew that God's spirit was with her all the time; she could actually feel His presence. Thus, the excellent physical care that she was receiving, coupled with the high degree of emotion that she sustained, provided her with a glow of health, peace, and a desire for those who had seen her to re-visit as often as they could. Dr. Hausmann was particularly impressed with Hannah. He had decided to suggest that she mate with some outstanding examples of *SS* men whom he had in mind.

"Yes," Hausmann said, overheard by Lotte while he was speaking with a colleague, "she is an excellent example of an Aryan woman. The man who sired her is from an excellent family, so you can imagine what a fine example of our species will be reproduced when she gives birth."

Lotte had mentioned this to Hannah during one of her visits, and Hannah was understandably excited about bearing a healthy child. Dr. Hausmann's words served to enhance her feelings.

Hannah would think of the convent where she had spent so many years in the service of the Lord. She, and most of the others at the facility, knew nothing of the disastrous Berlin air raid that August 23, 1943. She could not know that the convent had been closed by the authorities on August 16th and that the attack had reduced the convent to rubble.

One night, about a week before the baby's due date, Hannah woke up with pre-natal contractions. She lay in bed silently waiting for them to pass, but they did not and as they increased she rang for the night nurse, who hurried to her room. The nurse contacted Dr. Hausmann immediately; Hausmann was at Hannah's bedside within ten minutes. Her water had now broken and she was in pain. She was rushed to the adjacent clinical area where Dr. Hausmann was already in the process of washing.

"It's a breach baby," Hannah heard Dr. Hausmann say. "We must hurry," he continued, "we don't want to lose it. Everything will be fine, Hannah. We're going to perform a Cesarean."

Hannah's eyes opened slowly. She looked up at the white ceiling, forgetting for a moment where she was. She had given birth.

"My baby, my baby, did I have a boy or a girl?" she asked Lotte, who was the nurse sitting at her bedside.

"It was a boy, Hannah," Lotte replied.

"Is he all right?" Hannah inquired.

"Yes, he's fine, but I don't think Dr. Hausmann is too happy. You've upset his Aryan racial theories."

At that moment another nurse brought the infant to Hannah. He had dark, brown hair, and the Semitic overtones of the Mendelssohn family. Hannah took the infant to her breast, and was going to feed it.

"No, Hannah," Lotte said, "they're giving him some special formula. You're not to feed him."

A few moments later another nurse came into the room to remove the infant.

"Can I not hold him a little longer?" Hannah pleaded.

"No, I'm sorry," the nurse replied, "Dr. Hausmann wants to examine the child immediately."

Hannah was kept in the special area for four more days. She repeatedly asked to see her baby, but her request was never granted. On the fifth day she was transferred to her previous room. She had not seen Dr. Hausmann since he attended her at the child's birth.

Hannah was well treated and remained at the facility through that autumn and into the beginning of winter. She was permitted to see her child on occasion and various tests were performed on her body. None was painful, but Hannah felt as if she was being violated. In January, Hannah was told that at the end of the week she was to pack her things and be ready to return to Berlin. She pleaded to see her child once more, but she was always given excuses.

Lotte had come to say good-bye before Hannah's departure.

"Lotte, I'm so upset. I never knew it would feel like this—the feeling I have for my child. I want to see him so desperately, and now they're sending me away, as if I had delivered a package, and I'm now being dismissed."

Hannah started to cry. Lotte tried to comfort her and said:

"I do feel sorry for you, Hannah, but I'm sure the child will be all right. Don't let them see you crying. I once heard Dr. Hausmann tell a patient that tears were the residue of the weak."

"They are so heartless; have they no feeling for what anybody thinks?"

"Shh, Hannah," replied Lotte, "don't let them hear you. I think that the State is to be served by all of us, and that's what they think. They're letting me go home next week for a whole month. My mother has been quite ill."

"Oh, Lotte, I'm so sorry," replied Hannah, "and here I'm just thinking of myself. Where does your mother live?"

"In Dresden, Hannah. Possibly you can come and visit."

"That would be nice, Lotte. Good-bye and may God bless you."

"Oh Hannah," exclaimed Lotte, "that's so beautiful; people never talk like that anymore. Thank you, thank you for your beautiful wishes."

On January 15, 1945, Hannah boarded a train for Berlin. She wore the same gray skirt issued to her when she had left the convent. She had a deathly white appearance; her mind and body were exhausted, her prayers to the Lord for her son had gone unanswered.

31

Hannah sat in her seat as the train left the station. The weather was gray, damp and dismal, though relatively mild for a January day. The air hardly moved and the fog hugged the ground, suffocating the very earth from which it was born. Hannah looked out of the window; it was like looking through cobwebs. She sat back, exhaled a deep breath and thought that the worst must be over. She had planned to give her baby to her mother; and now her mother, and probably she, would never again see the child. After all, her thoughts continued, I couldn't very well raise a child of my own as a nun.

Hannah could hear the chugging of the locomotive intensifying as the train rushed through the fog-hidden countryside. The conductor, an elderly gentleman, opened the compartment door and saw Hannah sitting alone. He smiled at her and said:

"Your ticket, *Fräulein*, if you please."

"Of course," she responded as she handed him the ticket that the *Lebensborn* office had given to her. "Is it possible to get something to eat on the train?" she inquired.

"Most likely you can get off at the next stop and get something."

"And how soon would that be?" Hannah asked.

"In twenty-two minutes, *Fräulein*."

"Thank you," she replied.

The train slowly came to a stop precisely twenty-two minutes later. Hannah descended from the railway carriage, but she saw no vendors selling food. She walked into the station, which seemed rather deserted. The shrill shriek of the train whistle punctuated the relative silence as if to announce itself boldly. Hannah ran back to the train, and the compartment in which she was sitting. She opened the door to find that there were three new occupants. There were two *Luftwaffe* enlisted men and one elderly woman. The two servicemen sat quietly, one with crutches at his side. The airman with the crutches had a leg missing; the other's face was burned severely. They sat stoically as Hannah entered the compartment, the soldiers smiling upon seeing Hannah's pretty face.

The train started again. None of the passengers spoke. They all seem so weary, thought Hannah, but then I suppose I must seem that way to them as well.

Two military guards, obviously imbued with their own authority, opened the compartment door as one of them brusquely said:

"Papers, please."

All produced the necessary documentation. The guard, upon reading Hannah's, smiled at her and said:

"The *Reich* needs more people like you, *Fräulein*."

Hannah quickly looked at her papers and realized that the guard saw their place of issue and correctly assumed that she had come from the *Lebensborn* facility. Hannah said nothing and stared straight ahead. The guards exited as quickly as they had entered, followed shortly thereafter by the conductor. The accelerating train jolted as it quickly reduced its speed, wheels screeching, metal against metal with unimaginable shrillness that assaulted the passengers repeatedly. People held on as the train careened back and forth and finally came to a shuddering halt. Soldiers and others were running up and down like ants in a tunnel disturbed by the vibration of a passing footstep. Hannah sat quietly wondering what all the commotion was about. Dull thuds were heard in the distance; it was nighttime now, the weather had turned colder, the fog had lifted. She could see a red reflection against the sky.

"It's an air raid," said the *Luftwaffe* soldier with the crutches. "If they see this train it'll be bombed. We've got to get out."

Hannah helped the soldier from the train as the man with the burned face followed quickly. Suddenly the sound of the aircraft overhead increased and the whistles of the bombs, as if descending a musical scale without pause, came hurtling from the sky.

"Hurry, *Fräulein*, hurry," the lame man shouted.

They came to a tree and huddled against it as bombs hit the train and many of the freight cars in the front burst into flame and exploded. There was a chain reaction and the entire train became a ribbon of fire.

As the explosions continued, the soldier placed his body over Hannah's in order to shield her from the flaming debris that was hurtling in every direction. Hannah began praying silently. They both lay there, holding each other, the glue of fear pasting them together. The sound of the planes diminished as their droning engines receded into the darkness from where they had come.

"Are you all right, *Fräulein*?" the soldier inquired, as he looked at Hannah, whose face was visible from the light of the burning train.

"Yes," she responded feeling glad to be alive. "Yes, I'm fine . . . and how are you?"

"Just fine," he beamed as he answered her, still intertwined as if they were a pair of lovers.

Hannah, realizing the position of their bodies, slowly extricated herself from the soldier's grasp. The soldier, enjoying the closeness, was slow to relinquish his attractive prey.

"We must help those who need it," Hannah said.

"*Fräulein*, I doubt any on the train have survived. We must look for those who're hurt."

The two separated, Hannah helping the injured as best she could. The heat of the flames kept the couple from getting too close to the train. Suddenly there was an explosion from one of the cars, the shrapnel landing on the unsuspecting soldier. He started to scream as Hannah came to his aid. She grabbed an overcoat that was lying on the ground, probably from one of those who had left the train. She wrapped it around the man's body extinguishing the flames. By this time additional assistance had arrived, ambulances and fire engines were in the vicinity, doing their best to help.

"Are you all right, *Fräulein*?" asked a breathless ambulance attendant as he rushed towards her.

"Yes, yes, I'm fine, but please help this man."

The soldier, now unconscious was dispatched to an ambulance. Hannah just sat on the cold ground, now in a state of shock. The war had always raged around her, but it had never really touched her.

"*Fräulein*, what is your destination?" inquired a soldier who had collected the remainder of the train's passengers.

"Berlin," she replied.

"Come with me. There's a train on another line that is still operating. I can put you on that."

The soldier herded several passengers into a truck and it sped off into the safety of the night. Half-an-hour later Hannah and the others were discharged at a small village depot; ten minutes after that another engine slowly lumbered to a stop. The few passenger cars on the train were filled with soldiers, aged civilians, and several women. They all sat silently with faces that mirrored the grimness of their situation. Hannah, standing in the aisle, started to fall asleep almost immediately.

"*Fräulein*, please take my seat," offered a young soldier.

"Thank you," she responded, grateful for the offer.

Hannah slept deeply; she did not awake until the sun streamed in through the window. She looked outside, recognizing the southern suburbs of Berlin. Hannah became excited about being home and looked forward to seeing her mother, the sisters and Mother Superior at the convent. Upon arriving Hannah exited quickly. The guard at the exit platform checked her papers. She had eaten no food since she left the *Lebensborn* facility. Hannah purchased some buttered bread, cheese, and a glass of milk. She said her customary prayer in silence and slowly munched the food. She then went to telephone her mother from the station.

"Hello," said the male voice answering the telephone.

"Good morning," responded Hannah, "might I speak to Countess von Wallenstadt, please?"

"There is none here by that name; there are no women in this facility," was the response.

"Do you know where Miss Mendelssohn is? She had been living at the villa."

"This is now an *SS* facility. Nobody by that name is here. Mendelssohn? Do you mean the pianist."

"Yes, yes," replied Hannah with anticipation.

"There is nobody here like that. Who is calling? What's your name?"

Hannah thought for a moment, but as innocent as she might have been, she was wise enough not to continue the conversation any further. She replaced the receiver on its cradle and left hurriedly. At this point she felt it best to go directly to the convent and make inquiries about her mother afterwards. She boarded the S-Bahn. It was now 8:30 a.m.

Hannah gasped audibly as the train left the station. The city seemed to be a bombed-out shell. She could not believe what she saw and tears filled her eyes. Hannah buried her head in her hands, blocking out what she had seen, wishing all would be well when she again opened her eyes. She did, but what she saw was the same. An old man sitting adjacent to her said:

"Are you all right, *Fräulein?*"

"Sir, I can't believe Berlin has been so devastated."

"Haven't you seen the city lately?" the gentleman inquired.

"No, I've been in the country for the past year."

"Well, most people are leaving the city, not coming to it. The Berlin *luft* is not what it used to be. You might have been better off had you stayed away. So much has happened during the past year. Do you come from here?"

"Yes, sir," Hannah replied.

"You will adjust, *Fräulein*. We Berliners are a strong lot. I've lost a son on the Eastern Front, my nephew and his family died during an air raid last month, but we all continue. Sometimes I think those who die are the lucky ones. I don't think we'll get off too easily, if at all, when the Reds get here before the Americans.

"What are you talking about? Are things so bad? Do you really think that Germany will lose the war?" questioned Hannah in innocent, unabashed astonishment.

"*Fräulein*, you must have been far from the war. I cannot see Germany winning the war at this point," the gentleman whispered, "unless the *Führer* has some trick up his sleeve and will unleash it at the last minute. I think it's gone too far against us at this point."

The train had stopped at a station and the passengers started to leave.

"Why aren't we continuing?" asked Hannah.

"It is best to go to the air raid shelter, *Fräulein*. The American bombers start their pummeling about 9:00."

"And this happens every day?" asked Hannah in amazement.

"Yes, *Fräulein*. We have the Americans by day and the British at night.

"Sir," continued Hannah, "I am sorry for your family losses."

Hannah's mind could not accept what she had seen, her comment seemed out of context, but the gentleman replied:

"Thank you, *Fräulein*. It hasn't been easy, but I manage."

"There is always God to turn to," replied Hannah.

"Sometimes I think He has forsaken us," replied the gentleman, "but then again, maybe we're getting our retribution for starting the war."

"Sir, God will always be with us."

"I wonder, *Fräulein*, sometimes I wonder."

Hannah followed the crowd to a nearby air raid shelter as the sirens started to sound. Many people just ambled on, seemingly oblivious to the threat. She sat in the shelter and prayed silently as she felt the explosive shocks of the Allies' wrath. The vibrations intensified, becoming stronger and stronger, and then seemed to lessen until they were no longer perceptible. Hannah prayed silently during most of the time. She prayed for the salvation of her country and peace. The "all-clear" sirens sounded at 11:34 and Hannah left the shelter. She sniffed the air, acrid with the smell of the bombs' residue. Several buildings were burning a block away.

Buses started running almost immediately and life returned to "normal" rather quickly. Hannah arrived at the convent, crossed herself and said a silent prayer as she approached the gate. There was rubble all around the area, and she realized that there was emptiness where once stood the seemingly indestructible walls. Hannah was shaken and distraught, but her feelings were quickly interrupted when a deep, inquisitive voice intoned:

"Can I help you, *Fräulein*?"

Hannah turned around quickly to see an *SS* man standing behind her.

"Your papers, please, *Fräulein*."

Hannah produced the papers issued by the *Lebensborn* administration. The officer scrutinized them carefully and stared at Hannah.

"What is your business here, *Fräulein*?"

"I've come to see the Mother Superior who's an old friend of mine," she said somewhat haughtily, her proud, upper-class Berlin background throwing itself at the officer. "Do you know if she survived the attack?"

"This convent had been closed, *Fräulein*, even before the bombing. Your friend, the Mother Superior is very much alive. She has been arrested and sent to Moabit Prison."

"Praise be to God that she is alive . . . Arrested? Arrested?" Hannah inquired, almost shouting at the officer, "Why?"

"Why? We do not have to give excuses why, but the convent was sheltering Jews. *Fräulein*," the officer continued with a seductive smile. "Might I call upon you some evening?"

Those horrid *Lebensborn* papers, Hannah thought. They're going to plague me.

"Good day, sir," she replied sweetly, feeling that to be the best response.

"May I give you a lift someplace, *Fräulein*?"

"No, thank you," she said.

"No matter, wherever my destination it would be a pleasure to make a detour for you."

Hannah thought it best that she make a speedy exit.

"Well, sir, I have to go to the hospital. I might have tuberculosis."

The officer clicked his heels said the usual: "Heil Hitler," and headed for his automobile.

Hannah laughed to herself, proud that she had enough wit to carry out this deception.

"I shall go to my home in Grunewald; it's my home, even if the military has it now," she said loudly, in a strong, determined voice.

Hannah boarded an oncoming bus and headed for her childhood home. She was a bit anxious as she rounded the corner, which she had done so often in the past. She hoped the house would still be intact, and she was happy to see that it was. She walked through the villa entrance. The sign on the front door indicated that the building was the property of the *Gestapo*. Hannah knocked at the door forcefully. There was no response; she repeated the knock, still no response. Hannah walked towards the rear of the house. She paused on the north portico to look through the French doors. There was no sign of life; the house was empty. The rear door was locked as well. The *Gestapo* have probably left, she thought. Suddenly Hannah realized that the key to the cellar might still be hidden in the spot where she had placed it when she was a child. The *Gestapo* are so thorough, she posited, they've probably changed the lock. There was the key, underneath a stone that had been untouched for years. Hannah picked it up, placed it in the lock, turned it and the door opened.

She walked into the cellar, the smell of mildew invading her nostrils. There was a large cupboard where Helga used to hide treats from Hannah. She headed for the cupboard and opened it. There was tinned food, sets of china, silver flatware, and hard candies. Hannah took some of the hard candies and went upstairs. She went through all of the empty rooms on the ground floor her footsteps intruding upon the silence which was now resident in the house. Hannah saw the rooms as they once were—filled with antiques, the old Mendelssohn piano, the concerts given in the home, her practice with her mother, the happy times spent with Paul.

She walked upstairs slowly, each step flooding her mind with the memories of her past life. Hannah entered her childhood room. The sun shone through the window giving her a warm, comfortable feeling. She was a little girl again. She spent a long time in her mother's room where as a child she would often come to visit. They would have tea in the afternoon and talk about different things that a mother and daughter might discuss. Hannah's eyes started to fill with tears. She went to the secret wall behind which her mother had hidden a volume of *Phaedon*; it was still there.

Air raid sirens sounded in the distance, closer sirens echoed the previous ones. Hannah ignored them until she began to hear the dull, explosive thuds getting nearer. She went to the basement, curled up in a corner, and began to pray. The villa shook and kept on shaking as the planes dropped their missiles of destruction. She choked as the fine powder from the concrete ceiling filled the basement. She took off her coat and pulled it on top of her for protection. The vibrations lessened as Hannah prayed silently until the all clear was sounded. She exited from the cellar, choking and gasping for air. There was not much respite outside the villa. She smelled burning trees and the acrid smoke filled her nostrils. Hannah locked the door behind her and ran from the villa grounds onto the empty street, the distant sounds of fire engines and ambulance horns in her ears. She made her way to Avus, a broad boulevard that intersected the Grunewald.

Buildings were ablaze on both sides of the avenue. Trees just burned until there was nothing left to burn.

It was then that Hannah decided to go to Charité Hospital. She stopped at Haus Dahlem, a convent. This was an orphanage and a home for unwed mothers and poor mothers-to-be, operated by the Mission Sisters of the Sacred Heart; it was but a short distance from Grunewald, in Wilmersdorf. Hannah finally reached her destination and rang the bell.

"Sister," she said to the nun who answered the door. "I am Sister Ursula from the Convent of the Daughters of Charity. I am a nurse on my way to Charité Hospital. I would like to pray in your chapel before I continue."

"Of course, Sister. Please come in," was the immediate reply.

Hannah went into a small chapel that barely had a roof. She settled in a pew to pray. The late winter light illuminated the area where she sat, as if the angels of the Lord had come down from heaven to this hell on earth. She prayed silently and left the chapel. My beautiful city has been ruined, decimated by a dictator's maniacal quest for power. And who suffers, but the people. The same people who voted this Führer into power. Did they ever foresee what would happen to their country? And those awful Allied planes, why don't they leave us alone? Hannah's heart ached for her mother. If only I knew she was safe, she kept on thinking. It's the not knowing that hurts so much. However, I am a woman of God and I must place my trust in Him. Hannah did not want to go back on the streets. She felt she was probably the only person alive. She was quite mistaken and far from alone, for outside the streets were quite lively. She walked into a scene of activity with people milling about, buses operating and many people running to purchase food. Hannah boarded a bus in the direction of Charité. At the next stop army officers boarded the bus.

"All papers, please," they ordered.

"Papers?" said a passenger. "We're just going to Steglitz. What's going on?"

"We're looking for a saboteur suspected of blowing up some buildings," was the reply.

"In this air raid?" replied another passenger. "Are you sure the government isn't doing this so we think the Allied bombers aren't hitting any targets?"

"Silence," came the curt reply. "Comments like yours don't help us."

"Sorry," came the response, "but things are so tough, we have to joke about something."

The officer checked the man's papers and moved towards Hannah.

"Papers, *Fräulein*, papers."

Hannah kept on going through her pockets unable to find the *Lebensborn* papers. They had fallen from her pocket when she used her coat to shield herself at the Grunewald villa. What she did feel, deep in an inner pocket, were her former papers that would readily identify her as a half-Jew. She felt it quite unwise to show these.

"I am sorry, sir," she said, again emphasizing her upper-class Berlin accent. "I used my overcoat to shelter myself from some debris and everything has fallen from the pockets."

"Where do you live?" was the brusque reply.

"I've been out of the city. I went to my home and it was deserted. I'm a nurse and I am going to Charité Hospital. I can get proof of my identity and obtain duplicate papers there."

The air raid sirens sounded.

"Go to the shelter at the next stop," commanded the officer.

The bus discharged its passengers who quickly exited to the shelter. Hannah slipped away undetected and, as the sound of bombs heralded the arrival of enemy aircraft, she made her way into another shelter to wait out the air raid. When the all clear sounded she left hurriedly and eventually boarded another bus to Charité. The bus, threading through streets which were still open, arrived at the hospital about two hours later.

Hannah entered the hospital. There were wounded people

lying all over the halls. Some were moaning in pain, others staring with lifeless eyes in a trance.

"Sister Ursula, Sister Ursula. Is that you?"

Hannah turned around to see the face that matched the voice that she knew so well. It was that of Dr. Ellabo.

"Why aren't you wearing your habit? Never mind, so many things have happened since I last saw you. Sister, we need all the help we can get. Please come with me to the third floor so I can discuss what has to be done. All the hospitals are filled with wounded—troops and civilians alike."

Ellabo rambled on and on, sometimes hardly making any sense. Finally he looked up into Hannah's eyes.

"Forgive me, Sister, for prating so. I've been working straight through for days with very little rest. I haven't even inquired as to how you are, but there's so little time for the niceties which are probably so important these days. People just want to survive. They're terrified of the Russians. I'm thinking of leaving and heading towards the West, towards the Americans and the British. The Russians probably won't know I'm a foreigner and they'll slaughter me like the rest of the Germans. Sister, if you want to survive I would suggest you do the same thing. The Russians will have no respect for you, whether you are a nun or not."

A cold chill went through Hannah's body. It was traumatic to have had sex with Paul, whom she knew and cared for, but to be raped and possibly killed by a stranger was inconceivable. The thought vanished quickly as Hannah immersed herself in the nursing she did so well. She worked in the hospital until ten o'clock that evening and she was able to get a ride to the Convent of the Sacred Heart. Mother Superior Cunegundes had heard of Hannah's visit previously and she welcomed Hannah to the convent where she was immediately re-outfitted with a habit. Hannah worked long hours at Charité, and put in long hours at the convent orphanage as well.

On February 13, the British bombing of Dresden occurred, followed by the American bombers the next day. Hannah heard the news at the hospital. She said a silent prayer for her *Lebensborn* friend, Lotte.

The time passed quickly in a blur. Hannah and Ellabo worked around the clock, as Berlin was pounded by the Allied bombers.

On April 14, General Eisenhower determined that Berlin was a military objective no longer. It would be the Russians who would enter the city. The worst fears of the Berliners were to be confirmed.

32

The Russian offensive had stopped for the winter; they were encamped on the eastern side of the Oder River. Oddly enough, it never occurred to the Germans that Berlin would ever be taken, so there were no real fortifications around the city. Except for the building of those which had started the previous year; they too had stopped for the winter.

On April 16, the Russians launched a massive attack from the eastern side of the Oder River. The people in the eastern part of Berlin could hear the heavy thuds of the artillery in the distance. There was no doubt as to what it was; the expected was finally occurring. About eight o'clock that morning calls started coming in from the East that the battle had begun. The radio had an announcement that there was an attack, but it was mute about the intensity; word spread throughout the streets quickly. Military support was lacking; other than top echelons, there were few troops in the city. At this point there were insufficient supplies to build any additional, worthwhile fortifications. Old trucks, buses, anything that could be used, was being piled up in the streets to resist the oncoming Russians. It was like building a wall of toothpicks to hold back the oncoming deluge.

Hannah and Ellabo had not even heard the news, they were so busy caring for patients; the city's other inhabitants just went about their business as usual.

Hannah had arrived at the hospital at seven o'clock that morning. The Führer's Order of the day, held back until the certainty of the Russian invasion, had stipulated that all must fight to defend the city. It stated that those who did not would be considered traitors and killed.

Goebbels had the population convinced that they would be either annihilated by the Russians or transported to the East as their slaves. The population of Berlin was traumatized at the thought of these Barbarians occupying their city. Many of the people, like so many of the Jews before them, had cyanide capsules at the ready. They would commit suicide before they would succumb to Russian atrocities.

It was Saturday, April 21, the day after the *Führer's* birthday. Hannah and Ellabo were working in the hospital. At 9:25 that morning the 363rd air raid on the city took place. There was, as after every air raid, an additional influx of patients into the hospital. At this point, Hannah had to sit down She was light-headed from lack of food, tired from lack of sleep, and generally demoralized. She prayed, as she always did, for renewed strength in order to do the job for which the Lord had chosen her. Hannah's spiritual strength overcame her physical weakness; she rallied and returned to her work renewed. At 11:30 that morning Russian artillery shells started to pound Berlin with relentless intensity. The battle to take the city had now begun in earnest. The artillery shelling was more devastating than the air raids. The shelling was so intense that it was difficult to venture outside without being killed or wounded. People spent all of their time in shelters with either a minimum or no supply of food and water. The U-Bahn stations were overfilled and the smell of feces and urine permeated the very walls; infants and children died in their parents' arms, older people would just die. Disposal of the bodies was difficult and the smell of death was everywhere.

On May 1, Berlin was completely surrounded by Russian and Ukrainian troops. Most of Charlottenburg, all of Moabit and Schoenberg were now in Russian hands. Many *Volkssturm* units (those composed of men who had been considered too old for military service) were dispatched towards the East to help defend the city. They along with the Hitler Youth were fighting feverishly, often to the death. The hospitals were filled with the wounded. Hannah would be tending a fourteen year old boy in one bed and a seventy year old man in another. She knew the end was near.

Mass desertions of the city's defenders had been taking place. Those who were caught were executed on the spot by the Nazis; those who fought were annihilated by the Russians. Hannah and Ellabo worked feverishly; they could not leave the hospital confines. They and their colleagues worked frantically, forcing themselves to contain their emotions in a state of limbo. They were now working out of the lower floors or the basements. Hundreds of patients had died or had been killed by the shelling. Life went on in slow motion. Amidst all of this devastation word had leaked out that the *Gestapo* was making a systematic sweep to destroy all those with even a drop of Jewish blood. Hannah had heard Ellabo mentioning this, and even though rumors always circulated throughout the city, this news shocked Hannah. She did not have her *Lebensborn* papers, and the location of the *Lebensborn* home was now occupied by Allied troops. Hannah knew the ruthlessness of the *Gestapo*, and even with what was going on they might well trace her true identity.

"Dr. Ellabo," said Hannah a few hours later. "I am concerned with the *Gestapo* sweep to destroy the Jews."

"Yes, it is regrettable, Sister," he replied in a non-committal fashion. "I don't think the city can hold out much longer." Then, he cupped his hands and whispered in Hannah's ear, "I'm planning to leave to head West as soon as possible. I suggest you do similarly."

"Well, it might be the best course of action for you, but I'm concerned because I'm considered part Jewish," Hannah continued. "I think, Dr. Ellabo, that I might be one of their victims. I cannot take any action until I consult with Mother Superior. I'm a servant of God and the church. I don't believe I have the right to make these decisions without some consultations."

"How is it possible that you're Jewish, Sister?" he asked incredulously.

"My mother, although reared as a non-Jew was classified as being Jewish."

"I never would have believed it, Sister, but then you must leave here immediately," Ellabo counseled. "Why should you die at the hands of murderers who want your death because you are half Jewish?"

"Leave here? But where will I go? Who will take care of the patients?"

"Sister, your dedication is misplaced. I don't think there's much hope for any of us. The Russians will be here soon; we'll probably all be killed. I think our best course of action is to leave the area and head to the West. We'll be safe if we can make it to the American lines."

Hannah laughed.

"Dr. Ellabo, do you think we're just going to walk over the front into the arms of the Americans?"

"I don't know, Sister, but I think we'll gain nothing by remaining here to be fodder for the Russians. And you, Sister, have less of a chance if the *Gestapo* gets to you."

"Dr. Ellabo, I'm not afraid of death if I don't leave."

"That's your option, Sister, but time is of the essence. I suggest you *do* leave the hospital immediately, because you may be unable to return here. If I don't hear from you in a few hours I'll take off on my own towards Spandau."

Hannah paused and thought for a moment.

"Yes, Dr. Ellabo, you make good sense. I'll do as you suggest."

"Good luck, Sister."

"God bless you, Doctor."

Hannah turned around and left the hospital with him. The sky was a red blaze; the streets deserted. There was a brief lull in the artillery attacks and they were able to walk for almost a mile; then the shelling resumed, with even greater intensity. Hannah ducked into a U-Bahn station entrance. There was no additional room in the station, and by now people had crowded onto the tracks.

"Dr. Ellabo, Dr. Ellabo, where are you?" Hannah shouted, as she choked on the human stench, but he was not to be seen.

She remained in the station for two days, emerging on April 26, after having traveled less than one mile. Fires burned unimpededly since fire trucks had been ordered out of the city lest they fall into Russian hands; those police remaining were called to battle the Russians and looting had begun. Hannah decided to make her way towards the Dahlem Convent. Twelve hours later Hannah knocked at the doors. She requested an immediate audience with Mother Superior Cunegundes. Mother was in the wards helping screaming infants and pregnant women, the sounds of the attack and the intensity of the vibrations unceasing. Hannah explained her situation to Mother Superior.

"My child," mother intoned, "you must follow your own dictates at this time, but I am concerned for your safety."

"Thank you, Mother," Hannah replied, "but I do not think I'm any safer in the convent than I'd be outside."

Mother smiled, knowing Hannah was quite correct.

"I shall go to the chapel and pray before I depart, Mother."

"May God be with you, Sister," Mother replied and turned to continue her work.

Hannah prayed in the chapel and left the convent. A volley of shelling started and Hannah began to feel heat on her back; her trailing habit was aflame. She fought against terror as she methodically removed the robes; fortunately she was unscathed, but she was more upset in being clad only in her undergarments than with the possibility of having been burned. She decided to return to Haus Dahlem for more clothes. The bombardment continued and Hannah moved forward, as if doing a ballet between the hail of the shelling. Bodies were scattered everywhere; it was a gruesome sight. Hannah looked around her at the horrible scene, and as she began to flee she tripped over the body of a young, well-dressed woman.

"Forgive me, Lord," she murmured loudly.

She crossed herself, said a quick prayer over the body of the dead woman, and with the difficulty of moving a heavy, stationary object she took the clothes from the dead woman's body and quickly pulled them over her undergarments.

Hannah was quite near Grunewald at this point; she decided to go to the villa. I must see it, maybe for the last time, she thought. She arrived there about an hour later, to find the house in ruins. She looked at what remained of her former home. The top floor was gone, but the rest was still standing. She approached the front door, still intact. It was locked; and the key to the small door had long since disappeared in the confusion. How silly, she thought, there's no glass on the windows, I'll just slip in. It was getting dark, but even in Grunewald the fires from the city illuminated the area. Hannah flicked on the light switch, but there was no electricity; there had been none for days. She went to the basement cupboard that produced a few tins of tuna fish. Hannah searched for the opener, found it readily. She offered a prayer to the Lord for the tuna, which she ate with a silver fork on a porcelain plate of Rosenthal china. She then curled up near the cellar wall and, spent with exhaustion, fell into a deep sleep.

The Russians had now reached the heart of Berlin. At 1:30 that afternoon, on April 30, 1945, the Russian flag was raised over the *Reichstag*. The shelling continued over a city that lay desolate, with little left to destroy.

Hannah was so exhausted that she slept for two nights. When she awoke, on the morning of May 2, she stretched her body feeling renewed energy. She could still hear gunfire as it continued relentlessly. The smell of smoke was acrid and pervasive, but yet Hannah could detect a bit of sunlight burning through the fog. As Hannah turned around to stand up, she gasped. There in front of her was a Russian officer standing silently, staring at her.

"Good morning," he said in passable German. "Do you have any guns or military equipment which you are hiding in the house?"

"Sir," she replied, "we do not keep fire arms; this was my mother's house."

"And where is your mother?" the officer asked

"I don't know. She was deported because she was a Jew."

"Oh, I see," he replied with a degree of skepticism. "And what do you do?"

"I am a nun; a sister of the Daughters of Charity."

"A nun, and your mother is Jewish? What kind of fool do you take me for?" he replied with a great deal of anger in his voice.

"It's quite true, sir. My name is Sister Ursula," she said displaying the crucifix which was under her clothing. "My mother's name was or is, if as I hope she is still alive, Lily Mendelssohn, the pianist."

"I've heard Lily Mendelssohn perform before. She is, indeed, a gifted woman. How do I know what you're telling me is the truth?"

"I guess you don't, but I wouldn't lie to you."

"I don't know that either," he retorted

"Sir, I don't know what to say to you, but it is true."

The officer started rummaging through drawers and closets in the cellar looking for incriminating material. He pulled a piece of paper out of some rubble. It was the *Lebensborn* identification.

"What is this?" he said, attempting to decipher the wording.

Lord, Hannah thought, I doubt that the man will believe this story. I don't think that I would either; it's so farfetched. Fortunately for Hannah, the *Lebensborn* project was kept as secret as it could be, and it was doubtful that the officer would have any knowledge of it.

"What does this mean?" he inquired.

"I am a nurse, sir, and I worked at that facility," Hannah replied.

"Now you say you're a nurse? Before you said you were a nun," the officer continued. "What am I to believe? I will keep these papers and have them checked," he replied.

The Russian continued his search and came upon a large,

floor to ceiling closet that looked as if it might have held rifles. He opened it and pulled out some items.

"What is this uniform?" he asked pulling trousers and a jacket from a closet shelf. "I've never seen this type of German uniform before."

"I haven't seen it before either," Hannah said nervously.

The situation looked grim; she was expecting to be shot at any moment. Suddenly she remembered seeing a picture of her father dressed in the uniform.

"It must have been my father's," she replied.

"I don't believe any of this nonsense. I've had enough of this. You are probably a Nazi spy."

The officer raised his pistol, and the entire house shook as a nearby artillery shell landed in the area. The vibrations dislodged the closet, and as the officer turned around the entire closet fell towards him. He side-stepped it quickly as it landed next to him with a sharp crack. A worn photograph, pushed by the air contracting between closet and basement floor rose upwards, and like a gentle feather floated towards the floor. It landed next to a large, sheathed knife, which had been part of the uniform. The officer, gun still held in hand, gaze fixed at Hannah, picked up the photo and examined it. It was an old photograph of Lily and her husband, Hans. The officer handed it to Hannah. She looked at it with sad, tender feeling, kissed the picture and placed it in a pocket.

The officer had recognized the picture of Lily. He placed his gun in its holster.

"You must have been a pretty child, *Fräulein*. You look just like your father. I am honored to meet you."

The Russian officer walked towards Hannah, bowed, kissed her hand and left immediately. Hannah stood there for a few moments collecting her wits. She picked up the knife, and placed it in her pocket next to her parents' picture. Suddenly the telephone started to ring (most automatic telephones were operational). Somewhat surprised to hear this unexpected intrusion, Hannah following the sound of the relentless ringing, located the intact telephone under some rubble. My parents and the Lord have saved me from being shot to death, she thought, now what next?

"Hello?" she said.

"Is this Sister Ursula?" asked the voice at the other end of the wire.

"Yes," Hannah replied with a voice whose timbre sank and rose again.

"Sister Ursula, this is *Frau* Merth."

"*Frau* Merth? How did you know I was here?"

"I really didn't. I took a guess. I telephoned the hospital, but I couldn't get through. I just took a chance that you might be there. Trains are still running here."

"Here, where are you?"

"I'm at the very southeastern edge of Spandau, almost in Staaken. I have a small cottage. Try to come if you can. I can give you shelter, as long as the cottage is standing. I just hope the Americans get here first, then we'll be okay. Go to the town center and you'll be directed towards my cottage."

"Well," Hannah replied. "I've already met a Russian officer. He came into the house."

"Oh God," *Frau* Merth replied. "They're at Grunewald already? We're doomed."

"I'll try to get to you," Hannah responded. "Thank you and God bless you."

Hannah wanted to distance herself from the Grunewald villa before the arrival of any more Russian soldiers. She said a prayer, left the villa and just started walking towards the West.

As Hannah walked, there were other people by the thousands heading in the same direction. She felt she was watching a movie, for it was such a strange sight. Some people were well dressed, trying to cart everything of value along with them; others had nothing save the clothes on their backs, some hardly that. The infants' screams were barely heard against the sound of the guns; retreating German soldiers, many hobbling on crutches, others bandaged, were barely inching along. They were all headed for the bridges spanning the Havel River—to Spandau, the westernmost district of Berlin.

Shortly before 1:00 that afternoon, General Karl Weidling's request for a cease fire was honored by the Russians, whose guns fell silent two hours later. Colonel General Vasili Ivanovich Chuikov met with Colonel von Dufving, Weidling's Chief of Staff. The battle for Berlin had ended.

As the sound of gunfire diminished, the refugees, making their way towards Spandau, kept on trudging westward. Hannah finally reached the Havel River and crossed at the Pichelsdorf Frey.

Spandau seemed relatively untouched by the war, even though there were many factories in the area. Hannah came upon a church and she entered the building. It was quiet except for the snoring of people who had sought refuge within its confines. Hannah prayed, and she exited from the chapel, going into a small chamber in the front. She had hoped to see a priest, but there was none. She continued towards the exit passing a room with an intact piano that was located against the western wall of the church. Hannah went into the room, sat on the piano bench, and, for the longest time she just looked at the keyboard. Ultimately her fingers touched the ivory keys; she started to play a Mozart piece that her mother had taught her when she was a child. It was quite elegant in its simplicity and again the rush of her childhood memories filled her mind with a simultaneous happiness and feeling of *weltschmerz*. She continued to play, lost in the oblivion of her mind and her past; her thoughts haunting her into a more intense sadness. The music wafted out of the church, into the heretofore silent streets filling them with melody and beauty. It was so appropriate. Spring was in the air and flowers had started to bloom. Hannah finished the piece, let her head hang down and placed her hands over her weary eyes.

"*Fräulein*, I felt as if I had died and become resurrected," whispered a voice with a grateful solemnity.

Several people had gathered to hear the music; an old man approached the piano.

"My dear girl," he said, "What you have done has lifted my spirits from despair to hopefulness. I don't know what's to become of us, but I have hope for the future. There are things to live for no matter how bad our situation. I remember the days when I would go to hear Lily Mendelssohn play the piano. She was such a gift to the people of Germany. Lord knows where she is now. I hope she is alive and will come back to us to perform again."

Hannah smiled at the gentleman.

"Dear sir, the very fact that she is remembered by you will always keep her alive. May God bless you."

Hannah left the church and continued walking. There was no food or water available and she was tired. People were sleeping everywhere, but she continued trudging onwards, praying silently as she went. As her energy lagged, her spirits soared, for God had protected her and had kept her alive to continue to serve Him and help others. Finally she could go no further. There was one partially damaged house adjacent to the street on which Hannah was walking; she decided to go there to rest. She went inside and heard a rustling, maybe a dog or cat was running away. All was quiet. She sat down on the floor, her back to the wall, and as her eyes closed she heard someone say:

"Hannah, I mean Ursula, I'm so glad to see you."

Hannah knew the voice immediately and with joy looked up to see Paul standing against the opposite wall. He was an imitation of the person whom she once knew. He was thin, battered, and he limped across the room towards her.

"Oh Paul," she sputtered, "I thought you were dead. It's so unreal seeing you here."

Paul caressed her tenderly and kissed her on the cheek.

"I'm still a nun, Paul. I've been exonerated for what I've done with you."

"Hannah," he said, "I love you. I've always loved you."

"And I, you, Paul," she replied with the intimation of a platonic love.

"No Hannah, that's not what I mean. I love you as a woman; I've always wanted you as my wife and to bear my children."

Hannah's body stiffened and she stepped back slightly.

"Paul," she replied, "I did bear your child in order to save my mother; not out of sexual desire for you as a man. I felt that I was martyring myself for my mother, sacrificing my virginity, so that God, to whom I am betrothed, would spare her."

"Hannah, God cannot lie with you and love you physically as I have."

"Paul," she said, distraught, "the love I have for God is on a much higher plane than the physical. It's spiritual, and I serve Him by also serving others. I saved my mother, and I don't begrudge you any pleasure that you might have received in the process, but that was not my reason for sleeping with you. You must understand that. And, Paul, speaking of my mother, did you ever find out what happened to her?"

"She was sent to the East, Hannah. I know of no other details."

Hannah's body froze. She said nothing and exhibited no reaction.

"Paul, she may be dead."

"I don't know, Hannah."

Hannah started to weep and large tears rolled down her cheeks. Paul embraced her and held her close to his body. Hannah appreciated the consolation, but then Paul said:

"I love you, Hannah. I want you. I need you. I will take care of you, my darling."

Hannah, upon hearing this pronouncement, momentarily forgot her concern for her mother, attempting to extricate herself from Paul's embrace, and said:

"But, Paul, you must understand that I didn't want to do what I did. I don't want to hurt your ego, but I did this for my mother not for you. Now please, we must stop this."

She pushed him away gently.

"Hannah, why do you think I've survived this war? To find you, to come back to you, to be with you." Paul's compassion was starting to turn to anger. "I've loved you since we were children. All I ever wanted was you. I felt that once we were together you'd realize you could have a life with me."

"Even as a nun, Paul, even as a nun?"

"Nun? What does that mean to me? It's something that *you* have chosen, but in my mind it is far from irrevocable."

"Yes, Paul, but your mind does not coincide with mine or my desires for the life I've been leading. I emphatically do not wish to be your wife, and I will continue to pursue my desire to serve my God."

"Your God? What God? Is this the work of God? To destroy our country and to bring us to the state in which we're now? Look at yourself. Look at me? Do we deserve this?"

"Paul, stop feeling sorry for yourself. Look at all the harm and tragedy that our country has inflicted upon others. Look at all the innocents that have perished because the *Führer* has felt that we're better than they. We're not, Paul. They're human beings like we. They have the right to live like we do. I heard that the *Gestapo* would hunt down every person with even a drop of Jewish blood and kill them. Paul, if my mother died because she was Jewish, where do I stand in this situation? I am a *mischling* and I would be killed for this. How do you feel about that, Paul?

"Hannah, I loved your mother and I love you. I would never have wanted any harm to come to either of you."

"But yet you serve in the *SS*, an organization that annihilates people because they are Jewish."

"Hannah, I never had anything against Jews. I was young, impressed by the uniform, the *espirit de corps* of the group and the joy of belonging to a cause."

"What cause? The cause of killing every person who doesn't agree with you? Blindly following a man who has brought this nation to utter destruction and defeat? Who gave him the right?"

"The people, Hannah, the people. They elected him and his victories were wonderful for our people and our nation."

"And his defeats, Paul. Are they so wonderful? And then you have the nerve to say, *our people, our nation*? No, Paul, I realized that these cannot be *my* people, those who killed my mother and want to kill me. And look at the cost of those victories in human lives. The Russians who were so ruthlessly slaughtered and who will now do the same thing to us.

You say the people elected the *Füehrer*? Well, then they supported him. I cannot say I'd want this destruction to happen to Germany, but who's to blame? Surely you can't blame God for something that Germany has brought upon herself."

"Look at you, Paul, in the uniform you once wore so proudly. Are you as glorious in defeat as you were in victory? How did you feel about those who were defeated before you? Paul, you personify everything that I do not want in my life. My father fought in the Great War that killed him, and we lost, and now you fight in this war. Look what it's done to you. I think it's best that we don't see each other again. I'm going to leave you now. I suggest you remove that uniform of yours before the Russians get here."

"What do you mean, you're not going to see me again?" shot back Paul. "I'm not going to let you go just like that. I love you too much."

Paul's eyes seethed with anger as he glared at Hannah; it was a crazed, irrational expression. He approached, as if to grab her. He seemed to be someone whom she had never known, but, in a way, always knew. She was frightened. Paul grabbed her by the shoulders and said:

"Hannah, please, please don't say you'll leave me. I have no country, no family, and I may be killed by the Russians soon. I'm proud of my country, and I've worn my uniform proudly during my life; I intend to wear it proudly in death."

"Proudly in death?" Hannah snarled with a sardonic laugh, "You fool, such false pride is an egotistic aberration under such circumstances. All who die in this life pass into the next; their lot will be determined by a power far greater than their transcending, or descending soul. What will yours be?"

Paul seemed to hear nothing that Hannah was saying. He glared at her lustfully.

"Hannah, I want to hold you, to kiss you. I need you," he pleaded.

He grabbed her body and held it.

"Paul, let go of me." Hannah struggled trying to push him away.

They were both tired and weak, but Paul was the stronger. He started to put his lips on hers. She gave him a shove that broke his embrace.

"Get away from me, you idiot, you're despicable. I would rather grovel with swine than be in the same room with you," Hannah shrieked.

"You bitch," he countered, as he slapped her face and pushed her away, "Go rot with the swine. I don't see why I ever bothered with you, why I even made up that story about your mother, so you would sleep with me."

"What?" replied Hannah incredulously. "You made up that story? What do you mean?"

"Just what I said," replied Paul. "I knew that Heydrich had plans for your mother's deportation; there was nothing I could do about that, although I would have done anything I could to protect her. As far as sleeping with you—I figured you would be noble and righteous enough to fall for the story of your mother being in danger—and you did; and you went to sleep with me without too much prodding."

"Without too much prodding? Paul, I loved you as a brother. I did what I did with good heart and spirit. I can't believe you would stoop to such depths of sin and depravity. I can't believe it, it seems inconceivable. You're sick, Paul, sick. I can't forgive you for what you've done, that's in God's hands now. As far as I'm concerned you can rot in hell."

"Rot in hell? Don't play that pious, innocent role with me, you whore. It gave you the reason you needed to go to bed with me. And don't say you didn't enjoy it. It's probably the best thing that ever happened to you in your entire life."

Hannah was livid and shaking. This couldn't be happening. It couldn't be happening. Paul rushed up to her, threw his body on hers, slapping her face wildly. As he felt her body struggling beneath him he kissed her again, and her struggling intensified. She felt he was suffocating her. What did he have to lose? she thought. He could rape and kill me with ease, and who would know the difference?

He pushed her dress up and started to force himself inside her. She felt him enter her body and she screamed both from pain and the emotional trauma.

"God help me," she murmured.

Each of Paul's thrusts increased with rhythm and intensity, each one tortured her unmercifully. She felt her mother's picture in her pocket, the knife from her father's uniform pressing against her body. She pushed her hand into the pocket, pulled out the knife and the picture came along with it. She adroitly unsheathed the knife and as Paul's body lifted to thrust himself into her again she held the knife above her body, holding it with all of her diminishing strength. As Paul began to exhale a sound of orgasmic pleasure, the knife went through the picture and through Paul's stomach. The sound of Paul's release became a deep-throated gasp as his body fell upon Hannah's, for as his blood spilled from his body, his sperm entered hers.

She felt oddly ambivalent. Hannah was a servant of God, but she was still a woman—a woman who had been deceived and defiled by a person whom she had trusted. Hannah thought of Paul's comment about being a nun. Did that mean she could have no anger? Did that mean she could not protect herself? Yet she still wanted to save him. A renewed strength came over her. As Paul lay moaning, his life eking away, she pushed his body from hers and stood up. I cannot leave him to die like this, she thought. She rolled him over as he lay there moaning. The knife had pierced her father's face on the photograph and she gasped as the aged paper started to absorb Paul's blood. Hannah watched as Hans von Wallenstadt's face became obliterated before her.

"Paul," she said, in a concerned, but professional tone. "I'll do my best to save you. I'll see if I can get someone to help."

Hannah had dealt with many injured people in the hospital, many who had horrible deaths. She was not unduly fazed by the sight in front of her. She raised Paul's head and placed it on a piece of ripped floorboard. As Hannah left the house she turned around to see Paul lying there, barely alive and oblivious to his surroundings. Hannah went outside to try and get help. She saw a telephone two blocks away and ran to it. It worked; she made a call to the police station. She was told there was no one available to assist at the moment, help would be difficult to obtain, but somebody would be there eventually.

Hannah returned to Paul and said disdainfully:

"How weak the strong can be in defeat; the strength of a woman is not to be taken lightly. Paul, you will not deceive me again. But, Paul, you are a human being, and I have more respect for the individual than you or your kind could ever imagine. Don't despair, help will be here as soon as possible. Can you hear me? Can you understand what I've said?"

Hannah had little feeling for what had occurred, but she stayed next to Paul to help him, more out of duty than from true concern. At one point she arose and went to the door. She looked through the door and listened, hoping to hear the sound of an ambulance or an automobile, but all was quite still. As she turned around to return to Paul she saw him remove his revolver from its holster. He turned his head to look at Hannah, raised his revolver, pointed it at Hannah who stood transfixed, without thought, without fear. Paul then turned the revolver around, pointed it against his head and, with the last remaining bit of strength in his dying body he pulled the trigger. Hannah watched. She crossed herself and hoped God would be merciful to Paul's soul. There was just numbness, not from this incident alone, but from all the war's intrusiveness into her life. She moved lifelessly, a casualty as much as those soldiers wounded in battle. Hannah said a prayer over the corpse and left the building. He didn't even ask me about our child, she thought.

At the point where she turned south, she saw the bombed ruins of another church with its roof open to the sky above, its walls almost non-existent. Upon the walls' remnant, just above a still-standing table, was a hanging cross with the dying Jesus, ready to fall. Hannah entered the sacred area with the devoutness that she had always possessed. Genuflecting before the symbol of Lord Jesus, she entered what was left of a pew to kneel and then to pray. She prayed to the Lord, her husband in life and in death, to accept her humble prayers. She prayed for her mother; she prayed for the infant son whom she had barely seen. She prayed for the father whom she had never known. She prayed for all of those whom she helped to nurse and who lived or died in front of her in Charité Hospital She prayed for Paul, whose dried blood coated her body. She prayed for Germany, that it might find recourse in the time to come. She prayed for all the souls of those whom Hitler had unjustly annihilated. She had a special prayer for Mother Superior who, in attempting to do what she thought right by helping Jews, found herself condemned by the very society in which she lived and had sought to help.

Hannah's prayers returned again to her mother. She raised her head with tear-filled eyes to gaze at the cross of the ever-beneficent Christ. As she did, she watched the cross on which he lay dying, fall to the ground and settle ignominiously in the dirt that surrounded the table. Hannah rose from the pew to resurrect the Christ, her beloved husband, from the ashes of the bombed church. She tenderly lifted the cross from the earth, placed it near her lips, kissed it and held it there.

Suddenly, she felt something snap within her, against the background of her cognition, against all the prayers she had just offered. Hannah felt her mind and body become consumed with an anger heretofore unknown. She threw the cross vehemently across the church. It sliced through the beams of the slowly descending sun. And, as the cross settled in the dirt, it glinted in the sun's last gleam, lying broken on the ground, enveloped by the twilight that followed.

"What blasphemy," Hannah cried. "There is no Jesus. Nietzche was right. There is no God. It's all a myth . . . a myth to make people believe, and believe in what? In what, is there to believe? All this nonsense about God? Would God permit these tragedies to take place against His children? No parent or husband would stand by to witness that. Why was nothing done? Why? I divorce you, God. I renounce you as an entity. You do not exist for me anymore, and I wonder if you ever existed at all. Damn you, damn you, go to the hell that has been prescribed for the blasphemous sinners. And your people? Why did you create them if they were ultimately intended to destroy each other? It makes no sense, no sense."

During all this time, while the moral fabric of the world outside her had been steadily disintegrating, Hannah's faith had been a carefully maintained wall—between herself and despair. And now it had been broken. *She* had broken it. She was overwhelmed emotionally and physically, but now past the breaking point. Sleep came quickly.

Hannah awoke the next morning to the chirping of birds. She left the church and, for the first time, noticed that spring had come. Hannah looked at the flowers, still wet with a dark, buttery dew. How odd, she thought, but upon further examination it was moist soot, the residue of the still smoking guns that lay miles to the East. Would historians ever reference this in their writings? It's we, the people, who live through this, who shall remember these small things and add this to memories that we would probably prefer to forget.

Hannah laughed to herself. She felt free, the yoke of oppression had been removed from her shoulders. She and the land in which she lived had passed the point of distraction and was going through a re-birth; a re-birth that was to have a tortuous delivery. Hannah placed her hand on her stomach and rubbed it as it growled for attention, and the pangs of hunger manifested themselves with ever-increasing frequency.

33

The air was cool with an occasional scent of the freshness of the new season. The moon illuminated the area, like a page in a children's story book. There were few people on the streets, but the one person whom Hannah asked, a disoriented, elderly woman, was able to direct her to *Frau* Merth's cottage. The cottage was dark. Hannah knocked at the door. There was no reply. She knocked again, and as she turned she noticed a white curtain moving inside one of the closed windows. A moment later the door opened and *Frau* Merth appeared looking quite happy.

"Oh, Sister, I'm so happy to see you," she said. "I was afraid to answer the door. I thought it might be Russian troops, but then again, they probably wouldn't bother to knock, would they?"

"Thank you, *Frau* Merth. It's a pleasure to be here, to be in a home that's still standing. I'm grateful for your hospitality."

"No, Sister, it is I who am grateful. I'm frightened to be alone now. It's never bothered me before, but I've heard so many stories about the Russians that I've become afraid. I'm happy you're with me and I hope you'll stay."

"*Frau* Merth, I have no other place to go."

The two women went into the kitchen, where in the darkness, illuminated only by the moon, *Frau* Merth poured water over ersatz coffee grounds that had been used many times before.

"Sister, I'm afraid to light a candle. I don't want to call attention to the fact that I'm here."

"I quite understand, *Frau* Merth."

They spoke for hours. Hannah told *Frau* Merth of her religious emancipation and then discussed her mother. *Frau* Merth also spoke about Lily and told Hannah of the situation in the Spandau area. Finally, as sleep overtook their thoughts, they retired. Hannah felt like a princess as she went into her own room and collapsed on a bed covered with clean, crisp linen sheets. A crucifix of the omnipotent Jesus was on the wall over the bed.

Hundreds of Berliners continued to stream into the area. They told stories of how people cut up Nazi flags and displayed red banners to appease the Russians, only to have the *SS* shoot those who did so. They told of deserting *Wehrmacht* soldiers whom the *SS* shot and then hung on the street lamps. They told of massive, repeated rapes by Russian soldiers of females anywhere from ten to seventy. They told of looting and destruction by the Russians of everything they could put their hands on. Women who resisted, men who seemed as though they might be guilty of anything, were shot on the spot by Russian troops. They told of suicides and killings.

The following day, the Russians entered Staaken. Hannah and *Frau* Merth were petrified; and a subsequent knock on the door intensified their feelings.

"Let me answer it, *Frau* Merth," Hannah volunteered.

"No, Hannah, I'll go. I'm an old woman."

"It doesn't make any difference, *Frau* Merth. Remember the stories we heard yesterday? They rape young and old alike. From what I've heard the Nazi troops spared none in Russia. They killed everybody. Maybe the victor is claiming the spoils. Please, I'll go to the door."

Hannah opened the door just in time to see a Russian soldier remove his gun to shoot open the lock. The soldier's breath smelled of alcohol; in the background Hannah could see other troops arriving in the area, going into all of the houses. The silence of the descending darkness was now punctured by women's screams flinging themselves from the night, voices of doom coming from hell itself. Hannah was terrified of rape. She had gone through enough and she thought death might be easier than to experience this assault on her being yet again.

"*Komm, Fräulein, komm,*" the soldier said as he approached Hannah.

Hannah was immobile. *Frau* Merth rushed to her side.

"Please leave us alone," *Frau* Merth implored. "We've done nothing to anyone. We are Germans. We are not Nazis."

"*Komm, Frau, komm,*" was the response.

It was obvious that the soldier did not know German, nor would it have made much difference if he had. He was then joined by four of his comrades, also quite inebriated. One of the soldiers looked around the immaculately clean cottage. A bouquet of several wild, spring flowers, resting in a glass of murky water caught his eye. Hannah noticed this. She went over to the glass in which they were placed, removed them, walked over to the soldier and handed them to him. She looked into his eyes, not with fear, but with composure and humility. She was a woman completely self-possessed and able to dominate both her internal fears and the external circumstances that created them. Hannah took the man's hand and kissed it. Tears welled up in her eyes and dripped down her cheeks, moistening the man's hand and the flowers he held. She again looked up into his eyes, her countenance, though serene, now hid a deep sense of fear of what might follow. She then knelt at his feet and remained there silently, as if possessed by a spirit. The soldier, probably thinking she was demented, threw the flowers in her face and threw his body on top of her. I will not be raped, I will not be raped, she kept on saying to herself.

"This is enough," shouted Hannah, and fresh from the episode she had with Paul, she vehemently shoved the weight that was on top of her. The drunken soldier, more asleep than awake, rolled away from her body.

Hannah then went to *Frau* Merth who was screaming and fighting wildly with another soldier. Hannah, with her renewed and seemingly invincible strength, pushed the soldier away, and grabbed *Frau* Merth, saying,

"Come with me," and they rushed out of the door to the amazement of the soldier.

The soldiers pursued the two women, determined not to be outdone by them.

"*Fräulein* Mendelssohn," boomed a deep voice, and it continued, barking orders, in Russian, to the soldiers who immediately disappeared.

Hannah looked up and faced the Russian army officer whom she had met at Grunewald several days previously.

"Is this your house, *Fräulein*?" he asked.

"No, sir, it belongs to my friend, *Frau* Merth."

Hannah introduced the officer to *Frau* Merth who, still shaken, breathed a sigh of relief after her narrow escape.

"Won't you please come in? I don't have much to offer, but I do have some tea," said *Frau* Merth.

"It would be my pleasure, Madam. Permit me to introduce myself. I am Captain Sergei Ivanovich Karasik."

It was now daylight. The Russian troops arrived in Staaken *en masse*. They were milling all over the place. Soldiers were entering houses, tents were being erected, the area's former silence was no more; there was continuous commotion throughout the area. Hannah heard women screaming, others sobbing, a shot rang out now and then. Captain Karasik was oblivious to it all. He issued some orders in Russian to some soldiers and the three went into *Frau* Merth's cottage. *Frau* Merth went to get tea. Captain Karasik watched as she put one scant scoop in a large earthenware teapot. She placed a can of flammable material underneath the chafing dish in order to heat the little water that remained. There was a knock at the door. A soldier entered bearing sausages, vodka, tea and other food stuffs. *Frau* Merth cried out, and went over to Captain Karasik to offer her gratitude. The three sat down to tea accompanied by cheese and crackers. The two women had not eaten in days. The group's discussion centered around Lily Mendelssohn-Bartholdy. The captain was intrigued by the stories which Hannah told. After a fast-fleeting hour the captain excused himself.

"It has been a delightful visit. I hope I may return," he said.

"It is our pleasure, Captain Karasik," said *Frau* Merth.

Captain Karasik continued:

"I am having a sign posted on your door advising that this building is off limits to our soldiers. In the meantime I will post a guard outside to ensure your safety."

That evening, May 9, 1945 at 11:15, Germany surrendered unconditionally to the allies. Thirty years prior to the day, German torpedoes had sunk the Lusitania. Hannah's grandfather, Solomon Mendelssohn-Bartholdy, is still entombed within its watery bowels.

As the days passed, more Russian troops continued to stream into Staaken. Hannah still heard screams of women being raped, still heard gunshots during the day and night. The plundering and rape continued unabatedly, save for *Frau* Merth's cottage.

34

The Russians went about securing their hold, not only on Germany, but on many of the eastern countries they had liberated and then occupied. In Berlin, the Russians set up an administrative authority, the Magistrat. Utilities were partially restored and ration cards were being issued.

On May 26, 1945 at the Titania Palast Cinema in Steglitz, the first concert opened with Felix Mendelssohn-Bartholdy's *Music for a Midsummer Night's Dream*. He had returned to Berlin after a 12-year absence. Culture continued to be re-established as the Russians rehabilitated an old theater and re-named it the Admiralpalast.

Against this background of reconstruction, the two women would scrounge the countryside daily looking for items that might be useful; their days were spent just trying to survive. Captain Karasik had not returned and the food that he had brought had been consumed days before. Although rationing had begun in Staaken, supplies were sparse.

"*Frau* Merth," Hannah said one day, "I think it would be wise for me to return to Berlin. After all, I am a skilled nurse and I might be able to earn a few *reichmarks* to help us through."

"But Hannah, it may not be safe yet."

"Well, I won't know until I try."

Hannah left for Berlin the next morning. She had to fight to enter the train, and once inside most people prayed that they could exit quickly. Berlin had little or no water available and less soap. It was difficult to wash one's body, let alone one's clothes. As a result, the trains reeked of perspiration and the smells of urine and excrement overlay, in dulcet counterpoint, the stench of sweat and unwashed clothes that had long since reached their absorption limit.

Hannah finally arrived at Charité hospital, now guarded by Russian soldiers. She could not get permission to enter and was told to return to her home. The hospitals were filled with battle casualties, and they were soon to be overwhelmed with women giving birth to half-Russian children and people sick from starvation.

She was relieved to return to Staaken and her travels to the Mitte, the center of Berlin, ceased for a while. The days continued as they had previously. Hannah often compared her life to that of a forest animal who would scavenge around for food all day and go to bed at sunset.

Again Captain Karasik appeared at the doorway of *Frau* Merth's cottage.

"Captain Karasik," said Hannah with a smile, "how wonderful to see you!"

"Thank you," he responded. "It is nice to see you again also. Shall we have some tea?"

And with that he snapped his fingers and an orderly walked in carrying a large package of food supplies with several tins of tea on the top. The ladies were ecstatic with joy. They were not only happy to have the food, but they were also happy to be able to entertain the Captain. Life was one of bare existence. The citizens of Berlin went about their daily lives that precluded the niceties of entertaining. Moreover, as a rule, there was little, if anything, to offer to guests.

The conversation at the tea table was quite generalized until Captain Karasik said:

"*Fräulein* Mendelssohn, we have started cultural presentations at the Admiralpalast. I thought you might be interested in performing there."

"Thank you," said Hannah with a somewhat chagrined countenance, "I would love to do such a thing, but I'm afraid I don't have much talent. I haven't played the piano in a long time, Captain."

"Well, let's see. Stop by the Admiralpalast tomorrow afternoon. I'll be there at 3:00."

Captain Karasik thanked the ladies and left. Hannah and *Frau* Merth opened the package that he had brought. It not only contained food, but soap and an envelope with some *reichmarks*.

"How nice, *Frau* Merth, he even gave me carfare," said Hannah with a broad grin.

35

Hannah arrived at the Admiralpalast as Captain Karasik appeared with a heavy-set, gruff-looking, Soviet woman army officer. She mumbled something to Captain Karasik in Russian and he asked Hannah to play a piece on the piano. Hannah sat down and rattled off a Chopin showpiece, one that she often played as a child for her mother's guests.

"That was quite nice," said Captain Karasik. "Can you perform ballet music to which dancers can practice?"

"I must tell you, Captain," answered Hannah, "that I am not a professional piano player, regardless of my mother's fame. I have always enjoyed playing the piano, but the war and other commitments have precluded the luxury of piano playing. I would be pleased to play from any music you might have."

Captain Karasik translated Hannah's remarks into Russian for the woman, who responded:

"We do not have much sheet music here, but we are anticipating some deliveries from Russia. We do have this, however. Would you like to try?"

She placed some Tchaikovsky ballet pieces in front of Hannah who glanced at it, then sight-read it as she performed various selections. She was quite nervous and her performance reflected her feelings; the sub-standard caliber did not go unnoticed by her audience.

The woman officer mumbled something to Karasik who said to Hannah:

"Well, *Fräulein* Mendelssohn, we shall contact you if we need you. By the way, do you sew?"

"Sew?" asked Hannah.

"Yes," replied Karasik. "We will be employing German women in different types of jobs and you might fit in well with your background."

Hannah thought his comment rather gratuitous, that because her mother was in the arts, Hannah would make a good seamstress. However, she was desperate, as were most Germans for income and she would do almost anything to earn some *reichmarks*.

"Yes, Captain Karasik, I, like all German women, have been taught to sew. I would be pleased to assist you in anyway possible."

"Thank you, *Fräulein* Mendelssohn. Would you care to join me and have some tea?"

"With pleasure, Captain," she answered, and they adjourned to a canteen in the adjacent room.

The two chatted amicably and during the conversation Captain Karasik said:

"Forgive me if I appear to intrude, but tell me of your mother's life and your own before the war."

Hannah, usually close-mouthed about these discussions, felt a delight in discussing the past, as if in so doing she was reliving all of the happy times that she and her mother had experienced.

"Do you know what happened to your mother, *Fräulein*?" he continued.

Hannah's face turned solemn and her eyes glistened with tears.

"I've no substantiation, Captain Karasik, but I've been told that she was sent to the East."

"War is nasty business, *Fräulein* Mendelssohn. I lost both my parents during the siege of Leningrad. They starved to death. It's a grim situation indeed. Germans now probably suffered less than the Russians did then. I know that here the aged and the non-employed receive less rations than others, and even the others' rations are sub-standard, but my mother and father had no food at all."

After their commiseration the two seemed to have developed a bond of friendship whose links Hannah would never have thought possible. War does bring about strange situations, thought Hannah, but she genuinely enjoyed Karasik's company and welcomed the civilized respite as a temporary escape from the oppressiveness of the war in her life.

It was almost the end of June and Staaken was scented with late spring and early summer flowers. Berlin *Mitte*, as well as the surrounding areas were scenes of utter devastation. The air there was still heavy with the smells of burnt buildings and the Berliners' state of mind was no different.

Life for Hannah and *Frau* Merth under the Russians had been difficult, but bearable. They were not molested thanks to the protection of Captain Karasik and occasionally he would invite them to share the Russian mess, which was but a short distance from the cottage. The Russians established themselves conspicuously in most of the areas they occupied. All of the eastern European countries came under Soviet domination and a military dictatorship was imposed.

The Russians finally granted Berlin access to the Americans and British during the first week of July. Marshall Zhukov was quite firm in specifying how things would be handled. The sectors of Berlin were divided between the three powers, the British assigning France a portion of their territory. Zhukov advised that the West would not be fed by the Russian-held area. Eastern Germany was primarily agricultural, the majority of industry being centered in the western part of the country. The Allied *Kommandatura*—composed of Britain, the United States, and the USSR was formed to resolve problems in the city.

Hannah and *Frau* Merth were happy that the Americans were taking over the area's western sectors. The American Zone excluded Staaken proper, which was Russian-occupied, although it included most of the southern parts of the city to the center of the *Mitte*. *Frau* Merth's cottage was actually on the border and fell under American occupation.

When the Russians departed, the extra bounties of rations which Hannah and *Frau* Merth had received went with them. The Americans had strict rules. There was no fraternization permitted. Germans could not eat or use the same toilet facilities as the Americans. This irked Hannah no end.

"Are we lepers?" Hannah said to *Frau* Merth. "It sounds like the Nazi oppression all over again. The Nazis, the Russians, the Americans. They're all the same."

"Things will change, Hannah," replied *Frau* Merth. "It's all so new. I'd better go out to collect some water."

"Let me do it, *Frau* Merth," Hannah offered.

"Well, why don't we both go?" countered *Frau* Merth.

The two women walked several blocks to the water source. They lined up to wait their turn to collect the water, which flowed slowly and unevenly from the neighborhood's sole operating spigot.

After several week's time Hannah received notice to come to the Admiralpalast. A Soviet car had pulled up in front of the house (travel was unrestricted amongst the zones until October 18, 1948). A letter from Captain Karasik was delivered asking Hannah to come to the theater the following Tuesday at 10:00 a.m. When she arrived Hannah waited in line with other women who, evidently, had received similar notices.

"Ah, *Fräulein* Mendelssohn, what a pleasure to see you," said the familiar voice of Captain Karasik.

"It's my pleasure," beamed Hannah.

"Will you honor me by joining me at luncheon?"

Hmph, thought Hannah, the democratic Americans treat you like plague victims and the despotic Russians invite you to lunch.

"Of course, Captain," she replied.

The two went into the canteen. Hannah reveled in the delights of consuming a bowl of potato soup—thick, rich and fortified with lard—accompanied by dark bread thickly spread with butter, followed by tea and more dark bread and butter with thick fruit marmalade covering it.

"You delight me in your appreciation of our Russian food," said Captain Karasik benevolently.

"Oh, I'm quite stuffed and happy," said Hannah, both of them attempting to be genteel about the limited rations available to German citizens.

"*Fräulein* Mendelssohn, I understand we have uncovered a caché of records which the Nazis did not destroy. I have not forgotten to check into your mother's situation."

"Oh, Captain, I'd be so grateful. Thank you so much. I hope I'll be able to hear something about mother. This entire situation, the war, before the war, it all seems so unreal, like a passing dream—even now this situation with Germany occupied seems incredible."

"What has seemed real to you, *Fräulein*?"

Hannah sat quietly, pensively, quickly reliving years of her life, and in a few seconds that seemed like an eternity, she replied:

"The real things, Captain? When I was a child, growing up at home, with the security of mother's love, the warmth, never even thinking of not having enough to eat, going to school, playing piano with mother. I used to love it when we would play pieces for four hands on the same piano. Oh, but I must be boring you, Captain."

"Certainly not," he replied. "I enjoy hearing about your mother, and you too, *Fräulein*. Please continue."

"Also, Captain, and the most important, God; God was very real to me—even as a child I felt close to Him—and of course this closeness resulted in my decision to enter the convent."

"Have you ever regretted that decision?" asked Captain Karasik.

"Going into the convent?" Hannah replied.

"Yes," he answered.

"No, not at the time. It was nourishing, sustaining. In a sense it was a continuation of my childhood. I had proper order in my life, warmth, love, and a strong commitment to serving both God and mankind; that's one of the reasons nursing held such a strong appeal to me."

"Will you go back to the religious life, *Fräulein?*"

"I think not, Captain. Too much has happened in my life personally to feel that I would pursue such a life again. I have disavowed God, for me He exists no longer."

"Well, *Fräulein,*" replied Captain Karasik, smilingly, "you have a great deal in common with the Russians."

Hannah grinned bemusedly but thought it best not to answer.

"Oh, enough about me, Captain. How have things been going with you?"

"They've been going well, thank you. My wife will be arriving in two weeks and I am quite looking forward to that."

"Oh," said Hannah somewhat surprised to hear of Karasik's marital status, "I'm happy for you."

The two conversed until Captain Karasik suggested they adjourn to another room to which he escorted her. There were several German women, sewing costumes and curtains for an upcoming performance. A German forewoman approached Hannah and directed her towards the group.

"Good-bye, Captain Karasik, and thank you for all your thoughtfulness."

Captain Karasik smiled, bowed slightly, turned around and left the room, whereupon Hannah joined the sewing bee. The only reward for so doing was the receipt of a few packages that she had to transport back to Staaken.

"Well, dear, it's better than nothing," said *Frau* Merth as Hannah gave her the food and told her of the day's events.

"*Frau* Merth, I'm going to Charité Hospital tomorrow. Possibly I can get some work there. I am a nurse, and I'd expect my services might be useful. Even if I receive a few *marks* and some food, that would help us out. I could use a nose clip, though."

"A nose clip?" *Frau* Merth asked.

"Yes," replied Hannah, "so I don't have to smell those awful odors in the trains."

Both women had a long laugh; longer than they might have had normally, but they relished the bit of humor in an existence that seemed to offer so little of life's niceties. Berliners had a knack for adding humor to the worst situations; Hannah and *Frau* Merth were no exceptions.

The next day Hannah braved the transportation system for the trip to Charité. At the Friedrichstrasse station, she was pushed and pummeled as people tried to exit and enter at the same time; her anger at this repeated treatment reached a high pitch and she yelled,

"What has happened to us? Our manners? Our gracious style? Have we become no better than the animals?"

There was silence for a moment and a voice with a typical low-class Berlin accent broke out with:

"*Fräulein*, they do better than us. They don't have to work for the rations they get at the zoo."

The whole car, including Hannah, started to laugh.

As Hannah exited at her stop she came face-to-face with a familiar countenance.

"Lotte," she exclaimed in surprise. "How are you? I'm so happy to see you. I thought you might have been killed when you went home to Dresden."

It was Lotte Schnitt from the *Lebensborn* home.

"No, thank God. My family was not in Dresden at the time, and we've not been able to get back, which is just as well."

"There's so much to tell you," Lotte continued. "Do you have time for a coffee, or what's supposed to pass for it nowadays?"

"Well, I don't have much time, Lotte. I'm going to see if I can get a job to bring in some money. Things are so tight."

"Yes, Hannah, these are terrible times in which we're living. Imagine, our country losing the war, and now we can hardly get enough food to eat. I still can't believe it."

"I think, Lotte, that life itself has become one big unreality, and we seduce ourselves into complacency by getting used to what we think is real. If, perish the thought, we had always lived like this, better times might seem unreal."

"Oh, Hannah, you're so philosophical. You were always reading and studying, and things like that. I see you haven't changed."

"I have, dear Lotte, much more than you might think. This war has done strange things to us all. Would you mind if we just sat on this bench and chatted? I truly don't have that much time now. Or, if you like, we can go into the zoo and stroll for a bit. It's probably warmer in the sunlight than it is here."

"Let's go into the sunlight; I'm tired of the dark. I was in a cellar, without light, for days while the Russians were coming in."

Hannah said nothing in response to Lotte's remark. She, like most German women, did not want to share and re-live the suffering they had undergone.

"Hannah," Lotte said when they were comfortably seated, "I have some news for you of your son."

"My son?" exclaimed the astonished Hannah. "What news, Lotte, I don't know how much more 'news' I can put up with?"

"Hannah, I left the *Lebensborn* home about ten days after you did. There were many children in the nurseries and many areas that were not open to us. During the confusion of burning records, and the mass rush to obliterate the very existence of the place, I mistakenly entered a room with several infants. They all were non-Aryan in appearance; their names were clearly listed on cards and von Wallenstadt was one of them."

"How did he look?" asked Hannah, anxiously.

"Just fine; they all seemed to be well-cared for."

"What shall I do? How can I find my child?"

"Hannah, I think I heard somebody say something about sending some of the non-Aryan-looking children to the eastern part of the country, but I'm unsure. Don't forget, too, Hannah, that you signed a form giving him up to the State, so you don't have any legal claim to the child."

"Lotte, there is no more "State" as we've known it. Nazi Germany has been conquered. There are new people in charge and new laws; that entire *Lebensborn* experiment was a travesty, as far as I'm concerned."

"Well, Hannah, if you say that, why were you there?"

"Lotte, it was a set of external circumstances which brought me there."

"Oh come, Hannah, we could all say that's the case."

"I'd better get moving, Lotte."

"Well, Hannah, I wish you luck. Where are you staying?"

"With a friend, Lotte, near Staaken."

"Look, here's my aunt's address; her house is still standing, and I'm there for the moment. I don't know what the story is from one day to the next, but maybe we can get together."

"Yes, Lotte, that would be nice. I hope to talk with you soon."

The women parted with a farewell hug. Hannah looked at Lotte's address. It was in Treptow, on the other side of Berlin from Staaken.

Hannah finally reached the hospital, which to her seemed like an endless journey. She walked towards the red brick walls of the 275 acre, 2,000 bed complex. The hospital sat there like a contented, aging dowager seemingly impervious to all the years of turmoil in the city that surrounded it. The wind was blowing from the west, the sun shone brightly under a clear sky, and even the River Spree, sparkling as it flowed past the building, took Hannah to a place that wasn't. The guard at the hospital gate brought her back to reality.

"Please use the other entrance if you are sick," he said.

"Thank you, I'm not ill. I'm a nurse and I've come to see if my services can be used."

"Are you a party member?"

"Party member?" queried Hannah. "I have no connection with politics."

"You had better discuss this with your block leader first," the guard intoned blandly.

"Block leader? What *are* you talking about?" said Hannah.

"Where do you live, Miss?"

"In Staaken."

"That's under Soviet command. See your block leader there."

"Listen," Hannah said, somewhat irritated at this point, "I've come to serve as a nurse, not a party member. Sick people aren't necessarily interested as to whether, where, or with whom I'm registered."

"That may be true, Miss, but the party is," the guard said firmly and emphatically.

"Sister Ursula, Sister Ursula," a voice called out.

Hannah knew at once to whom that voice belonged. It was Dr. Ellabo.

"Sister, it's so nice to see you."

The two embraced and greeted each other warmly.

"How have you been, Ursula?" Ellabo inquired.

"Managing, Dr. Ellabo, managing; others have it much worse than I, so I'm not really complaining. You needn't call me Sister anymore, I've renounced my faith and I'm a nun no longer—just an ordinary person. And you, what about you? How is everything at the hospital?"

"The usual routine, not a spare moment. But my dear girl, you are far from just an ordinary person, and I do have some very exciting news."

"What is it, Dr. Ellabo?"

"Ursula, I'm going back to Peru. I'm going to be repatriated."

"Oh, Dr. Ellabo, I'm so happy for you."

"You know, meeting you like this is as if fate has thrown you into my lap. I want you to go with me, Ursula."

"Go with you, Dr. Ellabo?" she said, her voice rising and ultimately the vibrations of her words choking her at the throat. "Go with you? In what capacity?"

"I want you to go with me as my wife, Ursula. I've always

wanted you, and as we worked together I grew to love you. I could never express myself when you were a nun, but it's providential that you left the order and now, running into you like this. It's as if this was pre-destined."

"I'm thrown off guard, Dr. Ellabo; stunned. I don't know what to say."

"Don't say anything now, Ursula. Tell me how to get to your place in Staaken. I don't work tomorrow until the evening. I'll stop by your place at about noon. Is that all right?"

"Of course," she replied.

Ellabo hugged her, kissed her on the cheek, and bounded off down the street. Hannah turned around and headed for the Friedrichstrasse station to return to Staaken.

"And how did it go for you today, dear?" asked *Frau* Merth.

"The strangest thing happened to me, *Frau* Merth. I've received a proposal of marriage from Dr. Ellabo. I met him outside the hospital. He's returning to Peru and he wants me to go with him."

"Oh, Hannah, I'm so happy for you. I hate to have you leave me, but I would want you to be happy. I'm so thrilled."

"Yes, *Frau* Merth," replied Hannah, "but I don't love Dr. Ellabo and I know I wouldn't want to be married to him."

"But Hannah," replied *Frau* Merth, "don't be hasty. You'd be able to leave Berlin and live a normal life. You'd be able to have enough food and stop groveling like an animal, never knowing what the next day will bring. Marriages used to be arranged. You could learn to love the man. Time works in strange ways."

"He's coming here tomorrow, at noon, for my response."

"I'm so excited, Hannah."

"*Frau* Merth, I hate to disappoint you, but I will not accept his proposal."

"Hannah, dear. Think on it carefully. It can and will change your entire life."

"I know that, *Frau* Merth, but I think it's better to be by yourself than with someone whom you do not love."

"Yes, Hannah. I guess I cannot argue with you on that point. I know what that's like and I believe I've said those words before."

"You never really talked about your husband, *Frau* Merth," said Hannah.

"There's not too much to say," was the reply.

36

Hannah saw Dr. Ellabo in the distance. *Frau* Merth had exited some fifteen minutes earlier. Hannah continued to stare as the figure came closer, much as if she was going to meet her executioner, only her "executioner" was coming to meet her. She greeted Ellabo warmly.

"Hello, Dr. Ellabo, how was the trip getting here?"

"Ursula, you must start calling me Juan. Second"—at this point he paused, came up to Hannah, surprising her by sweeping her into his arms and continued, "I could have been traveling 20 kilometers or 200, I was completely unaware of time or anything happening around me. All I thought about was you, Ursula, just you."

And, so saying he placed his hand in his pocket, took out a ring, and placed it on her hand and kissed Hannah on her closed lips.

"Ursula, I cannot tell you how happy I am. You will not be sorry. My family in Peru has money. We can open our own clinic and you can work with me as a head nurse or you can stay home if you like. I love you, Ursula, I love you deeply."

Hannah stepped back; she took both of Ellabo's hands in hers.

"Let's go inside, Juan, we can speak comfortably in the house."

It was a hot, dry day. The rays of the sun were strong and they reflected against Hannah's blonde hair, which to Ellabo's eyes formed a halo around her. She was depressed and near tears for Hannah respected Ellabo and did not want to hurt him. They sat in separate chairs, facing each other. Hannah looked at the ring.

"How did you come by this ring?" she asked. "I can hardly believe there are jewelry stores doing business."

"Ursula, when I left Peru my mother gave me her engagement and wedding rings. She was quite ill and didn't know if she would ever live to see me again. I am sure she's no longer alive."

"Juan, I am very fond of you, and I'd not want to hurt you in any way," said Hannah. "You know I've lived my life as a nun, dedicated to serving a God in which I no longer believe. I was not prepared to be married to any mortal except to have my spirit bound with the Almighty to whom I was betrothed. I divorced God, and we both know that divorce is prohibited in the church, but not only that, when I did this I felt that I was married to someone who never existed. Right now, at this stage of my life, I am unprepared for marriage, for another union. I've been too used and abused by men to consider this."

Ellabo interjected,

"Ursula, I think every woman in Berlin has been raped. I'm sure it was a horrible thing, but I love you and it doesn't make any difference."

Ursula continued, "The point I'm trying to make is that I'm not ready to marry you or any other man and I don't know if I ever will."

Ellabo's face changed and he became anxious and distraught.

"Ursula, I love you. I can wait until you are more mentally settled in order to return my love. I would not press you, I swear."

"No, my sweet, and you are so sweet to say that, but I just cannot. Please understand, Juan. I'd feel imprisoned and held against my will."

"Is there no chance for me? I won't return to Peru. I'll stay here with you. The war situation will settle and we can leave for Peru at some future date."

"No," Hannah said, "I'd feel more pressured than ever and I might tend to regard you more as a prison warden than a husband; that in itself would be tragic."

"But, Ursula, if I leave now I may never see you again. I would contact you from Peru, but, but, I just can't leave you."

Ellabo started to sob heavily, heaving his sorrow from his mouth with each exhalation.

"I love you, Ursula, I love you."

Hannah walked over to him and put her arm around his shoulder. She then stood in back of him, placing her hands under his armpits and gently guided him from his seat. He looked at her through his moistened eyes as if his life had ended.

"Ursula, I love you, I'll always love you."

"What can I say? Juan, please—take the ring."

"No," he replied vehemently. "It's yours. I'm not interested in any other. Please let it remain on your finger."

"I cannot," replied Hannah. "It indicates a commitment which I am unprepared to fulfill. Please take it back."

"No, I want you to keep it. You may change your mind. I can come back again before I leave."

"Juan, please don't torture yourself like this. Please, for your own sake, it would be best not to return."

"Do you mean that, Ursula?"

"Yes," she answered.

He approached her as if to hold her, kiss her, but she stood firm, looking at him with feelings of understanding, but determination. She pulled the ring from her finger and gave it to him. He turned around and left the cottage. She could hear him sobbing as he walked away.

37

"*Frau* Merth," said Hannah, placing the letter she had just read back in its envelope. "Captain Karasik has asked me to the Admiralpalast and he would like me to bring you along. Maybe he has a job for you?"

"For me? That would be so exciting. Perhaps I can earn a few *marks* and get some additional food."

The following day they made the trip to the Admiralpalast, but Captain Karasik was not there.

Hannah was ushered into one room, *Frau* Merth was escorted into another. She was quite happy, looking forward to the opportunity to be productive.

Hannah waited for an hour. Nobody had entered the room; after an additional half-hour Hannah rose and went into the corridor outside. It was late in the afternoon and the theater was all but deserted. She entered the room where *Frau* Merth had been, but it too was empty.

"Could you help me, please?" Hannah asked a woman who was sweeping the area. The woman smiled and Hannah continued, "I've been waiting for instructions which have not been forthcoming."

"I'm sorry, but I don't know anything about that. I'm just here to clean the place."

"Do you know where my friend *Frau* Merth is?" Hannah continued.

"I don't think that anyone else is here, but you're free to look around if you like."

Hannah searched the area, but could not find *Frau* Merth. She waited an additional hour, with concern increasing at each loud tick of the clock on the wall. I'm sure she wouldn't leave without letting me know, Hannah thought, but maybe they put her on a special project. I'll probably find her at home.

Hannah left the Admiralpalast and went to the Friedrichstrasse *Bahnhoff*. She was anxious to get home. The train arrived and she was swept into it by the waiting crowd. She reached Staaken exhausted and demoralized. *Frau* Merth was not to be found. Hannah sat by the window waiting for *Frau* Merth, but she did not return. Hannah felt that her only alternative was to go seek Captain Karasik's help.

It was 8:30 the following morning when Hannah heard a knock at the door. Excitedly, believing that *Frau* Merth had returned, she rushed to open it. It was Captain Karasik.

"Oh, Captain Karasik, I'm so glad to see you. I've been so upset. *Frau* Merth has disappeared. Nothing happened when you asked us to Admiralpalast."

"I'm aware of what happened, *Fräulein* Mendelssohn. Please sit down."

"What is it, Captain? Please, tell me."

"*Fräulein* Mendelssohn, I was able to research your mother's situation."

"Oh, Captain, what is it? Is she alive?"

"She was deported to Treblinka, *Fräulein*. She is dead."

"I had that feeling, but I had hope. In a sense the frustration I felt about it is gone, and I even feel better knowing, just knowing. What happened to her, Captain? And what is Treblinka?"

"Treblinka was the concentration camp to which your mother was deported. The details of her death are very sketchy. There's just an entry for her on the day she died."

"My poor mother," Hannah muttered, but she was beyond

tears at this point; she just seemed to place it in the back of her mind as she continued:

"But, Captain, what does this have to do with *Frau* Merth's disappearance?"

"*Fräulein* Mendelssohn," Karasik responded, "the officer in charge of Treblinka was Christian Merth."

Hannah sat there in a state of shock, more affected by this pronouncement than the news of her mother's death.

Captain Karasik continued:

"The visit to Admiralpalast was an easy way to detain *Frau* Merth."

"But, Captain, what's happening. Why is she being detained?"

"*Fräulein* Mendelssohn, I don't think you quite understand. She was married to this man. This man was responsible for the death of almost all the mentally ill people in Germany, even before the massive extermination of the Jews took place. Merth had committed crimes of horrendous magnitude; and if he's still alive he must be caught and brought to justice. One million years in a concentration camp would never balance the injustices and criminal acts which he has committed amongst Jews and non-Jews alike. Look at this man. This is the portrait of an inhuman fiend."

And so saying, Captain Karasik pulled out a picture of Merth. Hannah looked at it. The face was vaguely familiar. She knew that she had seen it in the past, but she could not place it. It was worrisome to her. Captain Karasik noticed the consternation on Hannah's face.

"What is it, *Fräulein*, what is it?" he inquired.

"I don't know," Hannah replied. "I feel that I know this man, that I've seen him someplace before."

"*Fräulein*, if you have any additional information, it's important that I have it right away."

"Of course, Captain, of course. I can assure you of my utmost cooperation. But Captain, getting back to *Frau* Merth. She and my mother were close friends. I'm sure she helped my mother in many ways. She never spoke about her husband, and when she mentioned my mother it was always with love and affection. She couldn't possibly be involved in her husband's crimes. Also, Captain, she's lost a son of her own, a young boy who was mentally retarded, and for whom she still mourns."

"How and when did she lose the boy?" asked Captain Karasik.

"I don't really know all the details."

Hannah told Captain Karasik what she remembered of *Frau* Merth's discussions with her.

"*Fräulein* Mendelssohn, from what you tell me, Merth was probably responsible for his own son's death."

"What? I can't believe something like this," Hannah retorted.

"Believe it," Captain Karasik replied, " Power and greed can reach beyond the limits of all human comprehension when they consume those who lust for them, and unfortunately the innocent are the ones that suffer."

"Captain, *Frau* Merth is a wonderful woman. She would never be friendly with my mother if she were anti-Jewish. Please, please make sure she's all right. She's been as good to me as my own mother would have been. Please, Captain. I've never asked anything for myself."

"I know that, *Fräulein* Mendelssohn," he replied.

"Captain Karasik, I do want to ask you two questions, though, as a friend. I hope you won't think it too presumptuous of me."

"What is it, *Fräulein*?"

"Well, Captain Karasik, I had a child whom I believe to be alive."

"I don't understand, *Fräulein*? How could you if you were a nun?"

Hannah explained the entire situation to Karasik.

"*Fräulein* Mendelssohn," Karasik said, "I'm devastated by this story; and how you have withstood all as well as you have. Your life has been remarkable."

"We've all suffered in this war, sir," Hannah continued, as

tears started to well up in her eyes. "You've been so kind to me. I wonder if you could make inquiries as to the whereabouts of my child. I'd never given him a first name, but I'm sure somebody has done that already, but the last time I heard of him, he still bore the name of von Wallenstadt. I've been told that he was shipped to the east."

"Yes, yes, dear lady. I will do my best and try to bring him back to you."

"Do you have children, Captain?"

"No, *Fräulein*, my wife and I have tried unsuccessfully."

"Captain, I have nobody left except *Frau* Merth, and she's aging fast. If something happens to me, and you find my child, please take care of him if I'm not around."

"Now, *Fräulein*, nothing's going to happen to you," Karasik replied. "*Fräulein*, you said you had two questions to ask of me. What is the second one?"

"It's silly, Captain, and at this point solicitous, but why have you been so kind to me and willing to go out of your way to help me as you have? We've all been petrified of the Russians; many Germans killed themselves rather than submit to what they considered would be Russian brutality. You could have killed me when we first met, but everything you've done has been with the utmost of kindness."

"*Fräulein*, I am a human being. I detest violence. I hate the Nazis. They killed my parents, much of my family and many of my friends. But when I see ordinary Germans up close, they're just human beings. They all say they've done nothing wrong. Maybe in their own minds what they did wasn't wrong. The Nazis must all be punished for their crimes against the citizens of the nations they destroyed, as well as their fellow Germans. As for you, *Fräulein*, your mother was a beautiful woman who brought the joy and beauty of her art to many people. To see her on stage, to hear her perform, was a magnetic event that awoke every feeling of sensitivity in my soul. You've given me the honor of being able to meet and help the daughter of this woman. It is a pleasure and a privilege for me to do so. And lastly, *Fräulein*—and there may be other reasons which I cannot mention at the moment—I am a Jew."

Captain Karasik smiled at Hannah as he looked into her eyes; eyes glistening with tears. He took her hand, kissed it, turned around and exited. Hannah started to sob uncontrollably, as more of the repressed feelings which she could not recognize flowed out of her being, an uncontrollable river that she could not dam. At last she regained self-control and without looking back she left the Admiralpalast to return to Staaken.

38

"*Fräulein* von Wallenstadt, *Fräulein* von Wallenstadt," shouted *Frau* Hermann the lady who lived down the road, as she knocked at the door.

"Yes, yes, what is it?" answered Hannah as she came running to answer the call.

"The Americans are looking for people to do work. They want people who can also speak English. There's a sign down the road."

Hannah left the house to read the sign, with *Frau* Hermann in tow.

"*Frau* Hermann, this might just work out," said Hannah with a smile of joy.

Hannah ran excitedly back to the house. She felt she had to get to the American headquarters as soon as possible or else the job would be gone. She changed into the best dress she had; it was the dress she had taken from the dead woman during the Russian bombardment. She washed her face with the leftover water from the previous day and headed towards the headquarters.

"Yes?" boomed the deep voice of the desk sergeant. "What do you want?"

"I'm here to apply for the position that was posted," replied Hannah in her British English.

"There are several," the Sergeant said, softening his demeanor when he heard Hannah's fine diction, and looked up to see a beautiful woman standing in front of him. "Go to room 122A, down the hall, turn right, and it's the first door on your left."

"Thank you kindly," answered Hannah, smiling as she realized the Sergeant was looking at her from head to foot, and most approvingly so.

"Where do you come from, Miss?" the Sergeant inquired, not so much from curiosity, but from a desire to continue the conversation with Hannah.

"I come from Berlin. Where do you come from?"

"I come from Long Island. I thought you might've come from England."

"No," replied Hannah, laughing and throwing her hair back, enjoying the flirtation. "Where is Long Island, Sergeant?"

"It's in New York, in the States."

"Sergeant," retorted Hannah playfully, "we Germans are not all dumb, and a few of us know that New York is in the United States."

"What's your name?" he asked her.

"My name is *Fräulein* von Wallenstadt, Hannah von Wallenstadt."

"Well, it's a pleasure meeting you."

"And, Sergeant?" Hannah queried.

"And what?" he retorted, looking back at her.

"And what is *your* name?"

"Hochman," he replied, "Herb Hochman."

"And are you a Hochman?" she asked.

"What do you mean?" asked the Sergeant, apparently confused by her comment.

"Do you know the meaning of your last name in German?"

"No," he said.

"Loosely, it means high one. Are you true to your name, Sergeant?"

"Well," he said, equally enjoying the repartee, "we'll have to find that out, won't we."

Hannah shrugged her shoulders, her long hair falling back, and laughed. She did not remember when she had such an enjoyable, light-hearted laugh and she reveled in its delight.

"Sergeant Hochman, I'd better go to room 122A before the positions are all filled."

"Wait just a minute," he told her.

He picked up the desk phone and barked:

"Listen, Harry, come to the front desk for a few minutes right away. I have something to take care of."

Harry, a corporal, arrived at the desk promptly.

"Sit at the desk, Harry, I'll be right back," Hochman ordered.

"Come with me, Miss," the Sergeant said.

He took her by the arm and they paraded to Room 122A. Lines of people, job applications in hand, were waiting outside the room. Sergeant Hochman approached a private sitting at one of the desks.

"Jones," he barked. "Give this person the form to fill out."

Hochman leaned over, whispered something in Jones' ear and left the room. Hannah was directed to sit at the adjacent desk where she completed the form in English and returned it to Private Jones.

"Sit over there, *Fräulein*. We'll call you in a few moments," said Jones.

The few moments went quickly.

"Go into Room 122, Miss," Jones said.

Hannah walked over to Room 122 where another private sat behind a desk. He looked like the type of low-level English civil servant who wielded enormous control over the lives of the inhabitants of some colonial empire.

"I see your name is von Wallenstadt," said the private condescendingly. "Have you ever had any Nazi connections, been a member of the Nazi party, or a sympathizer?"

Hannah was rather put off by this condescension, but she wanted a job and she felt it best that she just play along.

"No," she answered tersely.

The questions continued and when the private was through he said:

"Go see Sergeant Hochman at the front desk. Tell him that we're going to assign you to the AFN."

"AFN?" inquired Hannah excitedly, "What is that?"

"It's our radio station, the American Forces Network."

Hannah reported to Hochman to tell him of her assignment.

"Great," he said.

"And it was so simple, I'm so happy."

"Right," replied Hochman.

"I'm supposed to start tomorrow."

Hochman gave an *Alice in Wonderland* Cheshire cat smile and repeated:

"Great," but Hannah could see through it and she knew that he'd arranged for her to get the job.

She smiled at Hochman and said,

"Thank you, Sergeant Hochman, for all your help," Hannah replied sweetly, and she meant it.

She responded positively to the sergeant's overtures. Hannah had little contact with Americans before. It was really a new situation for her; she liked their friendly and informal style.

Hannah started working at AFN, the radio station that had started on August 5, 1945 on the back of a truck. Hannah's duties were minimal. She dealt with Germans who came to make inquiries, but at the same time she loved to deal with the Americans. She always had a good GI lunch so hunger was no longer a problem. The soldiers at the radio station were always flirting with her, but it was harmless. She received many invitations to go on dates with the men, but she demurred. Hochman was a frequent caller who would "just be in the vicinity" and Hannah always welcomed his visits. During one of them he said trying to sound casual,

"*Fräulein*, I . . . I'd like to take you out this evening. Are you free?" he asked, stammering.

"One moment," she said, "let me check my calendar."

Hannah could see the boy-like anticipation and fear of rejection in his face. She didn't want to keep him in suspense any longer.

"Sergeant, I'd be honored to join you this evening."

Hochman knocked at the door of the cottage at 7:00.

"This is the first time I've been in someone's home since I've been here," he said. "Have you lived here all your life?"

Hannah laughed and replied,

"This isn't my actual home. This belongs to a friend of my mother's, *Frau* Merth. My home was destroyed by the Russians."

"Where did you live?" inquired Hochman.

"My mother's house was in Grunewald."

"The forest?" he asked.

"Yes," she replied.

"Grunewald is filled with GIs in tents now."

"I wouldn't know, I haven't been back there. It's difficult to get around the city and traveling is not pleasant. I'm going to make a trip to Berlin this Sunday."

"Sunday? I'm off Sunday. Maybe we can go together."

"That would be nice, Sergeant, but I'm going for a special reason and I think it best for me to go alone. Thank you, anyway."

She offered Hochman a cup of tea from the herbs that she had collected in the fields. He accepted eagerly; it was something he never had before. They sipped the hot liquid while Hannah told him the entire story of how she met *Frau* Merth, their visit to Admiralpalast, and *Frau* Merth's disappearance.

"So you see, Sergeant, I must go back to Admiralpalast to find out what's happened. The Russians are very secretive about everything and the sight of an American solider might not be in my best interests. Also, Sergeant," she said smiling, "you're not supposed to fraternize with German women."

Hannah laughed tossing her head back in her usual manner; Hochman just looked at her, enjoying her beauty.

That evening Hochman took Hannah to a local GI hangout where there was a group of Germans singing country and western music. This was an American-sponsored bar for the benefit of the GIs and Hannah marveled at the selection of food.

"Would you like some more?" Hochman said to Hannah as she finished the last morsel on her plate.

"Oh Sergeant," she said, quite embarrassed, "I'm so sorry to seem like a pig, but I was rather hungry."

"Did you have a tough time of it?" he asked her.

"Sergeant," she responded, "it wasn't easy for any of us. It wasn't easy under Hitler, it wasn't easy under the Russians, and it's not easy now. I don't single myself out necessarily, but I've never known hunger as I had recently. I'm still afraid that if I lose my job I'll be hungry again. I hope you'll excuse me, but it's best not discussed now. I'll try to be more polite in such instances."

"No, no, please don't misunderstand *Fräulein.* May I call you Hannah, if it's quite all right?"

"We're a bit more formal in Germany, Sergeant, but it's fine to call me by my given name."

"Great, but you must call me Herb."

"Okay," she said.

"Hannah, you're getting more American every day. Hang around us long enough and you'll be a real Yank."

Hannah laughed.

Hochman took her back to the cottage.

"Will you come in, Sergeant, oops, sorry, Herb?"

"Yes, I'd love to," he said.

"Some tea?"

"No thanks, Hannah."

Hochman moved in back of her and she turned around to find that she was encircled by his arms. They looked into each other's eyes, Hannah's telling him that it was all right to kiss her. He brought his lips close to hers and they slowly touched. She welcomed the kiss. It was warm, loving, stimulating, and most of all, it left her with an ecstatic feeling. As he continued Hochman reached over to open Hannah's dress. Hannah placed her hand on top of his and pulled herself back slightly.

"No Herb, please. I'm not ready for this."

"I'm sorry, Hannah," Hochman said apologetically. "I didn't mean to upset you."

"Thank you for understanding, Herb. I'm grateful to you for this evening. We both have to work tomorrow so we had best get some sleep."

"Good night, Hannah," Hochman replied, and he left the cottage.

39

It was Sunday. Hannah was on her way to the Admiralpalast. As usual, the S-Bahn was crowded. She was standing holding the strap, as the train stopped, just east of the Bellevue Station. Hannah was thinking of nothing in particular, just staring out of the window when another train, going in the opposite direction, slowly passed. She was staring into the train as it stopped. Hannah gasped; there in front of her was *Frau* Merth, surrounded by two large women. *Frau* Merth stared directly at her, but made no recognition of her presence. After thirty seconds or so, which seemed like an eternity, both trains started simultaneously. Hannah didn't know what to do, but she continued on to her original destination.

"Yes?" asked the imperiously commanding voice of the familiar-looking Russian officer inside the Admiralpalast.

"I'm looking for Captain Karasik," said Hannah.

"Oh yes, I recognize you. Captain Karasik's friend. He would always have refreshment with you."

"Thank you," replied Hannah, "I've come to see him."

"He's no longer in Berlin, *Fräulein*. I think he's returned to Russia."

"Oh," Hannah said dejectedly, "when will he be coming back?"

The officer laughed.

"I don't know, maybe tomorrow, maybe never. We don't know these things."

Hannah was tired and depressed. She returned to the cottage and fell asleep.

The next day, Monday, she was back at the radio station. Hannah loved the time that she spent there. She enjoyed the American popular music, she handled visitors quite well, and the GI crew loved her. They still tried to date her and she did go out with one or two, but it was for friendship as far as she was concerned. Word got around that she didn't go to bed with anyone and many GIs made bets as to which one of them would be the first.

Hochman was a frequent visitor to the cottage. They would date often. It was on one of Hochman's many visits to the cottage when he turned to Hannah and said:

"Hannah, I'm leaving Germany in two weeks and I'm going back to the States. I received my orders yesterday."

"Oh, Herb," she replied with deep sadness. "I will truly miss you. It just won't be the same."

"Hannah," Hochman replied. "I can't think of my life without you. I love you, I want you to come with me, I want to marry you."

"Herb, it's forbidden and we'll both get into trouble," she replied. The real reason was that the thought of marriage was just too frightening for her.

"Hannah, I'd do anything for you. I'll come back for you later if I can't marry you now."

He held her closely and kissed her, tenderly and sorrowfully; he might never see her again. A deep surge of desire arose within him and he felt the heat of passion filling his body.

Hannah willingly gave herself to him and he tasted the fruits for which he had waited so long, and they were sweet, and good, and right. Hannah felt similarly, not as if she was sacrificing herself for some cause, but opening her heart, mind, body and soul to a person with whom she wanted to give and share herself. They both felt it was their last meeting, and they relinquished themselves totally to each other. They spent the night in each other's arms, Hannah hiding her thoughts of Herb's departure. They spoke about so many things. She rarely discussed her past or her mother. Hochman realized it was too painful for her, but Hannah just felt it was best left unsaid.

Herb flew back to the States. Hannah's life was now without that previous inner glow that he kindled in her. She had not realized the strength of her feelings towards him until he was gone. She grieved, feeling that he was out of her life forever. It was several months after that when Hannah realized she was pregnant. She kept everyone of the letters that Herb had sent her, but she never told him of the child she was carrying.

She could not keep that secret for long. The GIs at the radio station soon realized what Hannah's situation was.

40

The knock at the cottage door startled Hannah from her sleep. It was one o'clock in the morning; she'd been dreaming that the Russians were after her, and that she, like *Frau* Merth, was to be arrested.

"What is it?" she asked behind the closed door.

The knock repeated itself and she opened the door slightly. She couldn't make out the face in the darkness, but the voice was unmistakable. Hannah quickly flung the door open and Herb burst into the cottage.

"Hannah, Hannah, oh Hannah," he cried as he held her and kissed her.

"Herb, Herb," was all she could say.

"Why didn't you tell me you were pregnant, Hannah?"

"Herb, I felt it was useless and that I'd never see you again, and I didn't want to put you in any position where you'd be embarrassed."

"But Hannah, I love you. I'm thrilled about it."

"But Herb, how did you know? Who told you?"

"The guys at the radio station went to see the Commanding Officer and he pulled a few strings to get me back. I have to leave in three days."

Hannah's joy turned to sadness as she said,

"Well, at least we'll have a few days together."

"Will you marry me, Hannah? I love you desperately and my life without you is empty."

Hannah smiled from ear to ear, turned to Herb and said:

"My dearest, it would be my greatest pleasure to be known as Mrs. Herbert Hochman."

Herb applied and received permission to marry Hannah. It was a simple, swift civil ceremony, and the lady who, several months ago, was not permitted to use the same rest room facilities as the Americans was now the wife of one. Hannah was laughing and happy; and Hochman beamed with pride as they entered the GI's tavern where his buddies and Hannah's friends from the radio station waited to celebrate the marriage.

It was two days later; Hannah was all excited. She was waiting for the jeep to take them to Templehof Airport to fly to the United States. Hannah had cleaned the cottage thoroughly, packed the few belongings that she possessed in a small bag and looked expectantly out of the window. She noticed the man who delivered the post coming up the walk, just as Herb's jeep pulled up outside the cottage. The postman handed her an envelope, she thanked him as she hastily stuffed it into the pocket of the jacket that she was carrying. Herb jumped out of the jeep and ran to embrace her.

"Darling, I'm so happy," she said as she turned to Herb who was beaming as much as she.

Herb said nothing, but just held her close and beamed all the more. They would be flying to the States in just two hours.

The airport was bustling with activity. They were to board their aircraft in fifteen minutes. Hannah had never flown and that added to the overall excitement. She looked at Herb as she said:

"I'll be right back, dear. I must go to the Ladies' for a moment."

As Hannah returned from the Ladies' Room a familiar voice called her name. She turned around to see Dr. Ellabo.

"Juan, I thought you were back in Peru."

"I had a great deal of difficulty with the Russians and the Americans, but it's finally coming to pass. How are you, Hannah?"

"I'm well, Juan."

An announcement came over the loud speaker.

"That's my plane, Hannah. Good-bye and good luck."

"Good-bye, Juan."

Ellabo stretched out his hand and grasped Hannah's hand in his. Hannah gently withdrew her hand, leaned over, kissed him gently on the cheek, grasped his hand in hers, kissed it, turned around and walked slowly away from him. Ellabo stood there, wistfully, for a moment, his eyes following her every step. Ellabo turned, walked in the opposite direction to board his flight. Ten minutes later Hannah boarded another transport with her husband.

"Are you happy?" Herb asked.

"My darling," she replied. "I have a husband whom I love, I'm going to have his child, and I'm looking forward to my new life."

Hannah felt melancholy as the plane left German soil. She took a last look at the devastated city below. It mirrored her own tragedies and experiences, which kept going through her mind repeatedly.

"Don't worry, darling," Herb remarked as he stroked her distraught face. "Everything will be fine."

"I know, Herb," Hannah smiled, "I know." She closed her eyes and within a few moments she was asleep.

The drone of the airplane engines seemed to echo through Hannah's subconscious. She was frightened, fearing it was an air raid. She woke up with a start and was reassured to see Herb sleeping in the adjacent seat. The airplane was cold and she buttoned her jacket, feeling the unopened letter that was delivered earlier. She had completely forgotten about it in all the excitement. The letter had no return address, but it was postmarked from the Western sector of the city.

Hannah opened it and saw a familiar hand. She read it slowly.

My dear Hannah,

Forgive me for any concern that my disappearance may have caused you, but it was not prudent for me to contact you. I am giving this letter to a confidant with the hopes that you will soon be receiving it. The Russians are rather suspicious about everything, and I'm afraid they might not permit me to send this.

I'm writing to you from Charité Hospital. I'm told that I have a cancerous tumor in my brain and I do not expect I'll be around much longer. Please don't feel sorry for me. I am ready for my death, and I'm welcoming it as a relief from the sordid existence that I've lead during the past years.

Hannah, I must write this to you before I die in order to confess the sins that I have committed.

My friendship with your mother was initiated by the *Gestapo*, for whom I was working at the time. It was a seemingly innocent way of entrapping Jews who might have been involved with activities against the *Reich*. Your mother was on a special list of protected Jews, issued by Himmler personally, who were not to be harmed. These people were spied upon to ensure they were not doing anything against the government. Your mother was quite innocent, but some high-ranking person, I don't know who, wanted to make trouble for your mother. We knew of the existence of a group that helped Jews to leave Germany, the Baum group. We had arranged for your mother to use their services, but something happened—one of those rare administrative mix-ups. The *Baum* people were captured and it seems your mother was not with them.

I continued to see your mother from time to time and I grew to be quite fond of her. She was a rare, kind, extraordinary woman, who in spite of her talent and renown was loving, considerate, and quite giving. She understood the loss of my child, as any mother would, and I related to her quite strongly. I truly came to feel quite close to her, and I decided that I would never do anything on my part to hurt her. She was ultimately sent to the East because she had played the music of Felix Mendelssohn-Bartholdy, which, of course, was strictly forbidden. Even so, I had the feeling that she was to be protected.

I continued my work with the *Gestapo*. I wanted to make amends to your mother by looking after you. And, Hannah, please believe this, I grew to love you as if you were my own daughter.

I can read your mind, asking me why I did this? I don't have to tell you what crazy times we lived through. I was never particularly fond of Jews and I became caught up with Hitler's ideology about them. I was a proud German who celebrated the victories and progress that Hitler brought to our country. We went through so much deprivation until he took over.

I came to realize that these Jews, whom we called *untermenschen*, were really the *übermenschen* and that was why Hitler was afraid of them. They actually were a small part of the population, but yet they achieved greatness far beyond their numbers. I recognized all that they brought to Germany and the jealousy of others that ultimately prompted their removal from our society.

I had thought that the *Gestapo* had destroyed all their records before the Russian invasion, but they did not and my file fell into the Russians' hands. I grew to hate the *Gestapo* all the more after that. They were so thorough in everything they did, but their irresponsibility in not destroying the records gave the Russians a great deal of information about many Nazis, the *Gestapo*, and how they were killing all of those people before the

Russians came in. I realized they were nothing but a bunch of legalized thugs—but Hannah, all too late I'm afraid.

When I went with you to Admiralpalast I was sure that Captain Karasik was going to be giving us work to do. He was so good to us. I was arrested and imprisoned by the Russians. Ultimately I agreed to work for them against the Nazis. I would have been shipped to a Russian labor camp if I didn't agree to this, and I doubt I would have survived very long. It's so ironic, Hannah, that we've gone from the dictatorship of Hitler to the dictatorship of Stalin.

I have completed a will, which the Russian authorities have on file, bequeathing all my worldly goods to you. I have few, but hopefully you will enjoy the cottage.

Hannah, I am not asking for your forgiveness, for I deserve none. I do want you to know that I love you and I want you to be happy in your life. Please believe this.

With affection,

Freda Merth

Hannah sat with her thoughts for a few moments. She turned towards her sleeping husband, filled with the warmth and glow of her love for him. She took *Frau* Merth's letter, ripped it into little pieces, and placed it in the small bag in the seat before hers. She held her husband's hand as he murmured inaudibly from his sleep. Then, without thinking, she took the other hand, crossed herself, said a "Hail Mary," and with a clear mind closed her eyes as the sound of the airplane engines lulled her back to sleep.

REFERENCES

Arard, Yitzak. 1987. *Belzec, Sobibor, Treblinka. The Operation Reinhard Death Camps*. Indiana University Press. Bloomington and Indianapolis.

Bajak, Frank. 1994. "Berlin Brigade's Role Lauded by Germans in Farewell Fete." AP, *The Washington Times* (5 February).

___. 1994. "GIs' Radio Station: 'Auf Wiedersehen.'" AP, *The Washington Times* (16 July).

Ballard, Robert D. with Spencer Dunmore. 1995. *Exploring the Lusitania*. Madison Press. Toronto, Canada.

Cargas, Harry James. 1990. *Shadows of Auschwitz, A Christian Response to the Holocaust*. The Crosswords Publishing Company. New York.

Clare, George. 1990. *Before the Wall, Berlin Days, 1946-1948*. Dutton. New York.

Daughters of Charity, More About the. 2000. Website: http://cptryon.org/vdp/tree/dc/more.html. (29 May).

Engelmann, Bernt. 1986. *In Hitler's Germany*. Pantheon Books. New York.

Evans, Richard J. 1994. "Are There Lessons in the Weimar Republic?" *The New York Times Book Review* (30 January).

Fleming, Gerald. 1984. *Hitler and the Final Solution.* University of California Press. Berkeley.

Gallagher, Hugh Gregory. *By Trust Betrayed.* Henry Holt and Company. New York.

Goldhagen, Daniel Jonah. 1996. "The People's Holocaust." *The New York Times* (17 March).

Goldsmith, Martin. 2000. PBS "Hewghouk" Interview. (20 November).

Gumbel, Peter. 1995. "A Village Divided." *The Wall Street Journal.* New York (5 December).

Herzstein, Robin Edward. 1980. *The Nazis.* Time-Life Books. Morristown, New Jersey.

Kamenetsky, Ihor. 1961. *Secret Nazi Plans for Eastern Europe, A Study of Lebensraum Policies.* Bookman Associates. New York.

Lifton, Robert Jay. 1986. *The Nazi Doctors.* Basic Books, Inc. New York.

Meltzer, Milton. 1988. *Rescue, The Story of How Gentiles Saved Jews in the Holocaust.* Harper & Row. New York.

Moss, Doley C. 1957. *Of Cell and Cloiser, Catholic Religious Orders Through The Ages.* The Bruce Publishing Company. Milwaukee.

Nash Nathaniel C. 1995. "Faith in a Scrap of Paper." *The New York Times* (25 June).

___. 1995. "Files Show Bank Aided Nazi Cause." *The New York Times* (19 March).

New York Daily News. 1945. (8 May).

Overy, Richard and Andrew Wheatcroft. 1989. *The Road to War*. Macmillan Limited. London.

Owings, Alison. 1993. *Frauen, German Women Recall the Third Reich*. Rutgers University Press. New Brunswick, New Jersey.

Pictorial History of the Second World War. 1947. Wm. H. Wise and Co., Inc. New York. (vol 2, p. 1004).

Posner, Gerald L. 1991. *Hitler's Children*. Random House. New York.

Rahner, Karl & Pinchas, Lapide. 1987. *Encountering Jesus—Encountering Judaism*. The Crossroad Publishing Company. New York.

Ryan, Cornelius. 1966. *The Last Battle*. Simon and Schuster. New York.

Simpson, Colin. 1972. *The Lusitania*. Little, Brown and Company. Boston.

Steiner, Jean-François. 1966. *Treblinka*. A Mentor Book, New American Library. New York.

___. 1967. *Treblinka*. Simon and Schuster. New York.

Tenenbaum, Joseph. 1956. *Race and Reich*. Twayne Publishers. New York.

Tuchman, Barbara W. 1962. *The Guns of August*. Macmillan. New York.

Turner, Henry Ashby, Jr. 1987. *The Two Germanies Since 1945*. Yale University Press. New Haven.

Tusa, Ann and John. 1988. *The Berlin Airlift*. Atheneum. New York.

Vexler, Robert. 1973. *Germany, A Chronology and Fact Book*. Oceana Publications. Dobbs Ferry, New York.

Whitney, Craig R. 1994. "Poles Review Postwar Treatment of Germans." *The New York Times* (1 November).

Whittaker, K. P. 1963. "Roll Your Tent Flaps, Girls!" Avon Books, New York.

Willenberg, Samuel. 1986. *Surviving Treblinka*. Basil Blackwell Ltd. Oxford, United Kingdom.

Wyden, Peter. 1989. *Wall, The Inside Story of Divided Berlin*. Simon and Schuster. New York.

___. 1992. *Stella*. Simon and Schuster. New York.

ENDNOTES

1 Deutsche Bank, Germany's largest, worked with the Nazi regime from 1933 expropriating Jewish businesses, which included the Mendelssohn Bank. One of the few clear objections raised was by Georg Somassen, a board member who wrote in a letter to bank officials in 1933, "I fear that we are only at the beginning of a conscious and planned development which is aimed at the indiscriminate economic and moral destruction of all members of the Jewish race living in Germany." (*New York Times*, p. 4, March 19, 1995.)

2 The two women were unaware of it, but as far back as July 14, 1933, the Nazis, in their obsession for purity of race, passed a law which sanctioned euthanasia; the program went into full scale operation after September 1, 1939, when war broke out. Patients were sent to observation areas for further examination; those to be killed to one of the six extermination camps within the *Reich*. It was from these beginnings that the concentration camps for the extermination of Jews and other "inferior races" came into being. Reinhard Heydrich came up with the idea of the "final solution" for Jewish extermination, and the task ultimately fell into the hands of Adolph Eichmann. (From Joseph Tenenbaum, *Race and Reich*, Twane Publishers, New York, 1956.)